**C. Daugherty**

er crime reporter and investigat
erty is the author of the international
series. She saw her first murder victim
rs old, and has been obsessed with the darke
nature ever since. Her *Night School* books, set in a
ng school for the children of the British elite, topped
charts and captured hearts in countries around the
Her books have been translated into 22 languages.
n Texas, she has lived in England for many years, where
currently working on a new novel. Find out more at
JDaugherty.com.

**Rozenfeld**

he was 9 years old, Carina Rozenfeld began writing
stories, because she thought dreaming at night wasn't
Later, she became a journalist for a French youth
ile continuing to write stories at night. After her first
re published in France, she became a full time author.
he has written nearly twenty popular books, including
selling trilogy *La quête des Livres-Monde* and *Les Clefs*
*el.* In young adult literature, she is known for her series
*Phœnix* and *La symphonie des Abysses.* She has won more than twenty literary awards. She lives in Paris, where she is now working on new science-fiction and fantasy books.

## Also by C. J. Daugherty

*The Night School Series*
Night School
Legacy
Fracture
Resistance
Endgame

## Also by Carina Rozenfeld

*Le Mystère Olphite*
La Quête des Livres-Monde
Le livre des Âmes
Le livre des Lieux
Le livre du Temps

*Doregon*
Les portes de Doregon
La guerre de l'ombre
Les cracheurs de lumière

*La Quête des Pierres de Luet*
La pierre d'Etlal
La pierre de Majilpuûr
La pierre de Goth

*Les Clefs de Babel*

*Les Sentinelles du Futur*

*Phœnix*
Les cendres de l'oubli
Le brasier des souvenirs

*La Symphonie des Abysses*
Livre 1 & 2

## Also by C.J. Daugherty and Carina Rozenfeld

The Secret Fire

C.J. DAUGHERTY
&
CARINA ROZENFELD

ATOM

First published in Great Britain in 2016 by Atom

1 3 5 7 9 10 8 6 4 2



A CIP catalogue record for this book
is available from the British Library.

ISBN: 978-0-349-002-21-7

Typeset in Bodoni by M Rules
Printed and bound in Great Britain by
Clays Ltd, St Ives plc

Papers used by Atom are from well-managed forests
and other responsible sources.

MIX
Paper from
responsible sources
FSC® C104740

Atom
An imprint of
Little, Brown Book Group
Carmelite House
50 Victoria Embankment
London EC4Y 0DZ

An Hachette UK Company
www.hachette.co.uk

www.atombooks.co.uk

THE SECRET CITY

# One

'Don't be such a baby. Try it again.'

Louisa lifted another heavy rock towards an already teetering stack. The stone was nearly as big as her head; her muscles bulged from the effort as she carried it across the dark, wet sand of the river bank, sending her elaborate tattoos rippling.

Once it was in place and balanced on the other rocks, she backed away rapidly, as if she feared the stack might explode.

Her arms crossed, Taylor watched this display in the glare of the bright afternoon sun. The old boathouse was the only building within sight. Beyond it, meadows shimmered green.

They were alone. A few rowers had sped by earlier – skimming across the water. But it had been a while since anyone had passed. The only sound was the wind, hissing through the grass, and bees buzzing among the wildflowers.

It was the perfect place to practise.

The afternoon had grown hot; blonde curls clung to Taylor's damp cheeks as she squinted at the stones dubiously.

'Come on, Lou. Why so many?'

Leaning against the wall of the boathouse, Louisa shot her a withering look. 'If I got paid every time you complained,' she goaded, 'I wouldn't be standing here stacking rocks. Now, are you going to focus, or what?'

Her blue hair caught the sun and converted it into bright azure sparks.

Giving up the fight, Taylor closed her eyes.

In the darkness behind her eyelids the alchemical world sprang to life. Molecules of energy danced around her, translated by her mind into tangible objects – waving golden strands of power from the high grass in the meadow behind the boathouse, silken copper cords from the molecules of light in the air.

It was the river that held the most potential – seen this way, it was a molten stream of amber lava, rolling slowly through the flower-strewn field.

Molecules are invisible to the human eye, but she'd taught herself to see them. She had to see what she was about to touch. To manipulate. To change.

Taking a deep breath, Taylor carefully selected one of the finer strands from the water and directed at the stones.

*Lift.*

When alchemy worked, she could sense it. A dizzying rush of energy filled her veins. A starburst of power.

She opened her eyes.

The tall stack of heavy rocks bobbed light as balloons, high above the slow-moving river, each rock neatly aligned with the one below it. A multi-layered stone cake.

Taylor surveyed her work with satisfaction. 'Did it.'

'Brilliant.' Louisa sounded unimpressed. 'Now set them down gently on the water.'

This was the bit Taylor had been struggling with all day. Picking them up was one thing. Putting them where she wanted them was much harder.

Frowning with concentration, she clung to the strand of energy and tried to lower the rocks gently towards the slow-moving waves.

*Float.*

She could almost feel the weight of the heavy stones. They seemed to fight her power. The pull of gravity was relentless.

Sweat beaded Taylor's forehead; her hands tightened into fists at her sides as she struggled for control.

For a second, the stack did as she demanded, wafting, light as rose petals, towards the grey-blue water. Then, without warning, the golden strand of molecular energy sprang free, dancing at the edge of her vision like a sprite.

'No!' Taylor reached out with her hands as if to physically stop what happened next, but it was too late.

The rocks shot out in all directions.

One heavy stone soared straight towards Louisa, who cursed and flung up one hand.

The rock seemed to hit an invisible wall above her. It bounced hard, before landing with a soft thud at the edge of the meadow.

Two other rocks splashed in the water far upstream. One disappeared on the opposite shore.

After that, even the birds fell silent, like they needed a second to marvel at Taylor's incompetence.

'Bollocks.' Taylor wiped the sweat from her forehead. 'Stupid rocks.' She turned to Louisa. 'Can't we light candles again? I love candles.'

The other girl shook her head. 'This is about control, Blondie. You've got this crazy natural ability. Now you've got to learn how to harness it before someone ends up dead.'

'Oh thanks, Lou.' Taylor pushed her hair out of her sticky face with a weary swipe of her hand. 'I feel so much better now.'

Before the other girl could zing back a tart reply, her phone rang. She gave Taylor a 'just a minute' signal and walked over to the boathouse to take the call in private.

Taylor watched her receding back with contemplative eyes. There were still things she didn't know – things Louisa hadn't told her. St Wilfred's College Oxford held hundreds of years of mysteries. And Taylor was at the heart of it.

With a sigh, she lowered herself onto an old bench, the rough wood worn smooth by years of wind and rain. The intense concentration involved in her training was hugely draining. She felt as if she'd run miles. Sweat streamed down her face, and her body felt weak. Her white t-shirt – with the slogan 'I like big BOOKS and I cannot lie' – clung to her torso.

Taking a swig from a bottle of lukewarm water, she looked back across the meadow. In the distance, St Wilfred's soaring stone spires rose high into the sky. It looked for all the world like a white castle glimmering in the sun.

She still couldn't believe this was her home, now. Every morning she woke up in her unfamiliar dorm room and looked around at the plain white walls and old-fashioned furniture, wondering where the hell she was. Then the memories would come flooding back. The fight in London. The Bringers surrounding her on the street, crushing her. Sacha roaring towards her on a gleaming motorcycle. The overwhelming surge of power when the two of them joined hands, and destroyed the demonic creatures together.

Her own phone buzzed in her pocket, disrupting her thoughts. When she pulled it out, a message from her mother glowed up at her.

`Missing you, honey. Call tonight?`

Something in Taylor's chest tightened and she held the phone close.

Louisa and the other alchemists had taken them to Oxford for their own safety. And maybe they were safe here. As safe, at least, as they could be. But it didn't feel like home.

She missed her mum more than she was willing to admit to anyone. She texted back:

`Yes! I'll call before dinner.`

She missed her home so much. She even missed her little sister, Emily. And she *really* missed Georgie. Her best friend messaged her constantly but they were miles apart now in more ways than one. Georgie was back in Woodbury, taking her exams and dreaming of the summer trip to Spain with her family that awaited her when it was all over.

Taylor was learning how to fight monsters.

Shooting a surreptitious glance at Louisa who was still talking on the phone, she took a deep breath and pushed the melancholy away. She couldn't let anyone know how she felt. They had to believe Taylor could do this. They all had no choice but to believe that.

Over by the boathouse, Louisa shoved her phone into the pocket of her cut-offs and strode back towards her.

'We have to head back,' she announced. 'Jones wants to see me.'

'Jones' was what everyone called St Wilfred's dean, Jonathan Wentworth-Jones. There wasn't much of a power hierarchy at the college, but when the dean called, you jumped.

Secretly thrilled to leave the rock-lifting behind, Taylor followed Louisa to the footpath stretching across the water meadow to the school.

The path was narrow, and crowded by tall grass and wildflowers that pressed in towards them, tickling the sides of her legs. As she walked, she twisted her unruly blonde curls up into a knot, letting the soft breeze cool the skin on the back of her neck.

It was the hottest July she could remember. Every day a scorcher. Like the world was about to end.

She was so lost in her own thoughts, they were halfway across the meadow before she noticed Louisa hadn't said a word. Normally, she'd have been insulting her for what happened with the rocks, and threatening hours of extended training. But she was silent; her face taut and thoughtful.

Taylor studied her curiously. 'What's going on?'

Louisa glanced up. In the bright sunlight, her eyes were the colour of warm toffee.

'It's nothing.' She shrugged, looking away. 'Jones is always worrying about something or other.'

Taylor could tell she was hiding something, but she let it go. She had problems of her own.

With every passing overheated day, her alchemical abilities strengthened. Maybe she couldn't control the stupid rocks, but there was no question she was getting better. Even now it was hard to focus on the solid path ahead because molecules of energy seemed to pursue her. Golden orbs of it got in her way. Fat, honeyed blobs and streams of it surrounded her. It was a constant distraction and made her dizzy if she looked at it directly while trying to walk, so she was teaching herself to focus on seeing the world as normal people saw it. Blue and pink flowers. Silky green grass. Sunlight.

At the end of the path, a weathered wooden door was set in the middle of a stone wall, dotted with deep-set windows. Ancient symbols had been carved deep into the stone above the door. When she'd first arrived, Taylor barely noticed them. Now she was constantly conscious of them – they were everywhere at the college. The sinister power of the ourobouros – a snake eating its tail. The simplicity of a perfect circle entwined with a triangle. The perfection of the all-seeing eye. There were dozens of them. Each represented an element of ancient alchemy – copper, mercury, tin – with corresponding power that repelled Dark energy. Gold, symbolised by the sun, and silver, by the moon, were the strongest symbols of all. Sun and moon carvings topped every doorway, every window, every wall.

Together they formed a protective barrier around St Wilfred's. Normally, this would be enough to keep the school safe. But things were changing.

Nothing was safe anymore.

The door had no handle. Louisa pressed her fingertips against the scarred wood. Seconds later there was a metallic click, and the door swung open.

On the other side, students and professors hurried across a grassy quadrangle, bounded on all sides by tall stone buildings. Above their heads, elegant towers and spires soared upward. It looked like a perfectly ordinary Oxford College. And in a way it was.

They stepped into the flow of students.

'Look, don't sweat the practice.' Louisa spoke so suddenly Taylor jumped. 'You'll get it. You're making progress.'

'I know,' Taylor said. 'I just wish it was faster.'

Louisa's smile was grim. 'It is fast. It just doesn't seem that way because we're in a hurry.'

A group of girls clustered together by a stone column and stared at Taylor. They made no effort to hide their interest, and the hiss of their whispers seemed to ring in her ears.

'Is *that* her?'

'I don't see anything special about her.'

This happened so often Taylor knew she should be getting used to it, but it still bugged her. Her cheeks flushed red, and anger swelled inside her.

Rumours about her and Sacha had swirled ever since they arrived at the college. They didn't know the whole story – Jones was keeping it quiet to avoid panic – but everyone knew the troubles they faced were connected to the two of them. And they weren't happy about it.

Before she could think of an appropriately cutting response, though, Louisa swung in front of her and faced the girls, arms folded, eyes blazing.

'What the hell has happened in your life to make you act like this? This isn't high school. Get going or I'll report you to Jones.'

The girls wilted in the heat of her glare. In seconds, the group had melted into the general hubbub of the quad.

'What morons,' Louisa grumbled. 'Come on.'

Grabbing Taylor's elbow, she pulled her down the stone walkway.

When they reached the steps of the tall, gothic admin building, shadowed by lizard-like gargoyles that leered down at the crowds below, Louisa paused.

'You could wait here, if you want, but I don't know how long I'll be.' She thought for a second. 'Why don't you check in with Alastair and the others?'

'Sure.' Taylor shrugged.

Louisa's expression grew stern. 'Go straight there, OK?'

Taylor bit back a sharp reply. She and Sacha were constantly guarded even on the college grounds, and they were both tired of being treated like children.

Keeping her expression smooth, she nodded. 'I promise.'

Once the other girl had gone inside though, she didn't head

to the lab, where the researchers were still experimenting on the bits of the dead Bringers they'd brought back from London.

Instead, she turned in the other direction, and headed off with purpose.

# Two

St Wilfred's Library was a round columned building, built of the same golden limestone as most of the buildings in Oxford. Its domed, copper roof gleamed green in the hot sun as Taylor slipped through wide doors encrusted with alchemical symbols into the cool dimness of the main reading room.

Inside, tables arced out from the front door in symmetrical semi-circles, each topped with two brass reading lamps, and surrounded by leather chairs. Most of the tables were empty. This wasn't because St Wilfred's students didn't study, but because this entire room was mostly for show. The workaday parts of the library stretched out beyond the decorative structure for more than a city block. Stacks of books were layered on thousands of shelves across four storeys, and there were more levels of books beneath the ground. It was a massive labyrinth of reading.

Despite the sheer size of the place, she still had a pretty good idea where she'd find Sacha.

With quick steps, she made her way across the hushed room, past carved marble columns thick as tree trunks, and headed straight for a set of towering double doors. These opened into a vast atrium. She could smell coffee brewing in the student cafe downstairs and for a second she thought longingly of their lush, chocolate chip cookies, but she didn't stop, turning instead towards the main staircase, which twisted up around a statue of four leaping horses.

They'd barely been at St Wilfred's three weeks, but already every part of this felt normal to Taylor. Faced with a complex new world in which everyone was older than them, more assured, and not, as far as they knew, facing immediate death, she and Sacha had quickly developed daily routines they followed with almost religious strictness. Every afternoon Taylor trained with Louisa. And Sacha buried himself in old French books in the library. Looking for answers.

Barely glancing at the lunging stone beasts, she sped upwards, passing loitering students and shuffling professors.

As soon as she reached the next floor, she turned right, heading straight into the stacks, where bookcases towered high above her on all sides.

In his usual black t-shirt and blue jeans, Sacha sat alone at the last table in a corner. He was bent over his books, his head resting lightly on the fingers of one hand. Strands of straight brown hair fell forward, hiding his face. His long legs were stretched out into the aisle.

If the alchemists' energy was warm and bright, Sacha's was

entirely different. His was an oasis of cool blue calm, edged with darkness. There was danger in him, and Taylor was drawn to it.

Ever since they'd killed the Bringers together they'd been connected somehow. They'd never talked about it, but she knew he felt it, too. She could see it in his face – a kind of thoughtfulness in his eyes.

But he didn't look at her now. He was so engrossed in his reading, he jumped when she dropped without ceremony into the leather chair across from him.

'*Merde*, Taylor. Don't sneak up on me like that.'

His silky French accent made each word sound so amazing that Taylor smiled involuntarily.

'Sorry.'

His gaze swept across her face, taking in her flushed cheeks and tangled hair. The irritation faded from his expression.

'How was training?'

She sighed. 'Pants.'

He frowned, sweeping a confused look down to her bare legs. 'Trousers? I don't know what you mean.'

She was teaching him the important bits of English – the parts they didn't teach you in school. Swearing. And things like 'pants'.

'Pants. As in underpants. It means rubbish.' She leaned back in her chair. 'Basically, I'm the worst alchemist in history. Rocks keep beating me. It's embarrassing.'

'You're good enough to kill Bringers,' he pointed out. 'Which is better than everyone else.'

She gave him a grateful smile.

'I wish you'd been out there to say that to Louisa.'

'Is it the same problem?' he asked. 'The control part?'

She nodded. 'Louisa says I'm a nuclear missile with no sense of direction.'

His lips twitched. 'Harsh.'

'Right?'

Sacha's face grew serious again. His fingers tapped the heavy book still open in front of him – the only sign he gave that he was concerned.

'What do you think it is? What's holding you back? I mean, I've seen you control your power and make it look easy.'

His voice betrayed no judgement, but Taylor hesitated. She was reluctant to say 'I don't know' to him. His life – everything – depended on her figuring out how to be a brilliant alchemist. And right now, she wasn't.

'It's hard to control it when there's no one standing there trying to kill me . . . I mean, us,' she said after a long pause. 'I'm better than I was, but I still lose control, and I don't know why. Louisa says I just need practice. But we haven't got much time.'

'You'll get there,' he said. 'Just keep trying.'

If he was nervous – afraid she'd fail and let him die – he was hiding it well.

Not wanting him to see how worried she was, Taylor picked a book up from the stack on the table. The title was in French, and it took her a second to translate it.

'*The Burnings of Carcassonne*.' She wrinkled her nose. 'Cheery.'

'Yeah . . . Uh, Taylor, I really don't . . .'

He reached out as if to take it from her, but she'd already flipped it open. The first page held an engraved image of a blazing pyre. A woman stood atop it, hands tied behind her back. Even in the rough lines of the engraving, her face was contorted with fear and pain.

Sacha said quietly, 'That book is quite disturbing.'

Taylor didn't reply. She didn't need to.

They didn't know much about the curse that threatened his life, but they knew it started with Isabelle Montclair, one of Taylor's ancestors. An alchemist who lived in France in the seventeenth century, Isabelle had rejected her upbringing and the beliefs of her own people and turned to demonology – which alchemists called 'Dark practice'. Like many alchemists of her time, she was burned as a witch. But two things made her execution different.

The person who burned her was Sacha's ancestor.

And, as she died, she'd used some unknown Dark practice to curse his family for thirteen generations.

Because of that curse issued long ago, over the centuries twelve first-born sons in his family had died.

Sacha was the thirteenth.

Taylor turned pages restlessly as if clues might leap up and offer themselves to her.

'Is there anything in here? About the curse?'

'Nothing new. The burning of Isabelle Montclair is mentioned, but the information is limited. It's never what we need.'

He slammed the old book shut so suddenly, Taylor had to yank her fingers out of the way.

'There must be more information somewhere about how to

undo a curse like this. There are thousands of books about alchemy and Dark practice in this library. The information we're looking for has to be here. It just has to be.'

Taylor could hear the frustration in his voice. She wished there was something she could say to make this better, but the simple truth was, they had to understand this curse if they were going to stop it from killing him. And the alchemists at St Wilfred's had been researching it for years without success. Sacha's birthday was seven days away.

It was all starting to feel hopeless.

'It's here,' she assured him, reaching for another book from the stack in front of him. 'We'll find it. I'll help you.'

Sacha didn't argue. But as she flipped through an old French book she could only barely understand, he didn't pick up another book. Instead he stood up and stretched, his black t-shirt riding from the top of his jeans to expose the tawny skin of his flat stomach.

'I've been looking at these books all day,' he said. 'I need to get out of here.' He glanced at her, a rakish glint in his eye. 'Let's go throw some rocks.'

# THREE

Ten minutes later, they were walking rapidly across the courtyard in the afternoon sunlight. Sacha slid his sunglasses on, ignoring the curious looks from the students they passed. Unlike Taylor, he very much liked the feeling of being watched and whispered about. He thought it was funny.

*There goes that French boy who knows the day he's going to die.*

What a ridiculous thing to be famous for.

'Louisa will *flip* when she realises we're gone.' Taylor looked as anxious as if they'd just stolen a car.

Sacha tried not to smile.

She obeyed all the rules, all the time. It was adorable and frustrating in equal measures. The world was literally ending and she still wanted to ask permission to go outside.

'If we solve your control problems, Louisa will forgive us,' he reminded her.

'I doubt that,' Taylor muttered. But she kept walking.

Blonde curls had sprung free from the clip holding her hair back, tumbling down to surround her face in a golden halo. Her cheeks were flushed from the heat.

She glanced up, catching him looking.

'What?' she asked, lifting a hand to her hair self-consciously.

Quickly, Sacha looked away. 'Nothing.'

As they left the quadrangle and turned into a shadowed archway leading past the science building, Sacha hurried his steps. He was eager to get out of here, even for a few minutes.

He didn't mind the stares but he didn't like this college. He didn't fit in at St Wilfred's at all. It wasn't really about the language – his English was good. It was simply the fact that he wasn't an alchemist and everyone else was.

He was out of place.

Reminders of his normality were everywhere. The professors conducting research in the library pulled books down without reaching for them. Earlier that day he'd watched one of them heat a cold cup of tea, as far as he could tell, just by glancing at it.

He knew there was more to alchemy than that, but he couldn't *see* it. Taylor had told him about streams of energy and molecules but these were invisible to him. All he saw was how different he was from everyone else here. How ordinary.

His otherness mattered. It made him feel left out, even when he was right in the centre of things.

When they came to a door hidden in the shadows at the edge of the quad, Sacha reached for the door handle automatically before realising there wasn't one. His hand hung in the air for a second, as if confused about what it was doing there.

'I have to do it,' Taylor said, a hint of apology in her voice.

He stepped back, watching as she pressed her fingertips against the door. Instantly, the lock clicked and the heavy door swung open.

Sacha had seen her do much more astonishing things than unlock a door, but he marvelled at how nonchalant she was about it lately. She expressed doubt constantly, but he could see her growing more unconsciously confident every day. She wasn't afraid of what she could do, or who she was anymore.

Following her through the door, he found himself standing at the edge of a broad green expanse of grass and wildflowers, wild and untamed. He stared at the field in open astonishment. Taylor had told him about it, but he had never seen it for himself. He was forbidden from leaving the college for any reason. The dean had been quite firm on the subject and Sacha had been kept within the university's walls since he arrived.

Now he felt like he was stepping into another world. Getting his freedom back.

Some of the tension that had kept him tight as a wire for days left his body. He stood still for a second, taking it all in. Already several steps down the path, Taylor turned to look at him.

'What's wrong?'

'Nothing.' Shoving his hands into his pockets, he stepped onto the footpath to join her.

He took a deep breath – the air smelled of sweet grass and wildflowers. The ground was soft beneath his feet. After weeks spent trapped in dusty old rooms, this was wonderful.

He could hear traffic sounds in the distance – real life was out there, somewhere. But it seemed far away.

'This is heaven, I think,' he said, tilting his face up to the sun.

Taylor glanced at him with a knowing smile. 'Glad to be out of the library?'

Still looking up, he nodded. The very thought of going back to those books made him want to start running and never stop. Finally, he lowered his gaze to hers.

'The worst part isn't the reading,' he confided. 'Or the students who gossip about us like they expect me to be able to fly or something. The worst part is the professors.'

'I know, right?' Taylor said. 'That guy with a beard . . .'

Sacha made a face. 'He is awful. I was studying on the ground floor in that room for a while but I had to move because he keeps sneezing. Really loudly. Each time he does it, he looks at me like it's my fault.'

She laughed. 'Seriously?'

'I think he's allergic to French people.'

She laughed harder then, and it struck Sacha it had been a long time since he'd heard her laugh like that.

Everything had been so serious lately.

'What about you?' he asked.

Her smile faded.

'You know about me.' She looked away. 'I come out here every day. I try really hard. And I mess up.'

They walked in silence for a while. Sacha shoved his hands back in his pockets, stealing sideways glances at her. Her brow was furrowed, and she seemed lost in her own worries.

He knew how much she wanted to succeed. He wanted to tell her not to be so hard on herself – it would be the kind thing to do – but if he was honest, each time she told him how something in her training hadn't worked, it hit him like a punch in the gut. However much she wanted to succeed, he wanted it – *needed it* – more.

He desperately needed her to be strong enough to fight the Dark practitioner. Strong enough to help him. He hated that he couldn't save himself. It wasn't fair that so much of the responsibility fell on Taylor's shoulders. They'd only known each other a few weeks, and now she had to save his life.

That was why he spent every day in the library. Why he buried himself in old French books.

He had to contribute something to his own salvation.

And he wasn't about to put more pressure on Taylor now.

'You're getting better,' he assured her.

She glanced up at him, doubt filling her cool green eyes.

'You *are*,' he insisted. 'You can't see it because all you notice are the things you can't do. I see all the things you *can* do. And you are getting better.'

They'd walked several steps before she replied, her voice so low he wasn't certain at first that he understood what she'd said. 'Not fast enough.'

Before he could think of a response to that she pointed ahead, changing the subject.

'That's where we're going.'

She quickened her pace, speeding to where a silver ribbon of river curved through the trees. Sacha hurried after her, down a few stone steps to a weathered stone boathouse near the river's edge.

A breeze rolled off the slow-moving water, blowing his hair into his eyes. The air smelled green and damp. It was cooler down here than up at the school.

'This is it.' Taylor threw open her arms. 'This is where I go every day.'

Aside from the boathouse and an old bench, there was nothing here except a muddy shore and a graceful weeping willow tree dangling its long branches into the water, which tugged and pulled at its leaves. It was quiet and isolated – the perfect place to train.

Picking a pebble up from the damp sand, Sacha flicked it sideways towards the river. It danced across the water before slipping quietly beneath the waves.

He turned back to Taylor. 'Show me what you can do.'

For a second he thought she would argue. Maybe even refuse.

But then she gave a small shrug and turned around, her gaze searching the shore. Finding what she sought, she held out one hand.

A heavy stone at the edge of the river rose with a jerk, floating weightlessly into the air. Taylor held it there, sweat beading her forehead for a few short seconds, then two things happened simultaneously.

She flinched and gave a small cry. And the stone fell hard to the earth, landing with a thud in the soft, wet dirt near the water.

'Oops,' Sacha said in the silence that followed.

'Yeah.' With a bitter sweep of her hand, Taylor wiped the perspiration from her brow. 'Oops.'

'That's what keeps happening?' he said, studying the heavy rock.

She nodded, her lips tight. 'Every time.'

It shouldn't matter that she couldn't lift the rock. She should have years to hone her abilities, to study, to learn. But she didn't have years. She had days. And it mattered.

Her family history made it clear Taylor could stop the curse that would kill Sacha, and end the Dark practitioner's demonic plans – everyone was sure of that. They just didn't know how.

That's why it mattered that Taylor couldn't set the rocks down properly. That's why people were whispering in corners about the two of them.

Everyone was scared.

The Dark practitioner was coming for them all. And time was running out.

Sacha pulled his hands from his pockets. 'Let's try something different.'

♊

They gathered the heaviest rocks they could find, stacking them at the edge of the water. It was hot work, and they were both sweating by the time everything was in place.

Then Taylor backed far away until she was nearly in the meadow.

Sacha watched her, bemused.

'You should hide,' she warned him. 'The rocks will go everywhere.'

He snorted a laugh. 'I'll be fine. Let's float some rocks.'

Squaring her shoulders, Taylor took a deep breath, and held out her hand. Sacha took it, lacing his fingers through hers. Her skin was velvet soft and cool, despite the hot day.

Tightening her grip, she held his gaze with eyes as green as willow leaves.

'Don't let go.'

For a second, fixed in that brilliant gaze, his voice failed him. He had to force himself to reply.

'I won't.'

Suddenly, a crackle of electricity raced through Sacha's body. He drew in his breath sharply.

He felt Taylor's body stiffen.

'*Now*,' she said.

Her voice had deepened, she stared straight ahead. He turned to see what she was looking at.

The rocks they'd stacked a few minutes ago were flying. Floating high above the water, lighter than air. Bobbing like kites.

Sacha's heart began to pound. He could feel the energy surging through him, flowing from him to Taylor and back, looping them together – the connection between them was a live wire. This was how it had felt when they fought Bringers together in London. Like they could do anything.

Nothing he'd ever experienced was as exhilarating as this.

'What happens now?' His voice sounded breathless.

'Now,' she said, 'we place them back down.'

Taylor's grip on his hand tightened painfully. She stared fixedly at the rocks.

The heavy stones began wafting slowly towards the river, perfectly controlled. When they reached the water, they separated into a line, and floated, duck-like, on the top.

'*Hallucinant*,' Sacha murmured, impressed. 'How did you do that?'

She beamed at him. Perspiration dotted her brow; the colour was high in her cheeks.

'I can't believe it. I've been trying for *days*. I couldn't do it on my own. But with you it was easy.'

'This is it,' Sacha told her. 'This is the part they're getting wrong. We have to do this together. I should be training with you all the time.'

'I think so, too,' she said. 'We could do this together.'

For just an instant, Sacha let himself feel the warm illusion of hope.

Maybe that was why he didn't notice the odd sound at first. A low rumbling roar, like ocean waves, rolling to shore.

When he did hear it, he turned towards the water, and tightened his grip on her hand.

'Taylor . . .'

Hearing the warning note in his voice, she followed his gaze.

The river had begun bending in their direction, pulling away from the opposite bank, and rolling across the muddy shore towards them. It seemed to lean towards them like a flower leans to the glow of the sun.

Atop the waves, the heavy rocks still bobbed happily.

Taylor blanched.

'Oh no,' she whispered and then, at the top of her lungs, 'STOP!'

She flung out an arm, focussing her power on the river.

The water kept rolling in their direction. The river bed was emptying, dark mud glistening in the sunshine. All the water flowing down the river was now flooding the beach, heading towards the meadow. Waves splashed at the base of the boat-house. It was unstoppable.

Sacha turned to look at her. 'Taylor . . .'

'I'm trying. Come *on*,' she begged the river, panic in her eyes. 'Please stop.'

'You have to release your hold.' Louisa's voice came from the meadows behind them.

They both turned. She stood, legs apart, hands on her hips. Her blue hair flashed in the light. She looked furious.

'You have to release your hold, or you're going to drown.'

# Four

'I can't do it,' Taylor said, her lower lip trembling.

'Find the power you were using to float the rocks and release it. And do it before it washes my sodding boathouse away.'

Louisa's voice was steady but Sacha suspected Taylor wouldn't miss the undercurrent of ice floating just beneath her words.

Turning back to the river, Taylor closed her eyes. She was breathing fast, gripping Sacha's hand so tightly he could feel the bones beneath her skin. She whispered something to herself he couldn't quite make out. Suddenly, he felt the connection between them snap and break. The power that had filled his veins with light, withdrew.

He felt empty without it.

With a sigh, the water slipped back to the river bed. The

rocks that had floated so improbably on the surface, sank silently to the bottom.

Taylor dropped Sacha's hand.

Louisa stomped across the dirt towards them. 'Dammit, you two,' she said. 'What the hell are you doing out here? I've been looking for you everywhere.'

'Did you see the rocks?' Taylor stuck to the positives. 'We did it. Perfectly.'

'And then you nearly flooded Oxford,' Louisa snapped. 'We've talked about this before. It's too dangerous for you to be alone out here. You know that. You should be accompanied at all times.'

'She is not alone,' Sacha said evenly. 'She's with me.'

Louisa swung her stern gaze towards him. 'And that's the other problem. Kid, you are a walking target with no ability to protect yourself. What the hell were you thinking?'

Sacha didn't flinch.

'I was thinking that perhaps I could help Taylor with her training,' he said coolly.

Louisa began a tart reply, but then stopped herself. When she spoke again, her voice was not unsympathetic.

'I get it, kid. I really do,' she said. 'But Taylor has to learn to do this on her own. She can't rely on your combined power to keep her safe. What if you're knocked unconscious and she has to fight this guy alone? What if you're taken hostage and she needs to rescue you? If she relies on this power thing you two have . . .' She swayed a hand back and forth between the two of them. '. . . she's vulnerable every single time you walk away. Which I want you to do right now. So I can teach her to fight for herself.'

Anger flared in Sacha's chest. He hated the way Louisa talked down to both of them. He hated that Taylor's training wasn't going better. He hated St Wilfred's and everyone in it. He hated that he needed them to save him.

'Stop calling me kid, OK?' he responded heatedly. 'You want me to act like a responsible adult? Then start treating me like one, or I can be the kid you pretend to see. I really can.' He took a step towards her. 'Is that what you want? To deal with a kid right now? Be careful for what you wish, Louisa.'

'Take a breath, kid.' Louisa rolled her eyes. 'Jesus.'

'Louisa,' Taylor snapped, stepping between them. 'Will you shut *up*?'

Sacha and Louisa glared at each other over her shoulder.

In all honesty, Sacha would have loved to have it out with Louisa right now. She'd been on his back since he arrived at St Wilfred's and he didn't understand why. Nothing he did was good enough. It was unfair.

The only problem was, this time, she had a point.

Taylor was the key to this battle. And she had to get stronger to be safe. He wouldn't always be there.

That didn't make any of this easy to take. He'd been through too much in his life to put up with being talked down to by a blue-haired, tattooed pixie.

'Louisa, you should apologise,' Taylor told her, still fuming.

Sacha took a step back.

'It's fine, Taylor. I'll go. I've had enough.' He fired a warning look at Louisa. 'But she needs to stop being such a bitch to me or I'm out of here. *Je me casse*.'

Without waiting to hear what either of them had to say, he

stormed back across the meadow with his head down, wishing for the hundredth time that he was back in Paris. He could go. They couldn't stop him – he had a return ferry ticket in his bedroom right now. But he wouldn't leave without Taylor, and he knew without even asking she'd never go.

Besides, he didn't even know where they were keeping his motorcycle. They'd taken the keys when he arrived, and told him it would be 'safely stored'.

He hated that, too. It was *his bike*.

Fuming, he kicked a rock off the path so hard it flew into the long grass. But that wasn't enough. He wanted to run. To punch someone.

Days like today made him long for his crappy old life. Maybe he had just been sitting around waiting to die. But at least he was free.

Now he felt like a prisoner.

It wasn't until he made it back to the door in the stone wall, that he realised his mistake. Only alchemists could open it. He couldn't get back in on his own.

Typical.

'I *hate* this place.' With a shout of futile rage, he slammed his fist against the wood.

The door didn't even shake.

Swearing under his breath, he stalked away, following the wall around the college towards the front gate.

He'd never been out here, so he didn't really know where he was going. All he could do was follow the wall surrounding the college. St Wilfred's grounds sprawled for some distance. It was fifteen minutes before he even reached the edge of the meadow. After that, the ground changed from soft grass to hard concrete. The sweet sounds of birds singing and insects buzzing were replaced by the rumble of cars and buses.

After a while, Sacha found himself on a narrow lane. On his right was the tall forbidding wall of St Wilfred's. Across the road, another wall faced the first – presumably the wall of another college, but he didn't know which. It was like walking in a valley of stone.

Up until now, he'd seen little of the town of Oxford. Now he found himself looking around curiously. Above the walls on both sides, he could see the spires of colleges and churches. He hated St Wilfred's, but the town was undeniably extraordinary – his father had lived here long ago, and loved it. Maybe he'd walked down this very street.

The thought was somehow steadying, and his anger began to ebb.

St Wilfred's wall curved to the right, and he turned with it. He began to pass more people – mostly students walking in pairs or clusters, talking and laughing. But also tourists, and locals.

From behind the safe wall of his sunglasses, Sacha watched them with an interest he would never have acknowledged. They looked so relaxed. So normal. They'd never seen a Bringer sliding towards them with death in its eyes. They didn't even know such things could exist.

*God, it would be nice to be that naive.*

It was hotter now he was out of the meadow, and he ran a hand across his brow. He'd been walking for ages. Where was that stupid front gate?

He had to be getting close.

He hurried his steps, pushing past a crowd of students talking and blocking the way.

Only when they parted to allow him to pass, could he see the college's tall gatehouse ahead, the red and gold banners at the top hanging limp in the heat.

Relief flooded through him. He was nearly there.

Just then, an ominous low growl rumbled through the air.

Sacha froze in mid-step. The sound wasn't loud but there was something strange about it. Something inhuman.

It grew louder. A creaking, almost industrial groan. Like something horrible was shifting, deep below the ground.

The fine hairs on the back of his neck rose. He turned around, seeking the source.

He wasn't the only one who'd heard it. Murmuring in confusion, the cluster of students looked around.

Sacha turned to warn them – of what, he wasn't certain. But he never got the chance to say a thing.

The ground shook with such violence he had to grab a lamp post to keep from falling. Then with stunning suddenness, the world around him exploded.

# FIVE

After Sacha stormed off towards the college, Louisa and Taylor stood by the river shouting at each other.

Louisa knew she'd gone too far, but she'd been searching the college frantically for them – the dean had called her 'irresponsible' for losing them – and when she'd seen them together where they weren't supposed to be, the tension and frustration of the last few weeks boiled over.

She regretted it instantly – the wounded outrage in Sacha's eyes and the puzzled disappointment on Taylor's face were all too clear. But the stubborn part of her (the part she held responsible for most of her bad decisions) wouldn't allow her to say she was sorry.

'Do you not *want* to be safe?' she heard herself snapping at Taylor. 'Do you *want* to die?'

'That's a stupid question.' Taylor folded her arms.

'Answer it.' Louisa doubled down.

'I will not.' Taylor's voice was taut. 'Besides. I'm the only person who can make myself safe.'

Louisa opened her mouth to argue. That was when the ground beneath their feet trembled.

Instantly, she forgot what they were arguing about.

'What the hell was that?' she muttered, turning to look back towards the college.

In the sudden silence, she heard a *whump*. And, a heartbeat later, an almighty roar.

Then faint, bone-chilling screams.

In the distance, amid the stone spires, a thin column of smoke had begun to rise, black against the crystalline blue of the summer sky.

'Lou . . .' Taylor's voice was low and terrified.

Before she could finish what she was about to say, Louisa was running towards the college.

'Stay with me,' she called over her shoulder without slowing down. '*Close*.'

The warning wasn't necessary – Taylor was right on her heels. But she wanted to say it anyway.

'What's happening?' Taylor shouted at her.

'I don't know.' Louisa's voice shook with each step. 'But it's not good.'

They ran so fast the wildflowers around them became a green-and-white blur. Louisa couldn't hear the insects anymore. The birds had fallen silent. There was only the harsh rasp of her breath and the shrill cries that grew louder as they neared the school wall.

Another massive *boom* shook the earth just as they reached

the gate, and Louisa felt it with her whole body. She could sense it now, in the distance. An oily sheen of Dark power.

The sky went dark. Grit and rocks showered down on them like hard, stinging rain. They huddled together outside the gate, shielding their heads with their hands.

When it stopped, Louisa reached for the door but Taylor grabbed her arm.

'Sacha.' Her eyes were wide. 'We sent him back.'

Louisa's stomach lurched. In the panic, she'd forgotten all about him.

Silently she cursed her temper. Why hadn't she made them all walk back together? How could she have been so stupid?

But she kept her expression steady.

'We'll find him,' she promised, with confidence she didn't feel. 'Taylor – I think it's *him*. Are you ready?'

Taylor swallowed hard. Then she nodded. 'I'm ready.'

She wasn't. They both knew that. But there wasn't time left to plan.

'Let's go.' Louisa pressed her hand against the door. It sprang open.

On the other side, St Wilfred's once orderly campus was in upheaval. Dust and smoke hung thick in the air, giving the scene a hazy, other-worldly feel.

'Stay with me,' Louisa shouted, and launched herself into the chaos.

Students, professors and staff stumbled in all directions, clutching each other, coughing. Smoke alarms shrieked their warnings from the school buildings.

The two girls stuck close together as they ran through the

crowds, until Louisa skidded to a stop, momentarily uncertain of where to go.

A porter, his black jacket powdered with dust, and his bowler hat askew, stood outside one of the side doors to the library shouting: 'The safe rooms! All students to the safe rooms!'

Terrified students flooded towards him, hurtling into the dim interior. Her jaw set, Louisa ran the other way, shoving against the tide, towards the tower of smoke. Her mind was whirling, trying to comprehend how everything could have gone so wrong in the few short minutes she'd been down by the river.

The Dark practitioner must have figured out Taylor and Sacha were here and decided to catch them off guard.

*Smart move*, she thought grudgingly, as the smoke swirled around her. *Now how do we stop him?*

The closer they got to the main entrance to the college, the more Dark power filled the air. Its presence filled her veins with ice.

It was happening too soon. They weren't ready. They'd thought they had more time.

She kept spinning around to check on Taylor. She was right there, face pale and drawn but matching her stride for stride.

A spark of pride kindled in Louisa's heart. She was tough, that one. Tougher than anyone knew.

The students were disappearing to safety in the basement of the library. Now the sirens were the only sound, their shrieks splitting the air like blades.

Louisa wasn't sure what to do. She had to keep Taylor safe,

fight whatever battle was happening and find Sacha. All at once.

It was impossible.

In an instant, she decided to keep Taylor with her and head to the fight. Something told her if there was trouble, Sacha would be there already.

The smoke was thickest near the main entrance, just next to the red brick tower, topped with the school's jaunty banners.

Louisa pointed. 'That way.'

When they reached the front gate, the dust and smoke made it hard to see. It was like walking into a toxic fog.

Coughing, they both pulled their t-shirts up over their mouths.

Only when they drew close could they see the extent of the damage.

One entire three-storey building was gone. Bricks and rubble lay strewn around an empty hole where the porters' offices used to be.

'What the hell?' Louisa muttered.

The destruction was stunning. Her mind kept putting the missing structure back where it belonged – steep roof, brick walls, leaded windows. But then she'd look again, and see . . . nothing.

It was as if a bulldozer had rampaged straight through.

A group of St Wilfred's faculty stood clustered in the broken space, facing out towards the street. Some wore the black gowns of professors. Others wore tweed jackets or blue jeans. A lightning storm of alchemical energy crackled around them as they formed a tight line. A fire crackled where the building had once stood, just to the left of them, and smoke swirled and eddied, darkening the sun.

'I don't see Sacha,' Taylor cried, scanning the crowd.

Louisa frowned. 'Me neither. Let's get closer.'

The two took off across the grass. Nobody seemed to notice as they skidded to a standstill behind the line of alchemists.

Only then did they see him.

Across the ancient narrow lane, the man stood, all alone. His grey hair, neat moustache, and erect carriage gave him the look of a retired general. He wore a natty tweed jacket and carried a black cane.

To any ordinary person, he would have looked completely unthreatening. But Louisa and Taylor could see what most could not – Dark power surrounded him in a way Louisa had never encountered before. It fairly poured from him.

'Oh my God,' Taylor whispered. 'That's him, isn't it?'

Louisa didn't answer. Her heart was hammering against her ribs.

She'd seen that narrow, icy face once before. In Taylor's hometown. He'd scared her to death then, and he frightened her even more now – because now, he was much, much stronger.

Stronger than the Bringers. Stronger than anything she'd ever encountered.

Was *this* what Dark energy really looked like? It looked . . . unbeatable. In that instant, she realised the alchemists were not standing in line – they were forming a barrier. They were trying to save the college.

They were trying to save everyone.

She grabbed Taylor's shoulders, holding her tightly. 'Stay back here,' she said. 'Don't let *him* see you. Keep an eye out for Sacha.'

When Taylor nodded, Louisa was relieved. She knew how much she wanted to help. Someday, Taylor would be a force to be reckoned with. But she wasn't ready yet. Not for this.

Leaving her safely behind the line, Louisa joined the other alchemists facing the grey-haired man. Each had a hand raised, focussing alchemical power at him to counter the waves of Dark energy he projected at them in a constant, overwhelming oily torrent.

It wasn't hard to find Alastair. He was ludicrously tall, and his perpetually dishevelled golden hair gleamed even through the smoke. Squeezing in next to him, she raised her hand, calmed her mind and focussed on pulling molecules of energy from wherever she could find them.

'Nice of you to join us.' Alastair spoke through gritted teeth, his eyes never leaving the man across the street.

Louisa steadied herself.

'I can't find the French kid,' she said, and directed all her strength at the Dark practitioner.

Alastair shot her a sideways glance, disbelief on his face. 'You can't be serious.'

A wave of Dark power hit Louisa like a punch and she grunted, absorbing it. It was a while before she responded.

'I didn't realise the apocalypse was today, Alastair. I didn't get the memo.'

Swearing, he turned back to face their target and redoubled his efforts.

'Here's the plan.' He spoke quietly. 'If we live, we'll find Sacha and be heroes. If we die, he's on his own.'

Grinning, Louisa sent a burst of alchemical power straight at the Dark practitioner. He turned sharply in her direction, his small, dark eyes travelling down the line of alchemists until he found her.

When their gaze met, he smiled a sharp, vicious smile. Then he lifted his cane slowly.

It writhed in his hand like a snake.

All thoughts of Sacha left Louisa's mind. She'd never felt numb with fear before, but right now she couldn't feel her hands.

What he was doing wasn't possible.

'Bloody hell,' she breathed, and sought all the power she could find. The muscles on her arms bulged from the strain. Next to her, Alastair was fighting to retain control. For the first time it really struck home: maybe they wouldn't get through this after all.

Everybody was struggling, and the man across the street knew it – a look of triumph filled his face. He raised the writhing cane higher.

Louisa's chest tightened as she stared at the serpent in his hand, its mouth opening, fangs extending, long and deadly . . .

That was when Taylor stepped forward to join the line.

# Six

At first, Taylor had set out to do as Louisa ordered. She stood back and watched the battle from safety. She stared in awe as the power flew between the two sides, flashes of molecular energy that left electrical burns hanging in the air like gun smoke.

As the fight intensified, the line had shifted, and suddenly she had a clear view across the street. She found herself staring at the man opposite. She couldn't tear her eyes away. He looked strangely familiar but she couldn't place him.

He was looking fixedly at Louisa now, and raising the cane, which seemed to writhe in his hand, like a snake.

But that wasn't possible, was it?

Taylor took a step forward. Then another.

His gaze shifted towards her. She saw his face register her – recognising her with a curious mix of glee and venomous loathing.

Only then did she feel the full, sinking impact of his Dark power. A freight train of soul-destroying hate.

She took a sharp breath. Before she could duck, hide – do something to escape that awful gaze – he directed the serpentine cane at her.

The oxygen left the air. Her heart slowed, each beat becoming heavy and painful.

Somehow she knew this was Dark power. Knew she should be fighting it. But she was drawn inexorably towards him. The man held out one hand in invitation. The other held the snake, its glinting eyes glowing red in the smoky light.

*This way*, it seemed to say. *You'll be fine here. This way.*

Her mind shut down. She needed to be with him. Her feet took her to him.

The man's eyes were locked on her. He ignored the other alchemists. She was his prize.

Some part of her still knew this. And yet she couldn't stop.

She was close now. She took another step. And another.

'Taylor!' Out of nowhere, Sacha shot through the line of alchemists, grabbing her around the waist with both arms, pulling her back. 'What the hell are you doing?'

For a blank, confused moment she wondered what he was talking about. Then, with visceral shock, she registered two things at the precise same time – first, the panic in the faces of the assembled alchemists as they trained their energies to shield her from Dark power; and, secondly, that she was standing at the edge of the street.

Sacha didn't wait for her to process this. Grabbing her hand, he dragged her back behind the line. Only when they were safe, did he let her go. His confused blue eyes searched her face.

'What the hell was *that*? What were you *thinking*, Taylor?'

Taylor shook her head, clearing the fog of Dark power. 'I don't know,' she said defensively. 'He did something to me. I can't . . . ' She stared at him in sudden realisation. 'Are you OK? Where have you been?'

'Looking for *you*!' he replied, with a burst of frustration. 'I didn't know what was happening or how to get back or where you were. It was terrible.'

In the stress of the moment, his French accent thickened, and he had to search for the English words. The vulnerability of that pierced Taylor's heart.

'I'm sorry,' she said with real remorse. 'We were looking for you, too. It all happened so fast.'

In the distance, she heard police sirens heading towards them. This fight needed to end, fast, or normal people were going to get caught up in it.

'What's happening?' Sacha asked, his brow creasing as he looked from the Dark practitioner to the line in front of them. 'Who is that guy and why aren't they fighting him?'

At first, Taylor was baffled that he would ask a question with such an obvious answer. Then she remembered he couldn't see the golden strands of energy duelling with the heavy Dark power – no normal person could see that. To him, it was just two lines of people, glaring at each other.

Quickly she described what was happening. The alchemists were pulling molecules of energy from everywhere. The air. The trees. The electrical wires overhead shuddered from the force of it. The Dark practitioner was sending a wall of viscous Dark power in return.

'I can smell it,' Sacha said, shuddering. 'It smells like death.'

'It is death,' Taylor told him.

'Who's winning?' he asked.

Taylor turned to look at the line of alchemists standing shoulder-to-shoulder. 'It's like they're equal. One of him. Against all of us.'

As if he'd heard her pessimistic assessment, the dean shouted encouragement to the line, and they redoubled their efforts. The Dark practitioner took a stumbling step backwards under the force of their attack.

'Wait, I think they've got him,' Taylor said excitedly, leaning forward to see what was happening.

The alchemists' combined power was blinding. The dean stood at the centre of them all, tall and slim, directing huge power across the road. Taylor couldn't imagine how the man was withstanding it.

Then the Dark practitioner spoke.

'This is just the beginning. You know me, Jonathan. You know what I'm capable of. I will destroy everything you care about.' His voice was ordinary, and somehow that made what he was saying even more disturbing. 'End this before it's too late. Give me the boy and I'll leave you in peace.'

Taylor's heart jumped to her throat. She felt Sacha stiffen.

The dean kept his eyes fixed on his opponent. When he spoke, Taylor heard uncharacteristic fury in his reply.

'You will *never* take him. And you will not destroy us.' He took a step forward, his eyes flashing. 'I know who you are, now. It is you who will be destroyed, Mortimer. You will be punished for what you've done.'

*Mortimer?* Taylor thought, her brow creasing. And the man had called Jones by his first name.

*They know each other.*

The Dark practitioner gave a low, humourless chuckle.

'Oh, Jonathan. I almost wish for your sake that was true. But I have much greater power now than you can imagine. I will have what I want. The costs no longer matter.'

As he spoke, the line shifted just a little. In the confusion, no one noticed a break had appeared. Quick as a whip, the man raised his cane and channelled Dark power in through the crevice. There was only a second, but that was all it took.

Realising their mistake, the alchemists rushed to seal the break. But they weren't fast enough.

An arrow of Dark power shot straight through, with tremendous speed.

To Sacha, it was invisible. He alone had no warning. No time to duck.

'Sacha!' Taylor lunged towards him.

She was too late.

It hit Sacha like a fist of iron. She watched in horror as his body flew through the air, landing with a sickening thud on the stone walkway at the edge of the quad.

For a split second, Taylor couldn't move. Her feet seemed melded to the ground.

As if from far away, she noticed that the Dark practitioner

was no longer standing across the street. She could hear the others exclaiming. Looking for him.

And then she was running.

She was vaguely aware of noises around her. Of someone hurrying after her. Calling her name. The first police cars screeching to a stop at the gate.

But she didn't look back. She threw herself to her knees beside Sacha's crumpled body.

'Sacha,' she whispered, her voice thin and airless. 'Sacha, no.'

His head was twisted at an unnatural angle. His eyes, open and sightless, stared over her shoulder. His skin was a bloodless grey; his lips faded to blue.

He was dead.

♊

Shivering, she knelt down on the walkway in the shade of the ancient building, Sacha's hand cold and lifeless in hers.

'Is he hurt?' Panting, Louisa dropped to her knees next to her.

'He's dead.' Taylor's voice was dull.

'*Dead?*' Louisa stared in disbelief. 'He can't be dead.'

Reaching across Sacha's body, she grabbed his other hand, pressing her fingers hard to the inside of his wrist.

There was a pause.

She dropped his hand abruptly. It landed on his chest with a hollow thump Taylor felt in her own heart.

'Don't do that,' she snapped, straightening his hand gently to what looked like a more comfortable position. 'He'll be fine.'

'Fine?' Louisa's voice rose. 'How can he be . . . Oh.'

Realisation dawned in her eyes.

There was a pause.

'So . . . What happens next?' Louisa asked carefully. 'Does he just . . . wake up?'

Taylor squeezed Sacha's hand. 'Yes. Kind of.'

Louisa stared down at him doubtfully. It struck Taylor that, even though she understood the curse, it still wasn't truly real to her. How could it be? Even Taylor found herself doubting it would really happen. That he'd really come back.

No breath lifted Sacha's chest. No red tinged his skin. His heart didn't beat. Everything that was Sacha had stopped.

She took a deep, steadying breath.

'He'll be fine,' she said again, reassuring herself.

'What's happened?' Dean Wentworth-Jones walked up behind Louisa and stared down at the damaged boy at his feet. 'We've lost Mortimer. What's wrong with him? Is he hurt?'

Louisa stood and dusted her hands against her shorts. She looked dazed.

'He's dead.'

'*Dead?*' The dean sounded shocked.

'He'll come back,' Louisa reminded the dean, although her words lacked conviction.

Taylor didn't want to hear the discussion of doubt and analysis that would inevitably follow. She felt oddly protective of Sacha.

'Could you just . . . leave us alone?' she asked.

'I beg your pardon?' The dean stared down at her with an expression of deep disapproval.

'This is kind of private,' she said, standing her ground. 'Could you go talk somewhere else?'

Jones looked at Louisa as if she could explain Taylor's behaviour, but the blue-haired girl just shrugged.

'I think not,' he said finally.

Taylor had never considered that he might refuse. Unconsciously, her fingers tightened around Sacha's cool, unresponsive hand.

She turned to look up at Jones. He was so tall, she had to twist her neck to see his long, aquiline face, narrow and (it seemed to her) arrogant.

'Excuse me?' she said.

'I believe it would be beneficial if we were to see how the process works.' The dean's tone was firm, clinical and void of any empathy. 'I think some of the others should see this as well. My assistant can handle the authorities. And Mortimer appears to have fled.'

Looking back towards the line, he motioned for someone's attention.

'Alastair,' he called. 'Come quickly, please.'

Taylor shot Louisa a furious look, but the other girl shook her head. The dean made the rules.

A fire truck had now pulled up, and was unfurling a long length of hose to spray the smouldering ruins of the building. The police were talking to a group of professors, who seemed to be explaining what had happened, no doubt making it sound like a disastrous – but perfectly unsuspicious – accident of some sort.

Alastair galloped across the courtyard to join them, his

shock of blond hair backlit to gold by the late afternoon sun. His face was ruddy from the fight.

'What's up?' he asked, looking from the dean to Louisa.

'I thought you should see this.' The dean nodded at Sacha's body. 'The boy's died. And we're waiting for him to come back to . . . well, life.'

Taylor turned away, so she didn't see how Alastair received this news. But she heard it.

'*Dead?* Oh Christ.' Alastair knelt next to Sacha's body, across from Taylor. Carefully, he lifted Sacha's hand to feel the lack of pulse for himself. Finding nothing he set the hand back where it had been with great care. His face crumpled.

'Dammit, Sacha,' he said. 'What the hell?'

'He'll be fine. Or so I'm told.' The dean seemed impatient with Alastair's display of emotion.

But the graduate student ignored him and looked across the motionless torso to Taylor.

'Will he really be OK?'

He looked scared, and she was touched by his gentleness, and by how genuinely upset he seemed. Out of everyone, he was the only one who'd reacted as she thought they should.

'I think so,' she said. Her throat was dry – her voice emerged raspy and afraid.

'How long will it be?' he asked. 'Before he comes . . . back?'

'I don't know,' she said. 'It changes, each time. It's getting longer. Last time it seemed to take forever.'

'That is most unfortunate.' The dean looked back towards the gate. 'The police and fire departments are here and we don't want them to notice this little situation.'

*Little situation?*

Taylor fought the urge to tell the dean exactly what she thought of him; but before she could say a single word, Alastair distracted her.

'How does it work?' he asked, drawing her attention back to Sacha. 'Does it hurt?'

Biting her lip, she nodded. 'I think it's very painful. That's one of the worst parts of it.'

'Shit.' He rocked back on his heels. 'That wasn't what I wanted to hear.'

Alastair swore a lot – it was one of the things Sacha liked best about him. The two of them were always hanging around together. Alastair had taken Sacha under his wing from the start and, to Taylor's surprise, Sacha hadn't seemed to mind. In fact, she got the impression Sacha was starting to see him as a surrogate big brother.

He'd even started swearing in English from time to time.

'We're here for you, Sacha,' he said now, resting one hand on his shoulder. 'We won't leave you . . . '

At that moment, Sacha's body arched backwards with such violence, Alastair gave a startled cry, snatching his hand away.

'It's beginning,' Taylor said grimly.

They watched with horrified fascination as Sacha's figure contorted, arching one way and then another. His body made awful wheezing gasps as his lungs struggled to fill. His long, slim fingers clawed at the stone beneath him. The lids of his eyes squeezed shut, his lashes black as coal against his dust-white skin.

'Bloody hell.' There was shock in Louisa's voice.

A second later, Sacha's eyes sprang open, brighter now, and staring at Taylor with sudden recognition. He opened his mouth so say something just as another spasm racked him and his face grimaced with pain.

'Dear God,' the dean murmured, moved, despite himself, to care.

Taylor had seen this process before but this, if anything, was worse than last time. She covered her mouth with her fingers, willing him to breathe, to *live*.

'*Merde*,' Sacha groaned, before adding with breathless lack of believability, 'Sorry. I'm . . . fine.'

Taylor wanted to speak, but her voice refused to work properly and the words she longed to say came out as a wisp of breath.

Across from her, Alastair's face looked pale and horrified. Louisa was speechless for the first time since Taylor had known her.

Sacha's body arched backwards again, further than seemed physically possible and then jerked forward forcefully, with a suddenness that made them all jump, until he was sitting bolt upright.

Sweat covered his face, and colour had flooded back into his cheeks.

*Please let that be the end*, Taylor silently begged whatever demon or deity was doing this to him. *Please stop.*

Whether or not her internal prayer was behind it, Sacha took a deep, shuddering breath, and turned towards her.

'Taylor?' His voice was hoarse. 'Are you OK?'

Relief flooded through her. She threw herself across to him and took his hand in hers. It was warm.

'Am *I* OK? I can't believe you'd even ask that,' she said, smiling through unshed tears. 'You nearly … You died.'

'I know. That old bastard killed me.' Rubbing the back of his neck, Sacha turned to Alastair. 'Who *was* that? And what the hell did he hit me with? It felt like a tank.'

'That was Dark power.' It was the dean who answered. 'And it is very interesting to me that you survived. It would have killed any one of the rest of us in an instant. This proves you cannot be killed by any means. Even Dark power.'

Turning, he motioned crisply to Louisa and Alastair.

'We have much work to do. Everything is moving very quickly now. Come with me.'

# SEVEN

'Are you really fine?' Taylor studied Sacha doubtfully. His skin was still unhealthily pale and, with his hair greyed by dust and soot, he looked ghost-like.

'I'm really fine,' he insisted.

The others had hustled off in the direction of the dean's offices; the rest of the professors were dealing with the fire department. Sacha and Taylor walked slowly across the empty college. His usual cool slouch was absent, and it seemed to her he moved with caution – testing each step as if afraid to find the ground unsteady.

'Maybe you should see a doctor – get checked out,' she suggested.

He shot her a look of withering disbelief.

She capitulated. 'Fine. Forget it. No doctors. Sorry I mentioned it.'

'Look,' he said, 'I'm just thirsty. Dying always makes me thirsty. Let's go get something to drink.'

Taylor knew they should be going back to their rooms – before she'd gone, Louisa had admonished them both to get inside right away. But she didn't argue with him.

The fire alarms had finally been switched off, and St Wilfred's grounds were uncannily quiet. With the stone spires and cloistered walkways, it was like being alone in a castle. It was nice to be by themselves.

'What happened back there?' Sacha cast a sideways glance at her. 'Why did you walk towards him? Was he hypnotising you or something?'

Taylor, who hadn't yet worked out that answer for herself, stared across the empty quad. Golden blades of late afternoon sunlight stretched towards them.

'I don't really know,' she admitted. 'I can't explain it. Whatever that was, I couldn't fight it at all. I don't even remember walking. I remember that cane, the snake, its horrible eyes . . . and all of a sudden I was in front of him. If you hadn't grabbed me, I think I might have walked right up to him. Sacha, he would have killed me.' She took a sharp breath. 'And I would have let him.'

Sacha stared. 'Why? I don't understand.'

'I don't know,' she said again, a defensive edge to her voice. 'I've never experienced anything like it. It was incredibly powerful. It took over everything. It's like I wasn't me anymore.' She shuddered. 'It was terrifying.'

More than a minute passed before either of them spoke again.

'At least you know what to expect now,' he said. 'Next time you'll be ready.'

All the tension of the afternoon coalesced into that one phrase. The one thing that wasn't true.

'I'm not ready to fight him, Sacha,' she said. 'He is unbelievably powerful. I can't even lift rocks. You have to accept it. I can't beat him.'

'Don't say that.' His voice was sharp. 'Don't say you can't.' She opened her mouth to argue but he talked over her. 'You're not weak. You can't be' – he raked his fingers through his hair with frustration – '*fatalist. Merde.* I do not know the English word.'

Taylor rounded on him.

'What do *you* know about it? I'm telling you he is unbeatable and your response to that is "*you're fine*"? That's just bollocks.'

They stopped walking.

'You're twisting my words. That is not what I said,' he argued.

'Yes it was.'

They glowered at each other.

'Well, maybe if you and the other alchemists didn't shut me out of everything, I might have more useful advice,' he snapped.

She rolled her eyes. 'What does that even mean?'

'You know what it means.' His voice rose. 'You go out and train without me, leaving me locked up in the library. You all stand around watching me die and come back like I am an experiment to be studied. It's horrible. Inhuman.'

'Nobody is experimenting on you.'

'Well,' he said, folding his arms. 'Not you. You're off with Louisa all the time, training.'

It was the wounded look in his sea-blue eyes that did it.

As quickly as it began, the storm passed. Taylor took a half-step towards him.

'Oh Sacha, I'm sorry,' she said. 'I don't know why I got angry. You're right. It is horrible.'

He let out a long breath.

'It's not your fault,' he conceded, softening. 'But I have to tell you the truth – I don't like it here, Taylor. Aside from you, the only person who's nice to me is Alastair. Everyone else treats me like a freak.' He kicked a pebble off the path. 'I hate it.'

'They treat me that way, too,' she said, thinking of the stares and the whispers.

'No they don't.' He held her gaze. 'You're one of them. I never will be.'

She couldn't argue with that.

'I meant what I said earlier,' he continued. 'I didn't want to be insulting, or pretend I know everything. But you *can* defeat him.'

Taylor's throat tightened.

She longed to believe him but she felt so defeated. Her actions had got him killed today. And the Dark practitioner had controlled her like a puppet.

'How do you know that?'

'I know *you*.' Unexpectedly, he reached for her hand, pulling her closer. 'I know how strong you are. That's all I need to know.'

They were so close she could feel the heat of his body. Smell his scent of soap and dust.

It was hard to breathe when he was so near – her lungs seemed to stop working properly.

He moved even closer. Near enough to hug. Or to kiss. Did he want that? Did *she* want that?

'Please don't be angry, Taylor . . .' he whispered, and she felt his breath on her face, warm and soft.

'I'm not angry.' Her lips parted to say something else, or to kiss him – she wasn't sure which. His proximity made it hard to think all of a sudden. His hand began to slide up her arm.

'Oh good, there you are.'

They jumped apart guiltily, and turned to see Alastair walking towards them from the direction of the administration building.

'I've been looking for you everywhere.' His tone was mild, but his eyes were knowing.

Taylor's cheeks burned.

'We were just talking,' she heard herself say, and she could have kicked herself.

His eyebrows winged up.

'I've been sent as a messenger boy,' he said, as if she hadn't spoken. 'The dean wants you to head over to his office. Says there's something you need to know.'

♊

When they reached the imposing lobby of the administration building, the sun was beginning to dip, sending long shadows across the grey marble floor.

The place was usually packed with professors and school administrators, but now the lobby had a hollow, empty feel. Rows of orderly columns held up an ornate plaster ceiling that soared high overhead. Enormous windows let in a flood of fading lemony light. Even the art was intimidating – the walls held huge oil paintings of tall-masted ships atop roiling grey-blue waves. Somewhere, in an office they could not see, a phone rang and rang, unanswered.

All the way there, Taylor remained silent, trying to figure out what had just happened. Had they really been about to kiss? Or maybe not? Was he just being nice?

Sacha's expression gave nothing away – he was walking alongside Alastair, always just a few steps ahead of her.

What if he was embarrassed? What if she'd misunderstood the signals and now he didn't know how to tell her he didn't like her that way?

*Oh God*, she thought with a sudden flash of icy conviction. *That's probably it.*

She didn't know what had made her think he wanted to kiss her. They'd never been anything other than friends. He'd put his arm around her from time to time when she was upset, but that was all.

She'd just misunderstood. Now he wouldn't look at her.

God, what was wrong with her? The school was about to be destroyed, they were all about to die and she was thinking about kissing Sacha who didn't even like her that way.

*I'm in shock*, she decided. *Or maybe I'm having a nervous breakdown.*

That would be her excuse if Sacha brought it up later.

*'Sorry I tried to kiss you,'* she would explain. *'I was having a nervous breakdown.'*

They hurried up the wide, sweeping marble staircase. Alastair and Sacha took the steps two at a time. Taylor fell behind.

By the time she reached the top, the others were already heading down the long corridor to where Louisa stood with the dean outside his office. As Taylor turned to follow them, her phone buzzed in her pocket. She pulled it out hurriedly and glanced at the screen. It was a text from Georgie:

`Bored and trying to decide what colour to paint my nails. Sunset Lava or Organic Fuchsia. HELP.`

The message might as well have come from another planet.

She shoved the phone back into her pocket without responding.

The hallway ahead of her was lined on one side with portraits of all the former deans at St Wilfred's. The first images were paintings of fierce-looking men and women in old-fashioned clothing. After a while, there were no more paintings – photographs took over. At first black and white, then, colour. The last image was of the current dean, who stood watching her now.

Tall and thin in a dark blue suit, Jones was a little apart from the students, hands clasped behind his back, his pale, angular face impossible to read.

Ever since she'd arrived at St Wilfred's, Taylor had been trying to decide whether or not she liked him. He was consistently polite but distant. She had the feeling he was watching her closely. Judging her.

She hadn't liked how he'd handled Sacha's death, but she had been impressed by his actions in battle. He'd been an avenging warrior – fearless and ferocious.

She'd never seen that side of him before.

'Good,' the dean said as she neared. 'We're all here. Now we can begin. I'm not going to make you wait to find out why you're here.' His cool blue eyes swept the circle of faces. 'Today, we learned who we are up against. We are up against Mortimer Pierce.'

He pointed at the photograph hanging on the wall next to his own image.

The man in the photo stood in front of a desk. He had thick dark hair and a thin moustache. He looked deeply ordinary. Taylor took a step forward to see his face more closely. The photo was more than a decade old. The man's hair was grey now, and his face no longer smooth and unlined. But, those were the same small, dangerous eyes.

She heard Louisa's quick intake of breath; Alastair swore under his breath.

So they hadn't known either.

Taylor turned to the dean, apprehension settling in her chest like a stone. 'Why is his picture on *this wall*?'

'Mortimer Pierce was Dean of St Wilfred's until fifteen years ago,' Jones explained calmly. 'He disappeared after he left the college. And now we know why.'

For once lost for expletives, Alastair stared at the dean with disbelief on his tired face.

'Tell me this is a joke, Jones. Come on.' But the anger in his voice said he already knew it wasn't funny at all.

'I wish it was,' the dean said quietly.

'*Dammit.*' At his sides, Alastair's hands curled into fists.

Louisa stepped forward, eyes blazing. 'How did we miss this?'

'We always knew we were up against an insider.' Jones' voice was steady. 'I never once suspected it could be Mortimer. How could it be him?'

For a fleeting second, there was real emotion in his expression, and he turned away, rubbing a hand across his face.

'All right, let's think this through.' Louisa took a deep breath. Calming down. 'This explains everything. How he got past our defences to Aldrich. Why he knows so much about how we work.'

'But it doesn't explain what happened today,' Alastair pointed out. 'His strength was exponential. That thing with the cane – that's not alchemical.'

'That was demonic energy.' The dean raised his head. 'It had to be.'

There was a pause as they absorbed this.

'Demonic . . .' Louisa exhaled.

'Incredible,' Alastair said.

Their earlier rancour was forgotten. They were a team again.

Taylor couldn't believe it.

'That's it?' She stared at them. 'You're all over it now? A dean of St Wilfred's turned Dark and you didn't know? A dean murdered my grandfather? And you *didn't know*?'

Her angry voice echoed in the quiet building.

Instead of replying, Jones pushed open the door to his office and motioned for everyone to follow.

'Come in,' he said. 'I'll tell you all I can.'

# EIGHT

The dean's office was cool and austere, with the clean, lemony smell of furniture polish. A modern desk dominated one end of the room; the school's red and gold flag stood in a corner nearby.

Jones directed everyone to a table at the other end of the room.

Sacha lowered himself into a chair across from Taylor and looked around guardedly. Taylor was biting her lip, her brow creased. Louisa and Alastair sat together at one end.

Alone at the opposite end of the table, Jones set a manila folder down in front of him.

'I will get to the hows and the whys in a moment, but first I want to tell you that our goal remains the same. We must understand the curse that threatens Sacha.' His gaze flickered in Sacha's direction. 'We must stop it from coming to pass. We are still fighting the same battle. Now we have something we lacked before: knowledge.'

He glanced at Louisa and Alastair. 'I know what the two of you are going to say. But for now, we must focus on keeping the college safe. We must continue to immerse ourselves in research. There will be no hunt for Mortimer Pierce in the short term – first we will need to understand the demonic power he used today. And prepare.'

'You can't be serious.' Louisa's expression was incredulous. 'We don't have time to read books. Mortimer Pierce has to be stopped. He's one of us. He knows how we work, our practices, our plans, where we *live*. He can walk right through our defences. We have to go after him *right now*.'

'I am fully aware of what Mortimer knows,' Jones said. 'Nonetheless, we must approach this situation in a calm and professional way. We have two hundred and fifty students who need us to keep them safe. You saw what we were facing out there today. We can't fight that. We don't even know what it is.'

'We will *figure it out*.' Louisa's voice rose sharply.

'At what point?' the dean asked. 'And at what cost?'

'The problem is, we haven't got time for anything else,' Alastair said.

'We must approach this rationally—' the dean began but Louisa cut him off.

'Your bloody rationality will get us all killed.'

'Oh, stop being so dramatic.' Jones' voice grew icy. 'Louisa, Aldrich may have been endlessly patient with you, but I am not going to let you say anything you want, whenever you wish. If you're in a meeting, you must behave.'

Louisa's face reddened. For the first time, Sacha felt sorry for her. The dean, he felt, was being unduly harsh. Also, he thought Louisa was completely right. They'd done nothing but research for weeks. It was time to fight or die.

Before he could say any of this, though, Louisa stood up, her hands on her hips. With the dark tattoos snaking down her arms and up her bare legs from her ankles, even in denim cut-offs and a vest she looked like a pagan warrior princess.

'Screw your rules.'

'Please sit down, Louisa,' Jones said. 'Let's keep this civilised.'

But Sacha could see she wasn't about to back down. Every muscle in her body was tense.

'Our lives are being destroyed and you want us to stay *civilised*?'

'As a matter of fact,' the dean responded, 'I do.'

'Well you're an idiot, then,' Louisa said. 'I'm not going to sit here and have a business meeting about Mortimer Pierce. I'm going to go find him.'

She stormed from the room without looking back, the angry thumps of her biker boots against the marble floor fading slowly in the distance.

Alastair half-stood, as if to follow her, but the dean stopped him.

'Please wait, Alastair.' There was weariness in his tone. 'I'll need you to tell her later what we discussed. She will want to know.'

Alastair hesitated then, with slow reluctance, sat again.

'She's not wrong, you know,' he said. 'You were too hard on her.'

'I will give her views due consideration,' the dean said with a sigh.

Sacha decided now was the time to enter this conversation.

'I just want to know how you are going to stop Mortimer Pierce. What if it had been Taylor he killed today, instead of me? This is . . . ' He paused, searching for the right English phrase. '. . . a mess.' It wasn't the phrase he wanted, but it would have to do. 'I thought we were safe here.'

'I'm afraid, Sacha, you are not safe anywhere. Not as long as Mortimer Pierce is alive.' The dean opened the file folder. 'You see, Pierce is one of the most brilliant alchemists I've ever met. He was a professor when I was a student.' His gaze settled momentarily on Taylor. 'Your extraordinary power, Miss Montclair, is a natural gift bestowed by your lineage. Mortimer's gift is the product of sheer determination and a brilliant mind. He truly understood the science of what we do. He read the histories of alchemy, studied the ancient manuscripts. His intellect was voracious. He became assistant dean while still in his twenties, and then dean fifteen years later. He was on a fast track to the very top. Until something went wrong.'

They'd all fallen quiet. Even Alastair had tilted his long frame forward as if hanging on every word.

'Our rules strictly limit how we can use our abilities, as you know,' Jones continued. 'We cannot influence government or courts. Our work must be benign and scientific. That has been the situation for hundreds of years. Mortimer broke those rules. He came to believe in a new natural selection. The extra gene we all share – he believed it represented evolution in practice. He once told me, "We are modern gods."' Jones shook his head. 'The more he studied, the more he believed in this mad theory. That we are not just unique – we are destined to rule. We alchemists are . . . God.'

His fingers toyed with the folder.

'Inevitably, he went too far. He challenged the board of governors. He threatened the life of a former dean who dared to speak out against the dangers of his teachings. Eventually, the board voted to remove his tenure and deny him teaching rights. The move was unprecedented. The greatest humiliation imaginable.'

Sacha waited for more, but Jones had fallen silent.

'When did he go Dark?' Taylor asked.

'That's the problem,' Jones said. 'We didn't know until today that he had.'

He picked up the top paper from the file in front of him.

'For a time after his dismissal, Pierce stayed in Oxford. In fact, we believe he lived here for three years before disappearing. He claimed he was relocating to London to pursue other interests, but I now suspect this was when he began researching demonic techniques in earnest. In the subsequent years, he visited alchemical institutes in Germany, Spain, Morocco and France, conducting research in their libraries. It seems obvious now that he was looking for something quite specific. A book that could tell him how to raise a demon.' He closed the file carefully, neatly. 'And what's more than clear, too, is that somewhere along the way he found what he was looking for.'

Hearing it explained like that made it all sound so simple.

As simple as a sharp knife sliding into a body. As simple as murder.

Taylor had been listening to all of this intently. 'You're saying he studied demonology. He found books telling him how to do it. He tried it, and it worked. Now he's one of them. It was that easy?'

Sacha could hear the shock in her voice.

'That is what we believe,' the dean conceded. 'The ancient books offer two paths to power. One is through science. The other is through Dark practices. Demonic power is an extreme form of this – one I've never seen used in this way.'

'Well . . . How do we fight that?' Taylor asked. 'Today it was like we just couldn't handle him.'

'This is why we must turn our attention to research,' the dean told her. 'To understand how to defeat him.'

'Oh for God's sake, Jones.' Alastair slammed his fist down on the table. 'You were out there today. You know we can't hide anymore. We can't wait for help or advice. It's too late. Louisa's right. All we can do is fight.'

'We will fight.' Jones looked unhappy. 'As soon as we have the weapons to do it with.'

Alastair held up his hands. 'And when will that be?'

'Soon.'

But Sacha could hear the doubt underlying that one word. And it seemed to him the dean didn't know what to do.

♊

After the meeting ended, Sacha and Taylor walked out of the admin building together, talking soberly. She tried to convince him to go to the library with her, but he made up an excuse to get out of it.

'I just need some fresh air,' he said. 'I don't want to go back in there yet.'

When she disappeared into the safety of the huge building, he headed towards the front gate to see for himself that Mortimer was really gone.

His phone buzzed. He glanced down to see a message from his sister, Laura. Seeing her name sent a sharp shard of homesickness to his heart.

`Are you OK?` *`Maman`* `and I are worried. Please stay alive.`

He texted back quickly – if he didn't reply he knew she'd pester him constantly until she heard he was okay.

`I'm fine. It's been a very boring day. I hate libraries more than ever. You stay alive, too.`

After sending the message, he put his phone away and tried not to think of home. Of warm Paris streets, and the soft sofa. Of watching TV with Laura, and then getting into trouble with Antoine.

It had never seemed possible that he would miss that life. But he did.

When he arrived at the front gate, workers in high-visibility jackets had already begun repairing the damage. Temporary fencing covered the hole in the wall. Lights had been set up to illuminate their work. The fire was out, but a faint acrid smell of smoke still hung in the air.

All the emergency trucks had gone, save for two vans from the gas company – the 'official story' was that the explosion had been caused by a gas leak.

Louisa and Alastair stood near the damage, heads close together, deep in conversation.

Alastair looked up as Sacha approached.

'Sacha.' He sounded surprised. 'What are you doing here?'

'Looking for the man who's trying to kill me.'

'He's long gone.' Louisa's tone was brusque. 'Unfortunately.'

Frowning, Alastair glanced over Sacha's shoulder. 'Where's Taylor?'

'Library.'

'By herself? Is Jones *deranged*?' He turned to Louisa. 'He's leaving them alone now? When Mortimer could be anywhere?'

'He's not deranged. He just doesn't want to see what's right in front of him.' Louisa raked her fingers through her short blue hair. 'One of us needs to stay with her. And it can't be me – I've got things to do.'

Their eyes locked. Sacha could sense an unspoken struggle between them. Finally, Alastair threw up his hands.

'I'll keep an eye on her.' He shot Louisa a warning look. 'But don't you dare go out on your own.'

'How could you suggest I'd ever do such a thing?' She was all innocence, but Alastair wasn't buying it.

'It's *dangerous*, Lou,' he said. 'If you leave the grounds, take someone with you. Don't go alone. Promise me.'

'I promise,' she said, not bothering to hide her irritation. 'All right?'

'Why don't I believe you?' he said with a sigh.

She smiled at him. 'You've got no faith. That's your problem, Alastair. Lack of trust.'

He didn't return the smile.

'You're going to get yourself killed one day, Lou.'

'Never.'

Giving up, Alastair turned and loped towards the library, his worry still evident in the set of his broad shoulders.

Louisa exchanged a few words with the workers, then turned to Sacha.

'Let's go,' she said briskly. 'We've got a demon to catch.'

# Nine

'Where are we going?'

Sacha couldn't keep a hint of puzzled irritation out of his voice. They'd been walking for ten minutes without stopping and he was still tired and weak from dying.

Louisa strode ahead across the darkened college grounds, her hair glimmering blue every time she passed through a pool of light before fading again when she slipped into darkness. Even in the shadows he could make out the tattoos that swirled up her arms and around her calves, inky black against her pale skin.

He didn't really know why he was following her. He was sick of all of her crap.

'First we're going to search the college and make sure Mortimer Pierce left nothing behind him.' Louisa spoke without looking back at him. 'No nasty little demonic presents.' She shoved open the door to the history building with such force it thudded against the wall. 'Then we're going to go find him.'

Sacha stared at the back of her head.

'Find who? *Mortimer*?'

'Who else?' She stormed down the long narrow corridor, past empty classrooms, looking in each one and then speeding to the next.

Still trying to process what she was saying, Sacha lagged behind.

'You can't be serious. We're going to look for him alone? You and me?'

Already at the end of the corridor, Louisa turned into the stairwell. Her voice echoed hollowly.

'Alastair said I couldn't go on my own. So I'm not. I'm taking you with me.'

It was too much. For Sacha, the anger and frustration from a long, exhausting day finally boiled over.

'Like hell you are,' he replied heatedly. 'I am not leaving this college to fight the man who just killed me three hours ago, all because you're not getting along with the dean, OK? *T'es complètement tarée, ma pauvre.* Fight him yourself.'

Turning on his heel, he headed for the door.

Louisa's biker boots thumped on the floor as she ran after him.

'Hang on. Don't take off. Hear me out.'

There was something new in her voice – a kind of plea.

Sacha hesitated. The door was right in front of him. He knew he should throw it open and storm out. Rush to the library and tell Alastair what she was doing.

But he didn't. Some part of him wanted to go with her, whatever the risk.

'We're not going to try to take him down.' Louisa stood in the dim corridor, watching him. The demanding tone had been stripped from her voice. She was just talking. 'All I want to do is locate him, then call the others to come get him. I can't do it alone, Alastair's right. I need someone to back me up.'

'That's it?' Wavering, he eyed her suspiciously. 'You swear it?'

She held up her right hand. 'Honest to God.'

Sacha couldn't figure her out. One minute she was treating him like a child. The next, she was doing things like this.

'I'm not going to fight him,' he told her.

'No one's going to make you.'

There was no hint of deception in her voice.

'Then why do you need me?'

She paused. 'I promised Alastair I wouldn't go alone. Anyone else would call him. Besides. You're the only person I know who can't die.'

*Well*, Sacha thought, *at least she's honest.*

He let go of the door handle. 'Fine. I'll help you.'

She looked relieved. 'Good.'

'But call me "kid" one more time and I walk.'

A slow smile spread across her face. 'It's a deal.'

They exchanged a look then, not of friendliness exactly, but of complicity. Like thieves who understand each other's reasons for stealing.

'First, though, we need to make sure the college is safe,' she said. 'I could use your help with that, too.'

He gave a careless shrug. 'Of course. I'm not busy, as you can see.'

She grinned. 'I like it when your English goes crooked.'

Turning she headed up the wide, empty staircase. He followed her, frowning.

'That was crooked?' he asked. 'What was crooked about it?'

'Hard to explain,' she called over her shoulder. 'English is a weird language.'

After that they got to work.

On each level, Louisa repeated the speed search process she'd done on the floor below, half-running down the empty corridor, quickly glancing in each room. Sacha followed her, looking for anything out of place.

He paused to peer into a shadowy classroom where rows of chairs were neatly aligned facing a podium. The rooms with their arched, leaded glass windows seemed a thousand miles away from his modern school back in Paris.

He'd never taken a class at St Wilfred's. All he'd done since they arrived was research his own history. Nobody else's seemed to matter.

Now looking at these rooms where students learned and laughed and grew up, he felt left out. Left behind.

'Hurry up, Sacha,' Louisa called, and he wondered if he'd ever heard her say his name before.

It was quieter up here. And darker. He moved cautiously across the old oak floors. To his right, Louisa peered into each room, her stance alert and cautious.

In the protective darkness, Sacha studied her curiously.

'I know why I'm doing this, but what about you?'

He expected her to tell him to mind his own business, or to make some insulting joke about French people not understanding things.

But she didn't do either of those things.

Stepping inside a small room, she motioned for him to follow. It was a professor's office, typically dishevelled, with books stacked nearly to the ceiling. A desk took up most of the small space, sagging under untidy stacks of paper. An umbrella leaned against one wall.

Louisa stood by the empty chair. In the gloom, he could barely make out the outline of her features – the blue of her hair, the glimmer of her eyes.

'I am doing this because no one else will.' Her voice was low but intense. 'And because Aldrich Montclair would want me to find the person who killed him. So that's what I'm going to do. And I'm going to make sure the bastard pays.'

She rested one hand on the back of the empty chair, touching it almost tenderly.

Suddenly Sacha knew whose office this was.

Stepping back, he checked the nameplate on the door: 'Aldrich Montclair'.

'This is Taylor's grandfather's office.'

It was so quiet, he could hear the brush of Louisa's bobbed hair against her shoulders as she nodded.

'It *was*.'

He looked around with new curiosity. He had never met Aldrich – knew very little about him. But Aldrich and his father had been friends. He found himself looking more closely at the black-and-white photos on the walls. He tried to read the words on the spines of the books stacked on the shelves.

Nobody had talked about it, but he knew it was very likely Mortimer Pierce had killed his father, too. He knew just how Louisa felt.

If she was getting revenge, he was going with her.

Abruptly Louisa let go of the chair, and pushed past him. When she strode down the hallway, Sacha was right behind her.

Her words floated back to him in the dark.

'Let's go get him.'

♊

At night St Wilfred's seemed even stranger to Sacha than it did during the day.

Unfamiliar faces in countless paintings peered out at him from the gloom as he walked with Louisa down a darkened corridor in the admin building.

He suspected the dean would not have been happy to know they were walking through this building at this hour, and he was certain he'd have been furious if he knew why. But Louisa didn't betray any doubts. Her steps were steady and quick as she led the way down shadowy concrete stairs into a basement level and through a heavy metal door.

The door slammed behind Sacha with a thud and he instantly regretted letting it close. The room on the other side was pitch black – too dark to see anything at all.

He promptly collided with something large, heavy and invisible.

'*Putain*,' he swore, grabbing his knee. 'Where are the lights?'

Louisa didn't respond. He couldn't see her. Couldn't even hear her footsteps.

He held his breath, trying to detect anything at all in the black cave.

Everywhere he turned he ran into things – heavy, huge things. And a faint but unmistakeable scent of petrol hung in the air.

In the silence, the faint click of the light switch seemed to ring out. The overhead lights buzzed, and flickered on.

Blinded, Sacha blinked. He was completely surrounded by cars.

There was a subterranean parking garage beneath the admin building – and he'd never known. In all the days he'd been at St Wilfred's he'd never been able to figure out where they kept his bike. Now he spun a slow circle looking for it.

He spotted it almost immediately, parked in a corner.

Happiness made his heart stutter and – forgetting Louisa and Mortimer – he raced over to check it, crouching next to it to run his hands across the glossy black metal curves, murmuring to it in French, 'God, I've missed you.'

To his relief, the Honda appeared undamaged. His two silver helmets had been left neatly on the seat.

Everything was there, except the keys.

Just as he clocked that, Louisa walked up behind him, a set of silver keys shining in one hand.

'Waddya reckon? Want to go for a ride?'

Sacha snatched them from her fingers.

'I'll take that as a yes,' she said dryly.

Handing her a helmet, he pulled his own over his head. The world shrank to the size of the visor's narrow eye-slit. He liked it that way.

Louisa climbed onto the back of the bike with ease – placing her feet in the right places without being told. She'd definitely been on a motorcycle before.

For some reason, that didn't come as a surprise.

Sacha turned the key and flipped the ignition switch – the bike roared to life.

He sat still for a moment, just listening to the rumble of the engine – the sound seemed to come from inside him. From his heart.

'*Alors*,' he said in French before remembering to speak in English. 'Where do you want to go?'

'Just get us out of here,' she said.

He guided the machine out of the parking spot, heading towards the closed garage door. Only then did it occur to him he had no way to open it.

He was half-turning to ask Louisa what to do when she reached over his shoulder. The door rattled upwards, and he saw the lane outside, stretching towards the lights of town. And freedom.

He popped the clutch and gunned the engine. With a roar, they sped off into the night.

# TEN

*Late in the night, Henri fell into a deep sleep from which he cannot be roused. It is a rest like the dead. The apothecary says only time will decide whether he wakes or leaves this earth into God's mercy.*

*At first light, we rode to the old church and sought the chamber he described in the ancient crypt. There we found all as he told it – the star, the dagger. Many signs of blood-letting and sacrifice.*

*The Brotherhood was most distraught at the sight. We have seen sorcerers and encountered many servants of evil in our time together, but never have we witnessed a sight of such devilry and Dark madness.*

*At our request, the white sorceress Marie Clemenceau joined us. What she saw in that unspeakable place turned her skin pale as milk.*

*'It cannot be possible,' she whispered, reaching down to touch one of the stains on the old stone floor.*

*'Tell us,' Brother Claude urged her, 'what does this mean? We must know the truth of what we face.'*

*When he showed her the ceremonial dagger – with its curved blade and handle of carved bone and jet – she flung her hands in front of her face and recoiled from the instrument.*

*'This is the Darkest sorcery,' she said. 'The most evil and deadly power. In this very chamber, a convocation would call on the devil.' She turned to me, her lovely face pained and fearful. 'Matthieu, you must stop this.'*

*'I promise I will stop it,' I said. 'But I must ask you a question and I require as true and honest an answer as you can give.'*

*Still trembling, she raised her face. 'I will answer truly.'*

*'Could Isabelle Montclair be the one communing with the demons?'*

*For a single moment her eyes held mine and I saw the truth there. Then, overwhelmed, she collapsed, and only through God's grace was I able to catch her before she struck the ground. I removed her from that evil place forthwith ...*

Pushing the book away, Taylor rubbed her eyes.

For hours she'd been reading the heavy, leather-bound book – an eighteenth-century translation of a French book from Aldrich's collection. It was the only known book that told anything useful about Isabelle Montclair. Even so, it was only so helpful.

She didn't think Aldrich had believed it was real. A few

minutes ago, she'd come across a terse note he'd left between the pages. 'Overwrought and unlikely.'

She ran her fingertips across his familiar jagged handwriting. He was right, as usual.

She'd have given anything for him to be here now. To tell her what to do. She felt so lost. Everything was so dangerous, and they were running out of time.

The library was filled with books – thousands of them – about alchemical history. They would never get through them all. Never find the right ones.

It was so frustrating.

She pressed her fists against her eyes.

'You should take a break,' Alastair advised from across the table.

Relaxing her hands, she glanced across to where he sat, a book open in front of him. He'd appeared about twenty minutes after she got here, and he'd been sitting there quietly for hours, making notes into his laptop.

The pale blue glow of the screen highlighted the circles under his eyes.

'You're tired, too,' she pointed out. She reached for the cardboard cup at her elbow. The coffee was cold and bitter, but she made herself drink it. She had to stay awake.

Picking up her phone she glanced at the time – it was after midnight. The last text she'd received had been from her mother two hours earlier:

```
Good night, darling. We miss you. xx
```

Her heart twisted in her chest.

Not for the first time it struck her that if her mother had any idea what she'd been up to today, she'd yank her back home so fast the dean would see nothing but the dust from her tyres.

But she didn't know.

She scrolled down to check her other messages. There was nothing from Sacha. She'd not heard from him since she left him on the steps of the admin building.

For a second, her finger hovered over the text button. Then stopped.

He was probably asleep. Dying always wore him out. She didn't want to wake him.

With a sigh, she dropped the phone back down on the table.

She stretched, loosening the kinks in her shoulders.

Alastair typed something into his phone before throwing it down in a motion that mirrored her own.

'Where's Louisa?' Taylor asked, guessing who he was trying to reach.

He glanced at her, surprised. His straight blond hair was always unruly but at the moment it was standing almost on end. He kept raking his fingers through it.

'Searching for Mortimer.' His tone said what he thought of that.

'What? On her own?' Taylor's eyebrows shot up.

'She's not on her own. She *promised me* she wouldn't go on her own.' But he didn't sound convinced. His fingers drummed the table next to his phone.

'Maybe you should call her?' she suggested.

He picked up his phone and held it for a second before setting it back onto the table.

'If she's in the middle of something it'll just piss her off.' He let out a long breath, and leaned back in his chair. 'I'm sure she's fine. She knows what she's doing.'

It sounded like he was trying to convince himself.

Taylor studied him thoughtfully.

'You really like her. Don't you?'

He shot her a withering look.

'You know what I mean,' she said. 'You're friends. Louisa doesn't have many friends.'

'No, she doesn't,' he conceded. 'And, yes. We're friends.' As he spoke, he picked up a pen and tossed it in the air. It spun for a long time – longer than should have been possible. 'Always have been.'

'She likes you, too,' Taylor told him. 'I can tell.'

Snatching the pen, he set it down on the table with enough force to make it bounce. 'Yeah, well . . .'

He turned back to his laptop, signalling an end to the conversation.

Taylor let it go.

For a while after that they got back to work, but Alastair kept picking up his phone. Glaring at it as if that would somehow make her text back.

Finally, Taylor set down her book.

'Look. Why don't you just go find her?'

He shook his head. 'Someone's got to look after you.'

'You know what? I really am capable of sitting in a library by myself. I've been doing it since I was six.'

She didn't try to hide her irritation.

His lips twitched. 'Steady. I know you can sit still all on your own. But things really are not safe right now.'

'You think I don't know that? I was there today. I've been here for weeks. I survived Bringers. I'll be fine with *books*.'

'I am fully aware of that.' His tone was measured. 'But Mortimer could walk into this college any time he wants because he is one of us. He could walk into this library right now. All he has to do is slip past the guards. And it's dark outside, Taylor.'

He was right. She leaned back in her chair.

'OK, OK . . . ' she said. 'I'm sorry. I don't mean to take it out on you. I just . . . I don't like that you let Louisa go off on her own because of me.'

'She's not on her own,' he said. 'I think, anyway.' He thumped his forefinger against the book in front of him. 'I just wish I could get something out of *this*.'

Taylor glanced at it – now that she could get a good look at it, she saw how old it was. The leather binding was worn and frayed. The cover bore odd symbols in badly faded gold. It wasn't in any language she recognised.

'What is it?' she asked. 'I thought it was Greek at first, but it isn't, is it?'

He shook his head. 'Not Greek. Something else. A very old alchemical language – well, that's what we suspect, anyway. We thought for a while it might have all the answers but we haven't been able to crack it.' He shoved it across the table towards her. 'Take a look. Maybe you can make sense of it. I'm losing hope.'

Hesitantly, Taylor reached out towards the book. She'd handled a few alchemical books and she knew what it felt like to hold them – a kind of low-grade electrical buzz. Like standing underneath a power line.

But this one was different. She could sense it even before she touched it. It hummed with energy. It seemed to draw her to it.

Slowly, with a kind of fearful fascination, she lowered her hands to the book. The air above it crackled. She had the strangest sense the book *wanted* her to touch it.

Her hands hovered, hesitating.

Alastair looked at her quizzically.

'What's the matter?'

'I don't know,' she whispered.

He straightened, instantly alert. 'What do you feel?'

'I can't describe it,' she said, her fingers still just above the leather. 'It's like it's . . . calling me.'

'Wait.' He reached for the book. 'Don't touch it.'

He was too late. The pull of it was impossible to resist. Her hands seemed to move of their own volition, leaping towards the book before he could take it away.

The energy hit her like a tidal wave. Her heart began to pound, her hair flew back from her face as if blown by a sudden wind. She drew back with a gasp, but couldn't lift her hands from the book – they simply wouldn't let go.

Alastair leaned forward slowly, watching her with fascination. 'What's happening, Taylor? What do you feel? Describe it.'

Her hands were vibrating. The book seemed almost to writhe in her grasp.

'It feels . . . *alive*,' she said slowly. 'So . . . much . . . power . . .'

Without warning, the book shot out of her grip and slid across the table.

Drawing in a sharp breath, Taylor collapsed back in her chair, clutching her hands to her chest.

'What was *that*?' She stared at the book.

'I have absolutely no idea.'

Cautiously, Alastair reached for the book, sliding it across the table towards him with the base of his pen.

'I've spent weeks trying to understand what the symbols in this book mean. I've picked it up and carried it everywhere. It's never done anything like *that*.'

They both stared at the book on the table between them. It appeared benign now. Nothing but paper and ink. But Taylor was staying well away from it.

Alastair considered her with a new curiosity. 'There has to be a reason why that just happened. It can't be a coincidence.'

Taylor stared down at her hands. The sensation of power and electricity still seemed to tingle in her fingertips. She felt shaken and somehow exhilarated.

'Maybe we should try that again,' Alastair said.

'The young lady must not touch the book.'

The voice – authoritative and German-accented – came from behind them. They both spun around.

An elderly man stepped out of the shadows. His face was lined and his hair white, but his carriage was upright, and he moved at a sprightly pace. He looked back and forth between them, his eyes dark and intelligent. 'Where did you get that book?'

'Professor Zeitinger . . . I . . .' Alastair sounded awe-struck. 'I found it. In the Bodleian. When I was researching for Aldrich Montclair. You know, the French curse.'

'No one informed me of the finding of this edition.' The professor's voice made the statement an accusation. 'Germanic alchemical texts from the medieval period are overseen by me.'

'But . . . Professor.' Alastair frowned. 'It's not German.'

'Of course it is German.' The professor jabbed his finger at the book. 'Are you telling me you don't know what this is?'

Alastair shook his head in bewilderment.

'No.'

'I've spent my entire career studying these symbols.' Zeitinger's voice was low. 'I have searched the world for this book for many years.'

Alastair's eyes widened.

'Professor. What is this book?'

'*The Book of Unravelling*.'

There was a pause, and then, unexpectedly, Alastair began to laugh.

'Bloody hell. I am such an idiot. Jones will garrotte me when he finds out.'

'*Unravelling* is one interpretation of that word, of course,' Zeitinger continued, as if he hadn't spoken. 'It could also be translated as Undoing. Reversing. Untangling. The language of the time was imprecise.' He peered at the two of them. 'This book was believed lost for centuries. Possibly destroyed. Are you telling me it was in the library all this time?'

Alastair opened his mouth to answer, then closed it again. His shoulders shook with suppressed mirth.

'What is so funny, young man?' the professor asked disapprovingly. His W came out as V. *Vot is so funny.*

Alastair's slapped his hand against one knee as he tried to get control of himself.

'It was,' he gasped at last, 'misfiled.'

'That is an outrage,' Zeitinger tutted. That only made Alastair laugh harder.

Mystified, Taylor looked back and forth between the two of them.

'I don't get it,' she said. 'What is this book?'

The professor turned his focus to her. Beneath thick, white eyebrows, his dark eyes were deadly serious.

'You are Aldrich Montclair's granddaughter, are you not?'

She nodded hesitantly. 'Yes ... '

His expression softened, infinitesimally. 'I am Professor Wolfgang Zeitinger.' He tapped the air just above the book cover, never touching it. 'Young lady, this book is the missing piece in a very dangerous puzzle. Your grandfather searched for it everywhere. It's likely he died for it.'

Her stomach lurched. 'I don't understand. Why would someone kill him for a book?'

'This book was written by a German alchemist who studied the Dark arts,' Zeitinger explained. 'He came closer than any of us to understanding Dark power. How it could be used. And how it could be broken.' He pulled his hand away from the book. 'For us, this could be the key to life. And death.'

He snapped his fingers. 'We must hurry. Give me something to wrap that book in – paper. Or fabric. No one should touch it.'

'Yes, professor.' Alastair rushed off in search of the supplies.

'I still don't understand.' Taylor stood next to the elderly man, trying to comprehend what was happening. 'What is it about the book that will help us?'

'The discovery of this book is incredibly dangerous,' the professor explained as Alastair returned and began wrapping the book in paper, careful not to touch it. 'If Mortimer Pierce learns the book has been found he will kill us all. It is only our own ignorance that has protected us thus far. And now we have lost that.'

When the book was wrapped, the professor picked it up gingerly, motioning for them to follow.

'We must hurry.'

♊

'Is it true?' the dean asked as he strode through the door of his office. 'Have you found it?'

He wore no tie, but, as always, his white shirt was crisp and his suit un-creased. Taylor, who had never seen him wearing anything else, was starting to wonder if he slept in a suit.

Alastair and Professor Zeitinger both began talking at the same time.

'We didn't recognise it . . . ' Alastair said.

'How could this have happened?' demanded Professor Zeitinger, still furious about the misfiling.

'Stop, both of you.' The dean held up his hands. 'How and why are insignificant at this point.' He turned to Zeitinger. 'Wolfgang. Is it the book?'

The professor held his gaze.

'It is the book.'

Jones ran a hand across his face. There was a kind of awe in his expression.

'Where is it?'

Zeitinger stepped to one side. The book lay on top of Jones' desk, papers spread around it.

Jones reached out hesitantly before drawing back his fingers again.

'I can't believe we finally have it.'

'It is a miracle,' Zeitinger agreed softly. 'I genuinely believed it was destroyed.'

'All this time . . .'

The dean looked at the elderly professor, who finished the thought for him.

'. . . it was right under our nose.'

'Taylor,' Alastair said, as if suddenly remembering something important. 'She reacted to it when she touched it . . .'

Jones' head snapped up. 'She *touched* it?'

Alastair winced. 'It was an error. We didn't know what it was. I had no reaction to it at all when I touched it. No one had, up to that point. Aldrich knew it was important but he hadn't identified it as *the* book.'

'What was the effect?' Jones asked.

'I saw it all.' Zeitinger stepped forward. 'The power of the book recognised the power in her.'

Jones' cool gaze swung to Taylor.

'When you touched it, what did you feel? Did any thoughts come into your head?'

Taylor thought of the rush she'd felt.

'Just power,' she said. 'And maybe . . . anger? It happened

fast.' She looked at the dean. 'Why is the book so deadly?'

'Most of what we know is apocryphal,' Jones said. 'By that I mean, it's part of lore, but no one is certain if it's true. We believe the book was written by a German alchemist named Cornelius von Falkenstein in the seventeenth century. His sister was drawn to Dark power, seduced by it. She attempted to raise a demon and was killed in the process. Falkenstein wrote this book as a kind of revenge. But the professor is the expert.'

He glanced at Zeitinger, gesturing for him to take over the story.

The professor stepped closer to the book. 'The two siblings were very close. Her death broke his heart. Falkenstein became obsessed with Dark practice. Not as his sister had been – he did not seek power. He was obsessed with destroying it.'

Although his voice was not loud, his words somehow filled the quiet space.

'He practised day and night,' Zeitinger continued. 'Documenting his successes and failures in an archaic alchemical code he invented himself, hiding his findings so that no one else might be injured by trying to replicate his work. The Alchemical Council – which at the time set out the rules and laws for our kind – forbade his experiments but he ignored their restrictions. His research went further than anyone had ever gone before, stepping to the very brink of madness.' His glasses glittered. 'In the end he was forced to stop. It was too dangerous. No one knew what he might unleash. We still don't know. Condemned by the Council as a madman, he was imprisoned in an asylum for the remainder of his days. His research was believed destroyed by those who suppressed his work. However . . . ' He glanced back at his desk, where the leather-bound book lay on the stack of papers, as innocuous as an encyclopedia. ' . . . persistent rumours always maintained that it existed. That it was never destroyed, but rather hidden in the home of one of the Council leaders.'

'Now we know those rumours were true,' the dean said.

Taylor's skin tingled, remembering the promise of sheer, unbridled power that had surged through her.

'Can this book help Sacha?' she asked.

'That is the hope,' Zeitinger said after a moment. 'But hope will only get us so far.' He turned to Jones. 'I should start work immediately.'

'Of course,' the dean replied. 'What do you need?'

'A room with a locked door. An assistant . . . ' The elderly professor glanced at Taylor. ' . . . and Miss Montclair. Who reacted to the book as if she recognised it. And it her.'

# ELEVEN

Sacha and Louisa roared through Oxford's dark tangle of streets.

Occasionally Louisa called out directions, but mostly she was silent as he navigated the bike. Her eyes searched the quiet medieval lanes that twisted and turned between high, stone walls, past churches with soaring steeples and the jagged spires of Oxford colleges.

She was hunting.

While Sacha could see only dark streets and bright lights, to her it was much more vivid and elemental – golden streams of alchemical power were everywhere, lighting up the night. It poured off the river, from the electricity wires, from the wind. The molecular energy was limitless and constant.

But it wasn't alchemical power she sought. She was looking for Mortimer.

‘Where are we going?’ Sacha shouted to be heard over the noise of the engine.

‘Take a left ahead,’ she directed him. ‘Then turn right after St John’s.’

‘What’s St John’s?’ he shouted back.

Louisa winced. Of course he wouldn’t know even an obvious landmark. He hadn’t left the college since he arrived.

‘Never mind,’ she said. ‘I’ll direct you.’

He was a good driver, she thought, alert and focussed, even after everything that had happened today.

It felt good to be on a motorcycle again after all these years. To hear the wind whistling around them, feel the engine rumbling beneath her so that she felt almost part of it.

It reminded her of Tom and the squat in Liverpool. In a flash she could see it – the dirty walls, scrawled with meaningless graffiti, bare mattresses on the floor, lit by electricity powered with a wire strung illegally from a nearby flat. The place had been a firetrap. Cold in the winter, smelly and hot in the summer. But for her it was safety. Safety from the foster family that tormented her.

Tom’s motorcycle had represented freedom, and she’d loved riding it. She’d thought she was safe.

Then everything went wrong.

‘Which way?’ Sacha shouted.

Louisa blinked. They were nearing a junction. It took her a moment to get her bearings.

‘Turn right.’

She tried to sound authoritative but she was kicking herself. This day was getting to her. She had to be more focussed.

What if she'd missed Mortimer back there while she was lost in the past?

*The past doesn't matter*, she reminded herself. *The past can't hurt you, if you don't let it. You stop the pain by forgetting.*

She leaned forward studying the city with new intensity. The streets were largely empty at this hour, although occasionally they passed a nightclub, and Sacha would steer carefully around large clusters of students, dancing, shouting.

At one point, a bearded hipster in a flannel jacket lunged drunkenly towards them on a brightly lit corner, hands reaching out for the slow-moving motorcycle.

'*Fous-toi, salaud*,' Sacha growled.

His fierceness seemed to penetrate the haze of alcohol. The man backed off warily as the bike sped away.

'I'm not even going to ask what you just called him,' Louisa said dryly. 'Turn left.'

Still grumbling under his breath, Sacha turned into the narrow, dark road she indicated.

There were fewer street lights here. Their headlight illuminated nothing but grey stone. Suddenly she knew right where they were, in the tangle of streets behind the Bodleian Library.

Louisa leaned forward, peering over Sacha's shoulder, looking into the shadows.

That was when she sensed it. Unmistakeable and putrid.

Dark power.

Her breath caught.

'Slow down.'

Responding instantly to the urgency in her voice, Sacha slowed the bike to a crawl.

'Turn right.' She closed her eyes, searching again for its source. It was hard to pin down. It was close and then far. Right around them and then gone.

It took her a moment to realise what it was.

*He's underground.*

They had to get off the bike.

'Park there.' She pointed to a space where the wall was indented – forming the perfect hiding space.

Sacha cut the engine. Leaping nimbly from the bike, she pulled the helmet off in one smooth movement and set it on the ground. Strands of turquoise fell around her face and she shoved them back impatiently.

Her heart was pounding. She knew just where he was. His energy had led them straight to him.

*I should call Alastair now*, she thought, with a twinge of guilt. *We can't take him alone.*

But she didn't reach for her phone.

Ignoring the warning voices in her head that told her she shouldn't be doing this alone, she strode to a low door tucked into the thick ivy covering a stone wall. It bore no number, but a symbol had been carved into the wood – a triangle with a circle inside it.

When she pressed her hand against the battered wood of the door, it swung open instantly.

She glanced back. Sacha was still astride his bike, the keys in his hand, watching her guardedly.

She was almost starting to like him. It had taken balls to

stand up to her tonight, and even more nerve to leave the safety of the college and go out after the man who had already killed him once today.

Maybe she'd misjudged him. At any rate, she was about to find out.

'He's nearby. I can sense him,' she said. 'Are you in?'

For a split second he hesitated.

Then he climbed off the bike and set his helmet on the ground. She saw him rest his fingers reassuringly on the side of the sleek, black motorcycle.

Then he straightened, and followed her through the door into the unknown.

♊

The door led to a stone staircase, which they followed down into a dark, narrow space. Water dripped somewhere in the distance, the air was dank and cool.

Louisa pulled out her phone and turned on the flashlight. A tunnel sprang into view.

She looked around cautiously – but there was no immediate sign of Mortimer's energy. Using her last sighting of it as a guide, she decided to turn right, towards the library.

'This way,' she whispered to Sacha, and her words echoed around her.

*This way . . . way . . .*

Every word was magnified. Each footstep reverberated off the ancient stone wall and ceiling. Even their breath seemed to reflect back at them – like the walls themselves were breathing.

'Where are we?' Sacha whispered.

She glanced at him.

'Medieval tunnels.'

'You think he's down here?'

He sounded doubtful, and she couldn't blame him. Now that they were here, she could find no hint of Dark power. In fact, she sensed nothing but the golden energy of water running beneath and around them.

Where was he? She'd been so certain.

'Let's go a little further,' she said.

It wasn't an answer, but he let it go.

Just ahead, the tunnel narrowed and Sacha dropped behind her. They walked for a while after that in silence. Then he spoke again, his voice low and serious.

'Can I ask you a question?'

'I can't stop you.'

'Why do you hate me?'

She kept walking. Were they really going to do this right now?

'I don't hate you,' she said shortly.

'Then why do you act like you do? This is the first time I can remember you not being a bitch to me. And I don't know why. What did I do?'

Louisa stopped and swung around to face him.

'Look, ki ... Sacha. Sometimes you need to be a bitch to stay alive.' Her voice echoed back at her off the stone.

*Alive, alive ...*

Sacha looked at her earnestly.

'I am not your enemy, Louisa. I'm on your side. Or at least, I'm trying to be. If you'd let me.'

Closing her eyes, Louisa sought scraps of patience.

'I don't hate you,' she said. 'I really don't. When we first met, I guess maybe I blamed you for all of this.' She gestured at the tunnel around them, the light from her phone swinging wildly. 'But I shouldn't have. I know that's not fair.'

It was as close as she ever got to apologising. Being sorry made her skin crawl.

But he didn't know her well enough to hear it as an apology. He stared into the darkness at the end of the tunnel.

'I blame myself, too.'

He said it so quietly, his words were nearly lost behind the dripping water and the sound of their breathing.

'I wish there was something I could do to stop this,' he continued, not meeting her eyes. 'I'd give myself up to Mortimer right now if it meant Taylor would live and this would be over. But it wouldn't, would it?'

He glanced up at her.

'No,' she admitted. 'It wouldn't.'

'So. All I can do is what I'm doing.' His voice held a weary maturity beyond his seventeen years. 'I want to live, Louisa. I want Taylor to live. And all of you. I want to fight with you. But if you decide you still hate me, I can't blame you.'

Caught off guard, Louisa struggled to think of something to say. Taking her silence as condemnation, he walked past her into the shadowy tunnel, his shoulders slumping.

'Forget it.'

She ran after him, raising her voice. 'Hey ki . . . I mean . . . Sacha. Look. I'm sorry. Wait up.'

She found him some metres ahead. He'd stopped next to an ancient wooden door.

'Hey. I didn't mean . . . ' she began.

Then she felt it. Very faint, from the other side of that door. But unmistakeable.

All thoughts of apologising evaporated.

'He's here.'

Pressing the palm of her hand flat against the door Louisa closed her eyes and concentrated. On the other side she could sense the energy of electricity in the walls, running water beneath her feet, molecules of air. No alchemists. No people.

But something dark and dangerous lingered there.

Adrenaline raced into her veins like fire.

*I've got you, you bastard.*

With delicate precision, she urged the tumblers in the lock to turn.

The door opened with a groan.

After the damp tunnel, the room on the other side seemed to shimmer like a mirage. It was warm and dry. Expensive looking rugs lay scattered on the stone floor. All of it was illuminated in the soft glow of modern wall sconces.

She saw Sacha's jaw drop.

It was time to call Alastair.

But when Louisa held up her phone, there was no signal.

*Of course*, she thought, her heart sinking. *We're underground.*

They were going to have to do this alone.

Putting her phone away, she stood in the doorway, scouring the air, the walls, *everything* for Dark power. It was there, but faint.

Stepping inside, she motioned for Sacha to follow. 'Come on.'

The tunnel was wider on this side. Their footsteps were

soundless on the thick pile of the rugs. Doors led off here and there – Louisa paused for a moment outside each one, and then moved on.

She kept losing all sign of the energy, and then finding it again, always faint. As if it was flickering.

It was odd. Dark power shouldn't work like that.

Doubt made her stomach curdle. This didn't feel right.

But what if this was just a matter of distance? They were still underground. What if he was above them? The levels of earth and rock between them could be making his energy impossible to read.

They needed to go up.

She began to run.

'Wait,' Sacha hissed, scrambling to keep up. She could see the bewilderment in his expression. 'What is this place? Are we back at St Wilfred's?'

'This is the Bodleian Library,' she told him, without slowing her pace.

'Why does a library need tunnels?'

She didn't have time for this.

'Do I look like a bloody librarian?'

They'd reached the door to the stairwell. Louisa stopped, pressing her fingers against it.

'Nothing in Oxford is what it seems,' she said. 'I thought you'd have noticed that by now.'

She shoved the door so hard it thudded against the wall. Ahead, a utilitarian staircase spiralled up. The only light came from the watery green glow of fire escape signs at each level.

In the hollow silence, Louisa kept trying to sense Mortimer. If he was in this building, he'd know she was here, the same way she knew he was here. She had to find him fast.

But his energy was still ephemeral – as if flitting in and out of the building. It didn't make sense. He couldn't be here and not be here at the same time.

At least she'd been right about the layers of earth separating them. She could sense the Dark energy more clearly now. They were getting closer. Too close.

She felt jittery, excited, scared. She shouldn't be doing this. She should have called St Wilfred's when she first got off the bike. Now her phone had no signal and it was too late for anyone to get here in time anyway.

The thought made her chest muscles tighten. She'd seen what Mortimer could do. She didn't think she'd win this fight.

That didn't mean she'd back down.

When they reached the ground floor, she shoved open another door. The room on the other side was huge – ceilings soared above row after row of towering shelves stacked with hundreds of thousands – maybe millions – of books.

Mortimer wasn't there.

Turning towards Sacha, Louisa pointed to a fire exit on the opposite side of the room.

'Look,' she whispered rapidly. 'He's close. It's too late to get help. There's a good chance Mortimer will kill me before I can kill him. You can't fight him. I think you should go now. Get back to St Wilfred's.'

His face hardened. 'No.'

'Sacha . . . '

'Do you actually believe I'd leave you alone with him?' His lips tightened. 'I'm staying.'

She really had misjudged him all along.

'Well, I guess you're as stupid as I am,' she said.

It was a compliment. And to his credit, he knew it.

'I guess I am. Hey, let's go down fighting.' His grin was rakish. 'I always wanted to say that just before a fight. Let's go down fighting, Louisa.'

'If it's all the same to you, I'd prefer to win.' She pointed to a long, dark corridor that exited the big room on their right. 'If you're not leaving, we need to go that way.'

They took off at speed. The hallway was lined on either side by offices. As they ran, she caught glimpses of tables in dark polished wood, towering bookcases, office chairs.

There was no time to look more closely, because she could feel the Dark energy all around them. From the strength of it, Mortimer should be right in front of them. But she couldn't see anything.

'Where is he?' Sacha whispered, as if reading her thoughts. 'Are we close?'

At that moment, the door next to them crashed open and a huge man stepped directly into their path.

'Yeah,' Louisa said. 'We're close.'

Her voice was calm but her heart was in her throat. The man was enormous. And he was suffused with Dark power.

They backpedalled wildly. Sacha swore, stumbling in his haste.

The creature must have been seven feet tall, with shoulders so broad he filled the entire doorway in which he stood. He wore all black. Louisa barely had time to take him in. In the shadows and chaos, she thought she saw strange symbols in the flesh of his neck and arms.

That was all she had time to observe before, with a roar, he turned on them.

She shoved Sacha with all her strength.

'*Run.*'

# TWELVE

Louisa's push sent Sacha sprawling out of the way, just as the creature reached for him with its huge, meaty hands.

By the time he'd scrambled to his feet, bewildered, the library had turned into a scene from a nightmare. Louisa darted back and forth across the shadows – a flash of blue, luring the huge creature (*Because it was a creature, wasn't it? It couldn't be a man. Not looking like that . . .*) away from Sacha.

'I'm the one you want,' she shouted at it, whenever its attention turned towards him for even an instant. 'Come get me.'

She held out her hand, focussing. Sacha couldn't see it, but he knew she was trying to summon alchemical energy to fight it.

The thing paused for a second, shuddering. Then, as Sacha watched, horrified, its gaping mouth curved into an awful smile. It swung at her with such force he could hear its fist whistling through the air.

Louisa dropped to the ground, rolling out of reach, springing to her feet some distance away, and held out her hand again, her face pure concentration.

Ignoring her, the thing turned towards Sacha. Swallowing hard he raised his fists, but his hands suddenly seemed like such tiny, feeble things compared to the creature's giant swollen appendages.

For a moment they locked eyes. Sacha thought he saw something like recognition in that grotesquely swollen face.

And hunger.

'Oi!' At the other end of the corridor, Louisa waved her arms wildly. 'Over here, *thicko*.'

In his fear and confusion, for a split second Sacha thought she was talking to him.

With an inhuman snarl, the thing lumbered heavily towards her. Each footstep seemed to shake the building on its foundation.

Again she waited, focussing her power. Again it shuddered. Then its huge fist swung towards her, faster than before. More viciously. At the last possible moment, she ducked.

Only this time she waited too long. Its fist connected with her shoulder. The force of the blow flung her into the air so hard she hit the wall before sprawling on the floor near where Sacha stood midway down the corridor.

As the creature paused, staring stupidly at the space where she'd been moments before, Sacha raced to Louisa's side.

'Are you OK?'

'Bloody hell,' she said, rubbing her shoulder. 'What *is* that thing?'

'I don't know.' He helped her to her feet. 'But I think it recognised me. Let's go in here.'

Together, they ducked into a dark doorway.

'What do you mean it recognised you?' In the shadows, Louisa's brow creased.

Sacha tried to explain. 'It looked at me like . . . it's hard to say . . . Like I was the one it was looking for.'

Louisa stared over his shoulder to the corridor beyond.

'I guess it makes sense,' she said. 'It probably works for Mortimer. Like the Bringers. Only much more stupid.'

'Why do you not use your ability to fight it?' he asked.

At the end of the hallway, the creature had begun to turn in their direction.

'I threw everything I had at it,' she said. 'The thing almost seemed to . . . I don't know. Like it.'

'How is that possible?' he asked, disbelieving.

'No freaking idea.'

Sacha didn't know what to think. If Louisa's abilities didn't work against it, the thing would kill them both. It was twice their size, and it seemed to be getting faster. And no one knew they were here.

They were alone with a monster.

'What are we going to do?' They stood together, watching the thing search for them.

'Give me a minute,' Louisa said. 'I'm working on a plan.'

But they didn't have a minute. The thing had spotted them. It began lumbering in their direction.

It was very dark, but it seemed to Sacha something was different about it.

'Is it . . . growing?' he heard himself ask faintly.

'It can't be . . .'

Louisa didn't have time to say more before the creature lunged at them with a guttural growl.

'Go left,' she shouted at him.

With no time to think, he did as she said, hurtling out of the doorway. When he didn't hear footsteps behind him, he turned back.

Louisa had run in the opposite direction. Now she raised her hand towards it, trying one more time.

Sacha thought he heard her mutter, 'Will you just bugger off?'

Again the thing stopped for a moment and quivered – it seemed to Sacha it could feel whatever she was sending at it. But it didn't hurt. Without warning it spun towards her, swinging hard.

This time, though, Louisa was ready. She leaped out of reach, running behind it at top speed, and ending up close to Sacha.

As it had before, the thing paused, a stupefied expression on its face.

Louisa was breathing heavily. Perspiration beaded her forehead.

'I'm throwing all the power I can at it. It's like it's just *absorbing* it.'

They watched as the creature shuddered. Its bulk stretched the seams of its black trousers and short-sleeved shirt. Now they could see more clearly the symbols branded on the skin of its arms and face.

'It *is* growing,' Louisa said, staring. 'Isn't it?'

Sacha wanted to say no. He didn't want any of this to be possible.

'Yes,' he said. 'It is.'

The creature peered into the darkness towards them. Its gaze locked onto Sacha. That sickening hunger filled its eyes, and it began running towards them.

'Sod this,' Louisa said. 'Let's get out of here.'

Grabbing the sleeve of his t-shirt unceremoniously, she yanked him with her towards the deeper darkness at the end of the hallway. Behind them, the thing gave a roar of rage and thundered after them.

It was getting faster, Sacha thought, but it wasn't fast enough to catch them. They ran through the darkness, past rows of doors until the hallway ended abruptly in an elegant circular atrium.

A blue wash of moonglow flooded in through skylights high overhead. In that ghostly light, Sacha could make out an elaborately tiled floor beneath their feet, and arched doorways leading in four directions.

Louisa pointed to the one on the left. 'That way!'

Sacha thought she looked pale and drained, but that could have been the light. There wasn't time to worry about it – the thing's footsteps were getting closer. They ran together into the shadows of the narrow hallway she'd indicated.

The hallway turned into another hallway, and then a third. Louisa led the way, turning left, then right, then left again. Finally, they couldn't hear it chasing them anymore.

'In here.' She skidded to a stop in front of a door. They

rushed into a room, shrouded in darkness, and she closed the door behind them and locked it.

For a second they stood still, trying to catch their breath. Sacha pressed his ear against the cool wood of the door. He could hear nothing outside.

'I think we lost it,' he said, relieved.

Louisa didn't reply. Instead, slowly, and with surprising grace, she slid to the floor.

'Louisa? What's wrong?' He crouched next to her, struggling to see her face in the darkness.

'I don't know.' Her voice was hoarse. 'I feel weak. I think that thing . . . I think it did something to me.'

Reaching into his pocket, Sacha fumbled with his phone until he got the flashlight to work.

The room sprang into view – a cluttered storage space filled with empty wooden tables, bookshelves and stacks of old chairs. When he looked down at Louisa, his breath caught. Her blue hair glinted around a face as white as paper.

'Oh *merde*. You look horrible,' he said. 'We have to get help.'

'I'm . . . fine,' she insisted. 'Just need . . . a second.'

Her words came in short bursts, her breathing was shallow.

Sacha crouched on the floor next to her. 'What is it, Louisa?'

'Been trying to . . . figure it. Every time I . . . try to manipulate . . . energy . . . it gets stronger. I get weaker.' Her hair clung to her damp cheeks. 'It's stealing my energy. Draining me.'

The first strands of real panic tightened around Sacha's lungs. Pressing the flats of his hands against his forehead he tried to think.

'We don't even know what it is,' he said, thinking aloud.

'And those marks on its body – like burns. What do they mean?'

Louisa pulled herself up a little. Sacha was relieved to see her breathing becoming more normal, although she still looked pale.

'It's Dark power,' she said, wiping the sweat from her brow. 'I can sense Mortimer on them. It's faint. But it's there. Whatever it is . . . it's his. And I can't fight it.' She pulled out her phone, her movements unsteady. 'I'm calling Alastair.'

Alastair must have answered right away, because she spoke quietly into her phone without preamble.

'Bodleian. Ground floor; medieval corridor. We need an extraction.'

Even with the phone pressed to Louisa's ear, Alastair's creative expletives were audible to Sacha.

Louisa's expression didn't change. 'Directions, please.'

He stopped shouting.

They spoke for less than a minute, Louisa briefly described the creatures. After that, she mostly listened, nodding her head.

'Quick as you can, Al,' Louisa said, quietly. It was the only sign of urgency she gave. Then she ended the call.

It struck Sacha that she looked a little better with every passing minute. Her breathing was normal now, and she was sitting easily. Still, she wasn't going to be able to fight at her usual level, that much was obvious. He needed to be ready.

Holding up his phone for light, he scoured the room, eventually settling on a battered chair with a sagging seat. Grabbing it by the back, he slammed it onto the floor as hard as he could. It shattered into several pieces.

Louisa pushed herself upright. 'What the hell are you doing? Trying to call every demonic bastard in the building?'

Sacha picked through the pieces on the floor, finally settling on a chair leg with a sharp, jagged point at one end. He tested the weight of it, swinging it in the air. It felt good in his hand.

He glanced over to her. 'If you can't use your power, we're going to have to do this the hard way, aren't we?'

She considered this. Then she held out her hand. 'Give me one of those.'

He picked up another jagged piece of broken wood. When he tossed it to her, she caught it easily.

She was shaky, but she was alert and on her feet.

'Alastair doesn't know what those things are but he's got someone looking into it now.' She bent her knees, testing her balance. 'He thinks there's an exit near us. If we're fast, we should be able to get to it.'

That was all Sacha needed to hear. He turned towards the door they'd come in through, but Louisa shook her head.

'Not that way.' She walked across the room to where a bookcase leaned against the wall. 'Help me move this thing.'

The bookcase was heavy but empty, and the two of them were able to slide it far enough to see behind it.

Behind it was another door.

Louisa pressed her ear against it for a long time, then straightened.

'Not a sound,' she whispered. 'Just follow me, OK? No matter what happens.'

Sacha wasn't about to argue. 'Agreed.'

She put her hand on the door handle.

'I just hope that thing came alone,' she said.

The door opened with a faint creak that seemed as loud as a shout in the stillness of the huge library.

They slipped out – Louisa first, Sacha right on her heels.

The long, wide hallway was empty as far as they could see in both directions. It looked fine.

And yet, apprehension settled heavily in Sacha's chest. Some animal instinct told him they weren't alone.

He turned to whisper a warning to Louisa but she was already on the move. Motioning urgently for him to follow, she darted to the right.

The darkness swallowed her instantly. Sacha sped after her, trying to move as silently as her.

Ahead, Louisa was a dark shadow in black shorts and a t-shirt, moving so fast it was hard to believe he'd just seen her collapse a few minutes ago.

They raced through the twisting hallways. There was no sign of the creatures.

Finally, after what seemed like forever, Sacha saw the pale green glow of an exit sign in the distance.

His heart jumped. They were going to get out of here.

Ahead, he saw Louisa increase her speed, flying towards the light.

She was moving so fast, she never really had a chance when the creature stepped out of a tall arched doorway, into her path.

'*Louisa!*' Sacha shouted.

But it was already too late. She ran straight into it.

Swearing under his breath, Sacha sped towards them.

The thing was holding Louisa, who struggled fiercely in its grip. She was fighting hard, but she looked so tiny, all of a sudden. The creature was *enormous*.

Desperately, Sacha danced around the two of them, looking for a way to help her.

As he moved, on the edge of panic, he slowly became aware of an ominous sound from the shadows.

*Thud, shuffle. Thud, shuffle.*

He backed away from it slowly, straining to see the source of the sound in the darkness.

Another of the creatures stepped out of the shadows.

There were two of them.

The second one looked like the first – not quite as big, perhaps, but he wore the same black trousers and pullover, had the same strange symbols scorched into his flesh. The same protuberant brow and swollen face turned towards Sacha as it scanned the corridor.

With his heart hammering against his ribs, Sacha spun to see if Louisa had spotted the newcomer just as she kicked the creature holding her so hard in the knee Sacha heard the crack.

With a roar of pain, the thing lifted one huge fist and punched her in the face.

'No!' Sacha cried.

He heard the thud as its knuckles connected.

Louisa's head snapped back. The chair leg dropped from her hands, clattering to the floor.

She didn't move again.

# THIRTEEN

'Louisa!' Sacha hurtled towards her.

The two creatures both swung towards him. Their huge, swollen faces held oddly identical expressions of dull surprise, as if they'd forgotten he was there and were delighted to be reminded.

The one holding Louisa reached out towards him with a growl of hungry excitement that turned Sacha's stomach.

It was like it wanted to eat him. Or worse.

In the thing's thickly swollen arms, Louisa was horribly still.

Gripping his chair leg, Sacha skidded to a stop. He had no idea what to do.

He couldn't take those things on alone. Louisa was twice the fighter he was, and she was an alchemist. It knocked her out with one blow.

It wasn't supposed to be like this, he thought miserably.

They'd just come to find Mortimer and leave. Now, his only weapon was a broken chair leg and he faced two monsters all by himself. Even if he managed to get Louisa from the creature, he didn't know where to go. He was helpless.

Again.

The floor shook. He looked up to see the newer of the creatures thudding heavily towards him. It was drooling.

Without thinking, Sacha braced himself, raising the sharpened leg in his hand. Adrenaline rushed into his veins, setting his heart racing.

Suddenly, he was angry. Mortimer had killed him once today. It wasn't going to happen again.

Anger has a wonderful side effect of clearing your thinking. The clouds disappear. And it becomes all about the fight.

Maybe he wasn't trained like Louisa. Sure, he didn't have the natural ability to manipulate molecules, like alchemists could. On the other hand, he very much doubted any of them had fought the toughest gangs Paris had to offer. He had. He'd stolen a car from a notorious crime boss and lived to tell the tale. He'd jumped off the roof of a five-storey warehouse and walked away.

Sacha knew how to fight.

'*Allez!*' Standing tall, he tossed the chair leg from one hand to another. Cocky. Fearless. '*Salaud.* I am not afraid of you.'

The creature's tiny eyes, half-hidden behind thick swollen flesh, glinted. It ran faster, thundering closer.

Still Sacha didn't move.

He waited as it closed in. Waited as it reached out its huge hands for him. Waited as its mouth gaped open, revealing blackened teeth. Waited until he could smell its breath – a fetid scent of rot and earth.

Only when its heavy fingers scratched at his shoulder did he move, feinting sharply to his right before cutting back hard to his left.

The things couldn't react quickly. Behind him, he heard it crash into a wall with a resounding thud that seemed to shake the building.

Without looking back, he hurtled himself towards the one holding Louisa.

It stared at him blankly, her unconscious body held loose in one hand, almost as if it had forgotten her.

With a cry, Sacha raised the sharpened chair leg and lunged.

The thing raised its free hand to block the blow, but its movements were sluggish. With all his strength, Sacha drove the sharp point into its chest.

It entered the bloated body with horrifying ease.

Landing lightly on the floor, Sacha crouched low, anticipating a blow.

It never came.

Instead, with an expression of astonishment, the creature stared down at the wooden spike sticking out of its body.

Dark blood oozed down its chest, slickening its hand, pooling around its feet.

The creature made a disgruntled, almost woeful sound, grabbing ineffectually at the stake with its free hand. This only made the bleeding worse.

Taking advantage of its confusion and pain, Sacha grabbed

Louisa's wrists, yanking her free of its grip. She landed in his arms.

The thing, its attention focussed on its wound, didn't seem to notice.

The other creature had now lumbered over to join the first, where it too yanked at the stake, in what looked like an oddly human attempt to help. Both seemed too befuddled by what had occurred to notice as Sacha carried Louisa down the hallway to the protective shadow of an arched doorway.

Her body was heavier than he'd expected – she was pure muscle. Her skin felt worryingly cool.

Laying her down on the wood floor, Sacha fumbled at her wrists, trying to find a pulse, but he'd never checked a pulse before and he didn't know how to do it. All he could feel was his own blood, pulsing too quickly through his veins.

'Louisa, please ... Please wake up,' he hissed. She didn't stir.

Unconscious, she looked much younger than she did when awake. And more fragile. At least she was breathing.

Sacha leaned out of the doorway to check on the creatures. The first one still clutched the end of the chair leg protruding from its chest. The other one was standing, hands loose at its sides.

This close, Sacha could see the marks on their flesh more clearly – the raised scar tissue around the edges where their skin had been burned. They'd been branded, he realised with revulsion, like cattle.

The wounded one crashed to its knees with a melancholy moan. Then, moments later, collapsed entirely, and lay still.

For a moment, the second creature stared at it, as if dumbfounded. Then everything changed. Roaring in rage, it abruptly abandoned its wounded compatriot, and thundered away, yanking open doors, storming inside, and then crashing out again in a frenzied search.

It was looking for them.

Forcing himself to stay calm, he leaned close to Louisa, slapping her cheek with his fingertips and whispering as loudly as he dared, 'Come on, Louisa. *Wake up.*'

On the second slap, she drew a sharp breath.

Her eyes fluttered open. 'What . . . ?'

Sacha was so relieved he could have hugged her.

Her hand flew up to touch her face, a purpling bruise had begun to bloom across her cheekbone.

'Balls,' she whispered. 'It got me.' Her voice was hoarse but strong.

'It did,' he agreed, one eye on the corridor.

The second monster was getting closer. The walls shook from its movements. It would get to them soon.

Louisa still looked shaky. They had to get out of there.

His eyes darted to the glowing exit sign at the end of the corridor. It wasn't that far – maybe fifty metres. They could make it. If they were fast.

'Things are a bit dangerous, Louisa,' he said, trying not to sound as urgent as he felt. 'We need to leave, now. Can you walk?'

Her eyes searched his face, missing nothing.

'It's coming?'

It was two doors away.

Sacha gave a careless shrug. 'You could say that.'

She held up one hand for him to help her up. He'd never known her to let anyone help her before. When she was on her feet, she spit blood on the floor and worked her jaw to test it.

'I don't think I'm broken,' she said, wincing.

She turned to look out over the corridor and her eyes fell on the dead creature, lying sprawled in a pool of dark blood.

'You've been busy.'

Before he could respond to that, a tremendous crash shook the walls, as the second creature burst out of a doorway, its swollen face red with fury.

Louisa's eyebrows rose.

'You didn't tell me he had a friend.'

'I was getting to that part,' he said.

The thing roared.

'Well, this has been fun but . . . ' Louisa pointed at the exit sign.

Sacha didn't need to be asked twice. They took off running, side by side. Sacha should have known better than to worry about her strength. She outpaced him, a blue-haired bullet shooting straight at the exit.

They had their differences, but he had to admire her sheer strength of will.

He could hear the creature snarl as it galloped after them. It sounded dangerously close, but he was already running full speed. His breath burned his throat, and his lungs ached.

Ahead, he saw the door – metal and heavy. And surely locked. He was wondering how the hell they were going to get out in time when, without warning, it swung open.

A tall, broad-shouldered figure faced them. Backlit by lamplight from the street outside, his dishevelled blond hair looked like a halo.

'*There* you are.' Alastair stared past them at the creature. 'Who's your friend?'

Sacha couldn't remember ever feeling happier to see anyone. He and Louisa shot past him out into the fresh air.

'He's meaner than he looks,' Louisa shouted breathlessly. '*Close the door.*'

Alastair slammed it shut, pressing his hand against the metal just as the thing smashed into it from the other side with an inarticulate howl of rage.

He flinched, his eyes fixed on the heavy lock.

The door held.

Gasping, Sacha bent over, his hands on his knees, struggling to catch his breath.

Now that they were safe, all his limbs felt weak – it was hard to stand. Louisa collapsed on the ground nearby, one arm thrown over her eyes, struggling to catch her breath.

The creature was banging against the door now, with such force it seemed to shake the foundations but the door didn't move.

Apparently satisfied that his work was done, Alastair strode over to Sacha.

'What the hell are you doing here?'

'Long story.' Still breathless, Sacha pointed to Louisa. 'Check on her first. She's hurt.'

Frowning, Alastair dropped into a crouch next to her.

'You look like hell, Lou. What happened?'

She waved his concern away. 'One of those things got me.' Gingerly, she pushed herself up until she was sitting. 'Sacha saved my arse.'

Meeting Sacha's gaze, she gave him a nod. 'Thanks, by the way. I owe you one.'

Pride sent heat rushing to Sacha's face. He tried to appear nonchalant.

'It was nothing.'

A series of heavy thuds interrupted them, as the creature threw itself against the exit. It wasn't giving up.

Louisa held Alastair's gaze. 'Will the door hold?'

'It'll hold.' He reached for her hand, pulling her up. 'But there are other doors. Let's get out of here.'

# FOURTEEN

Taylor woke from restless dreams to find herself in an unfamiliar room. Sunlight streamed through an arched window and she raised a hand to shield her eyes against it.

'Ah,' a German-accented voice said gruffly. 'She wakes at last.'

Startled, she jerked upright. Zeitinger sat at his desk on the other side of the room, an unlit pipe in one hand. Reaching down, she felt the soft leather of a battered sofa beneath her. Her gaze skittered across piles of books, crooked pictures on the walls, papers piled everywhere.

It came rushing back. The book. Her reaction to it. The German professor's insistence that it held the answers.

After leaving the dean's office they'd headed straight to Zeitinger's crowded little office, its bookcase heaving with heavy tomes, oil paintings of strange faces slightly crooked on the wall.

It looked so much like her grandfather's little flat that the sight of it had sent a stab of pain through Taylor's heart.

Once they'd arrived, though, the professor seemed to forget she was there – busying himself with his research, muttering to himself quietly in German.

She'd waited for ages for her part to play, but it never came.

Although she had no memory of falling asleep, at some point she'd drifted off. Glancing down, she saw that her legs were covered with a faded, red-and-green plaid blanket. It hadn't been there earlier.

It didn't appear the professor had slept at all. His hair was mussed, and he clutched the cold pipe like a lifeline. The book sat on the desk in front of him, open. A notebook covered in excited writing lay next to it.

'I'm sorry,' she said, rubbing her eyes. 'I didn't mean to fall asleep.'

'It is necessary to sleep,' he said gravely.

'Has anything happened?'

His nod held grim satisfaction. 'Progress.'

'Progress?' She sat up straighter. 'What kind of progress? Did you find something?'

He flipped through his notebook and she saw that page after page was covered in that same spidery writing.

'I have translated many chapters of the book, and can verify that I was correct.' He thumped his finger against the desktop. 'This is the book we sought.'

'Is it in there?' she asked excitedly. 'The cure for Sacha? Have you found it?'

'Not precisely.'

Some of her excitement ebbed away.

'What do you mean, "not precisely"?'

'The early chapters of the book document Falkenstein's struggle to understand Dark practice. This was as I expected.' The professor tapped the empty pipe against his hand as if emptying invisible ashes. The action was automatic and ruminative. 'It was complex and dangerous work that several times could have cost him his life. Or perhaps his soul. If you believe in such things.'

He blew on the pipe, tilting it to study it.

'Vell,' he said, his accent turning the 'w' into a 'v', 'what I now know is Cornelius von Falkenstein understood how Dark practice worked. Understood it better than any man. I think he stood on the edge of a very steep precipice and considered jumping. I think he was brave, and angry. Anger is useful but sometimes . . . it blinds us to what is worth living for.'

There was worry in the crease of his brow, in the way his gnarled hands toyed ceaselessly with that old, curved pipe as his small steady eyes met hers.

'My dear, Falkenstein proved Dark practice can be undone. But it will be dangerous. Very dangerous.'

Taylor's nerves tensed. 'Dangerous how?'

There was a pause. 'He believes undoing Dark practice will likely kill everyone involved.'

Taylor's mouth went dry.

'Everyone?' It came out as a whisper.

'Everyone.'

The floor seemed to sway just a little under Taylor's feet.

She would go through all of this to save Sacha, and then

they'd both die anyway? It couldn't be true. There had to be a way.

'But he did it, right?' Taylor pointed at the book accusingly. 'Falkenstein undid a Dark curse and lived.'

'Once.' Zeitinger's tone was sombre. 'He succeeded once. After years of trying. And we do not have time for many errors.'

'You think we can do it, don't you?' She pointed at his notes. 'You believe it's possible.'

He hesitated.

'I believe it is possible,' he conceded at last. 'But it will be the most difficult thing you ever do. You will need to be very brave.' He peered at her from beneath lowered white brows. 'Are you brave, Miss Montclair?'

She didn't think she was. Not at all. But she had no choice. If her grandfather had been right, and the curse had the potential to raise a demon that could kill everyone she loved, then this wasn't about bravery. It was about survival.

'I will be brave,' she said. But her voice didn't sound very convincing, even to her.

A flicker of sympathy crossed the professor's lined face. He set the pipe down on top of his notes.

'So.' He stood so abruptly his chair skidded back and thumped against the wall. 'We must begin teaching you Falkenstein's methods. I believe we are ready to understand how he worked, to prepare you for what awaits. First, though, I think you must eat so you do not expire. And I must speak to the dean.' He glanced at his watch. 'In one hour we begin.'

♊

Taylor ran all the way to the Newton Dormitory, and jogged up the stone staircase to her room. Her thoughts were racing.

*I can do this. But I might die. I can do this. But . . .*

Her phone battery had run out at some point during the night, and as soon as she reached her bedroom she plugged it in.

Grabbing a towel, she all but hurled herself into the shower, scrubbing her hair with more violence than was entirely necessary.

By the time she stepped out from under the water, she felt calmer. She could do this.

As she readied herself, she went over what she'd learned the night before, treating it like a science experiment or a fiendishly complicated calculus problem. If she approached it like an exam, it wasn't so frightening. She could handle an exam.

She'd finished dressing and was racing out the door when her phone buzzed loudly.

Her heart jumped. She hadn't heard from Sacha in ages. It was probably him, asking where she'd been.

She hurried back, letting the door swing shut.

But it wasn't his name she saw at the top of the message when she picked up the phone from the desk. It was her mother's.

`Hi honey. I didn't get a chance to talk to you last night. Have a great day. Do you think you can come home next weekend? I'm making lasagne. Bring your laundry. Ems sends love too. xx`

Unexpectedly, tears burned Taylor's eyes. She missed her mother so much it ached. She missed her room, her best friend, her annoying sister.

The worst part was, her mother thought she was safe here.

She held the phone up to her lips.

'I'm not safe,' she whispered. But nobody heard.

Swiping a tear from her cheek, she typed a quick reply.

`Hi Mum. Everything is fab. SUPER busy. Lots of studying. Don't know about the weekend, will ask. Have a great day! Hugs to Ems. xo`

So many lies in so few sentences.

Leaving her phone on the desk, she fled the room before her mother had time to reply.

♊

The dining hall at St Wilfred's was one of the most beautiful spaces at the school. The tables were long rows of polished oak, aligned with perfect symmetry, each surrounded by heavily carved chairs.

The school's red and gold crest was set out in stained glass in the centre of each of the towering windows lining the far wall. All other walls were panelled with polished oak, and dominated by huge oil portraits of past dignitaries, who stared down unblinking beneath the soaring, beamed ceiling.

The room was packed. The students' voices echoed deafeningly as Taylor walked in. Snippets of conversations floated around her.

'Will saw him – he said he looked inhuman.'

'They can't keep pretending it's not serious.'

'Why won't they tell us the truth?'

'It's about them, isn't it? That cute French boy and the blonde girl.'

As soon as the students spotted her, standing by the buffet table, a tray loose in her hand, a hush fell – the loud conversation was replaced with a hiss of whispers.

Keeping her head down, she resolutely piled her plate with eggs, bacon and toast from the buffet table at one end of the room, and poured herself a steaming mug of tea from a huge copper urn.

Their narrowed glares were intimidating and horrible, but she had to eat food and this was where they kept it.

Steeling herself, she took a deep breath and turned to face them. Those closest to her quickly turned away. Others were more brazen, openly staring at her.

When she spotted Alastair sitting with Louisa in the far corner, heads close together, relief flooded through her.

Motioning for her to come over, Alastair cleared books and notebooks to one side, and pushed a chair towards her.

When she was seated, he said, 'How'd things go with the professor last night?'

Taylor took a bite of egg and chewed it thoroughly. She thought it was probably best if she didn't tell them everything right now. They'd find out eventually.

'He says he's on to something,' she said vaguely. 'It's dangerous but he really thinks the answer's in the book.'

'Good,' Alastair said. 'That's good.'

He seemed to be only half-listening. In fact, they both seemed distracted. There was some unspoken tension in the air between them. Louisa, in particular, was unusually subdued, barely even looking at her.

'What's up?' Taylor frowned, searching their faces. 'Did something happen?'

Alastair made a 'tell her' motion with his hand.

'Mortimer has new minions,' Louisa said with clear reluctance. 'Big ugly ones. And they are hard as hell to fight.'

She turned to face her. The light streaming through the windows illuminated the bandage above her eye, and the ugly purple bruise on the side of her face.

Taylor's fork fell from her hand, landing on the table with a clatter.

'There was another attack?' She looked back and forth between them. 'What happened? Why didn't someone tell me? Is everyone OK . . . ?'

Louisa held up a hand to stop the stream of questions.

'It didn't happen here.' She dodged the accusing look Alastair sent her. 'I went out looking for Mortimer last night. I didn't find him but I found these new *things*.' She gestured at the stacks of books and papers surrounding them. 'Alastair and I have been trying to figure out what they are so we can know how to kill them.' She picked up her mug with a sigh. 'So far we're not having a lot of luck.'

'How bad were you hurt?' Taylor asked, examining her bruise. 'You look awful.'

'I wish people would stop telling me how terrible I look,' Louisa complained. 'It's bad for my ego.'

'The worst part isn't the bruises,' Alastair said. 'The worst part is there seems to be no way to fight these things.'

Picking up a paper that lay on the table between them, he turned it around so Taylor could see the fuzzy black-and white image it held. It appeared to have been taken by CCTV. It showed a hulking man, freakishly muscled, with strange symbols on his face and arms. His enraged eyes peered out from between bulging flesh.

Taylor turned to Louisa.

'*That's* what hit you?'

Louisa nodded. 'Not much of a looker, is he?'

'What's wrong with it?' Taylor stared at the huge creature. Even in the grainy image, its eyes were dark pits of hatred and torment.

'We've been up all night researching it.' Alastair took a gulp of coffee. 'It looks as if it was once human – until Mortimer used some intense Dark practice on it.'

Leaning forward, he tapped at the marks on the creature's skin.

'These symbols scorched into its flesh. They're used in a ceremony of reanimation.'

'Reanimation?'

'Bringing something back from the dead.'

'Bringing something back . . . ?' Her jaw dropped. 'But, that's not possible . . . is it?'

He rubbed his eyes tiredly.

'None of this should be possible,' he said. 'But here we are.'

'Mortimer can bring people back from the dead?' Taylor

couldn't seem to accept this sickening idea. 'But that means he could have an army of these ... zombies.'

'He could, but we don't think he does.' Louisa leaned forward. 'If he had an army, he'd send an army. He sent two. But there's only one left now, thanks to Sacha.'

'*Sacha?*' Taylor stared. 'What was he doing there?'

Louisa avoided her eyes.

'It was my fault,' she confessed. 'I took him out with me to look for Mortimer and—'

'You did *what*?'

Taylor couldn't believe what she was hearing. She'd thought he was sleeping and all the while ...

Panic swept over her. 'Where is he? Is he hurt?'

'He's fine,' Alastair interjected soothingly. 'Only Lou managed to get herself bashed around.'

Taylor's surprise morphed into confused anger.

'I don't understand. What was he doing there? Mortimer could have taken him. That was so dangerous.'

Louisa ducked her head. She looked incredibly guilty.

'I know it was stupid, OK?' she added with a hint of defensiveness. 'I don't know how to drive. I needed his bike.'

Taylor's jaw dropped, but Alastair jumped in before she could remonstrate further.

'It was a terrible idea. And a pretty terrible reason to have a really crappy idea. But, at least now we know what we're up against.'

Casting him a grateful look, Louisa redirected the conversation away from herself.

'These things have some major mojo courtesy of our friend

Mortimer,' she said quickly. 'He's pimped them up in his own special way. They go straight for our abilities. We direct power at them, they suck it up. It weakens us temporarily, making it hard for us to keep fighting. Easier to kill.'

'How does that work?' Taylor asked. 'Is there a way around it?'

It was Alastair who responded.

'Dark practice is the counter to our abilities in every way,' he explained. 'It is yang to our yin. It's intended to copy what we can do but it's a corrupted, demonic version of us. Mortimer has designed these things very efficiently to do that. When we fight them we make them more powerful.'

'They get bigger,' Louisa said darkly. 'Physically larger. They grow off this power. I'm sure of it.'

'I just don't see how that can be,' he said, shaking his head.

'You didn't fight them.' Louisa cut him off, and he shot her a glare.

'I would have if you'd just called me.'

Taylor got the feeling they'd been having this disagreement for a while.

'If we can't use our abilities,' she said, interrupting before the dispute became a row, 'how do we beat them?'

Holding up the picture, Louisa studied the bizarre, hulking figure.

'You kill them like you kill a human,' she said without sympathy. 'It's the only way. Fast and brutal. Go straight for the heart.'

# Fifteen

Taylor spent the rest of the day fretting impatiently in Professor Zeitinger's office.

She still hadn't spoken to Sacha. After breakfast she'd run up to his room to look for him, only to find it empty. Since then, she'd been stuck with the professor.

She wanted to talk to him – to hear his side of the story. To make sure he really was unhurt. Maybe even to ask him why he'd done such a risky thing.

But she couldn't.

It wouldn't have mattered, except she didn't know why she was there. Most of the day passed with Zeitinger muttering and making extensive notes in his tiny cramped handwriting.

After a while, she began searching for routes of escape.

'Maybe I could just dash out . . . ' she suggested as noon came and went.

Glancing up at her disapprovingly, the professor shook his head.

'We are close,' he kept saying, tapping the book with his empty pipe. 'Very close.'

Then he would delve back into his work. The office, at the top of the history building, was quiet, the only sound his pen scratching across paper. Sometimes he talked to himself when he uncovered something interesting.

'Ingenious, Herr Falkenstein,' he said once, with what sounded like genuine affection.

Outside, Taylor could hear shouts and laughter. Occasionally she caught the sound of running feet from the classroom floor beneath them. She felt cut off.

She was half-dozing on the sofa when the sound of Zeitinger's chair sliding back sharply woke her with a start.

'Now. We will try an experiment.'

Taylor sat up straight.

'I'm ready,' she said, not bothering to disguise her relief. 'What do I do?'

Over the tops of his reading glasses, he fixed her with a severe look.

'This will be dangerous, Miss Montclair. Everything to do with this book is dangerous. Especially for you. Do not take this lightly.'

The professor cleared a space on his desk, his movements methodical, until he'd freed a space of papers and clutter.

'For me it is a book of historical reference. For you?' He slid the book towards her. 'It may open the gates of Hell.'

He spun the open book around to face her.

'Please.'

Taylor stepped slowly towards him, all her earlier eagerness gone. 'What was that about Hell?' she asked with sudden doubt.

'This book contains a means of demonic communication.' All the warmth that had softened Zeitinger's countenance was gone now, he was deadly serious. 'Falkenstein's research revealed a gateway – a means of contact. But it works only for those with whom the demons wish to communicate.' He leaned across the desk. 'Last night they showed me they want to talk to you.'

She swallowed hard.

On the dark desktop the book lay open. The pages facing her were aged a dull ivory – the colour of old bones. Each page was covered in symbols. Some were recognisable alchemical symbols, others were different. The sinuous lines, and dark curving arrows seemed both familiar and yet dangerously out of place. Like an old enemy, encountered unexpectedly.

'What do I do?' She could hear the uncertainty in her own voice.

'These symbols carry a message,' the professor explained. 'I'm going to tell you what to say. The book itself will recognise you. I suspect the demon will as well.'

He made her memorise a sentence, saying it over and over until she could do it perfectly.

'If Falkenstein is right,' he explained, 'when you begin the rest of the answers will come to you. They may not be the answers you expect.'

Then he stepped back, giving her room.

'When you are ready.'

An icy dread in the pit of her stomach, Taylor reached gingerly for the book. She didn't want to do this anymore. But she had no choice.

Just like the night before, she felt the book before her fingers reached it. It had its own gravity, pulling her irresistibly. An icy breeze blew her hair back as her hands neared the paper.

'Now!' Zeitinger shouted.

Over the noise of the wind she called out: 'Lord Abaddon. I, Taylor Montclair, descendant of Isabelle, humbly beg entry. Hear me.'

She touched the pages in front of her.

All the breath seemed to leave her body. The room disappeared. Now she was falling – feet over head. Tumbling into nothing. She couldn't see anything. Couldn't feel anything except air rushing past.

She tried to scream but made no sound. She reached out but there was nothing to hold.

Then . . . darkness surrounded her, and she was still. Time stopped.

There was absolute silence. No laughter from outside the windows. Zeitinger and his office were long gone. She was utterly alone. She could not even hear the sound of her own breathing.

She was neither falling nor standing. She was nowhere. She was nothing.

An awful sense of loneliness swept over her. Of isolation

and pain. She was filled with an unspeakable agony. And a vindictive, murderous rage.

Every negative emotion she'd ever had was magnified beyond human capacity. She hated. She wanted to kill.

These weren't her thoughts, she told herself. This was something else. Something demonic.

She tried to remember who she was, and what she believed, but the real world seemed too far away to be real. *This* was real. This hate.

She didn't know how long she'd been there – it felt like a lifetime – when something spoke.

'Daughter of Isabelle Montclair. You dare petition me?' The voice was deep and hollow. It seemed to come from everywhere. From everything.

And she knew what it was.

'I do.'

Her voice sounded confident and seething. She didn't know how that was possible. It was as if someone else spoke through her.

'What do you seek?'

'Power.'

Her reply came without hesitation but she didn't know why she'd said it. The professor hadn't told her what to say if questioned.

Yet it was the truth. She was hungry for power. Starving for it.

'Why do you seek it?' the voice asked.

Again, the answer was already there, waiting for her.

'Vengeance.'

'Against whom?' The demon's voice was as emotionless as her own.

'Those who desire to harm Sacha Winters.' She knew, somehow, that fact would anger the demon.

She was right.

A roar of fury deafened her. She recoiled, but there was nowhere to hide.

'Sacha Winters is mine. You shall not save him.'

She longed to say nothing. To somehow get out of this. And yet the words came.

'I will save him.' She said each word with cold clarity. 'And I will destroy anyone who tries to harm him. Hear my words, Abaddon. You will not have him.'

The enraged roar came again. 'Lies.' A rabid fury gave his voice a razor's edge. 'You dare to tamper with the Dark arts, Daughter of Isabelle? You dare to enter my realm and challenge me?'

Terror ran through Taylor's body. She'd gone too far. Why had she said those things? Why was any of this happening? Why couldn't she stop herself?

The part of her that was reason and calmness was silenced here. All that was left was rage.

Then she heard her own voice again. She sounded fearless.

'Know it is the truth, Abaddon.'

She never got to say more. Something reached from the darkness and grabbed her arm, talons digging into her skin and muscle. Seconds later, something ripped at her left hand. The pain burned like fire.

She screamed, struggling in the unseen grip, but she couldn't move. Something held her immobile.

'I leave my mark on you,' the voice told her. 'Remember this: If you dare to challenge me, you will die.'

She fought with every muscle, unable to breathe. To think.

Then someone slapped her face, and she fell again, into darkness.

'Miss Montclair!'

It was Zeitinger's voice. His thick German accent.

She wasn't cold anymore. Something hard was beneath her. The air was warm.

Shivering, she forced her eyes open.

Golden afternoon sun streamed through the window, and she squinted into the light. She lay on the floor of Zeitinger's office. The professor's worried face loomed over her.

Taylor scrambled back until she was pressed against the sofa.

'Where is it?' she asked, eyes darting around the room. 'Where is that thing?'

'You're safe.' Zeitinger held up his hands. 'I promise it cannot get you here. Tell me what happened.'

Stumblingly at first and then faster, she told him all she could remember. Falling. The darkness. The strange fury. The sense of being somehow possessed. Pain.

It was then that she realised her left hand still burned painfully. Looking down, she gasped.

She had three fresh cuts on the back of her hand. Blood ran down her fingers. It looked like something had *clawed* her.

'Oh my God,' she whispered. 'He said he was leaving his mark on me. It was real.'

'Very real, I'm afraid.'

As she sat there, staring in numb disbelief at her hand, Zeitinger disappeared. When he returned a few moments later, he bent one knee stiffly and crouched beside her, applying antiseptic to her wounded hand, before wrapping it in a clean white cloth, and tying it snugly at the wrist.

Taylor sat impassive throughout this. Too stunned to speak. Distantly she noticed that the book still lay on top of his desk, but someone had closed it. It seemed to her that even the cover pulsated with malevolence.

Remembering how she'd felt while talking to the demon – the sudden ravenous hunger for power, the total loss of her moral compass, the furious spirit that seemed to control her – she felt lost.

'What exactly happened to me, professor?' Her voice was low. 'When I was talking to that . . . demon, I said things I don't believe. I wasn't . . . me.'

Zeitinger did not appear surprised.

'It is precisely as I suspected. The demon knows you. There is a connection.' He struggled to his feet. 'Please.' He gestured for Taylor to sit on the sofa. 'Tell me again what it said. Leave out nothing.'

They went over her experience again and again, Zeitinger at his desk, at first taking notes, and later simply listening, the pipe half-forgotten in his hand. Taylor sat on the sofa, clutching the plaid blanket to her chest, trying to remember every nuance. By the time he was satisfied, the sun had set.

'I still don't understand my own feelings. The things I said.' Taylor cradled her injured hand.

'The things you felt – the power, the anger – that is within you now,' the professor told her gently. 'It is in all of us. We are all a mixture of good and evil. The demon found the anger in you, and drew it to him. You were in its world. Darkness is what dwells there.' He set down his pipe. 'Do not expect to find rainbows in Hell, Miss Montclair. They are not there.'

She held up her arm. 'He left his mark on me. What does that mean?'

Zeitinger hesitated.

'It means he's taking you very seriously. He wishes to make you easy to identify, wherever you might encounter him again. And for others to know that you are his.'

'I don't—' Taylor tried to interrupt but he talked over her.

'The important thing, for now, is that the experiment was successful,' he said abruptly. 'I know what we need to do to fight Mortimer Pierce. Now, we need the boy.'

Her brow creased. 'Sacha?'

'Please.' Zeitinger's glasses glittered. 'Find him. Tell him to bring the book of his family. He will know the one I mean.'

'What does his book have to do with this?' Taylor asked, confused. But Zeitinger made an impatient gesture.

'Bring the boy, and I will tell you both.'

As she hurried from the building a short while later, Taylor felt dazed. Beneath the makeshift bandage, her hand throbbed.

She didn't know what time it was, or what Sacha was doing right now. She didn't have her phone with her. For want of a better plan, she decided to start at the dorm.

It was dark now, and all the lights in Newton Hall were ablaze. When she reached Sacha's floor, the corridor was quiet. Most of the doors on the hallway were covered in personal notes and pictures. Some had white boards, where friends could leave messages, often obscene or insulting.

Sacha's door alone was completely empty. Nothing hung on the dark, aged wood except the room number: 473.

They had this in common. There was nothing on her door, either.

She tapped hesitantly. 'Sacha. It's me.'

The door jerked open.

He wore a grey t-shirt and scruffy jeans. His feet were bare.

'Taylor, where have you *been*? I've been calling and calling.' He seemed genuinely relieved to see her.

'I've been with one of the professors, Zeitinger.' Her eyes searched his face for signs of damage. 'Are you OK? Louisa told me what happened.'

'I'm fine,' he said impatiently. 'Why didn't you answer your phone?'

'My battery ran down – I had to leave it charging in my room.'

'*Bon sang*, Taylor,' he chided her. 'You scared me. Don't do that.'

After the day she'd had, his concern filled her with warmth.

She wanted to tell him everything – about the professor and the book and the demons. But Zeitinger had seemed in such a hurry. It felt like there wasn't time.

'I'm sorry. I'll get my phone later. Look, you need to come

with me.' Her words tumbled out in a rush. 'Zeitinger – the professor – he found something. He wants you to bring that book. You know, the one about your family?'

He frowned. 'Why does he need that?'

'I don't know. He just said for you to bring it.' As she spoke, she held up her hands in a vague gesture. Spotting the bandage, Sacha grabbed her wrist.

'You're hurt? What happened?'

'It's a long story,' she said. 'Can I explain on the way?'

She could see he wanted to know everything right now, but still, he dropped her hand and stepped back, giving her space to enter.

'Give me a second. I have to put on some shoes.'

His room was smaller than hers and much messier. Clothes lay discarded on the floor. Books and papers were piled up on the narrow bed, covering the dark grey duvet. An open laptop glowed on his crowded desk.

Seeing her eyeing the clutter, Sacha shrugged.

'The cleaner is on holiday.'

His accent made the 'h' disappear. *Oleeday.*

It was adorable.

'Oh, mine, too,' she assured him airily. 'Can't get the staff.'

He glanced at her with an ironic smile. 'Your cleaner is not allowed holidays, I think. Your room is always perfect.'

Taylor, who was fighting the urge to stack the papers on his desk, didn't argue.

Dropping down onto the rumpled bed, Sacha pulled on socks and a pair of black Converse high-tops.

'The book is here.' He pulled a slim, ancient volume from

the top of the stack on his bed and handed it to her.

As he laced up his shoes, Taylor looked at it curiously. He'd told her about it long ago – it was a hand-written history of his family.

*Why does the professor want this?*

Jumping to his feet, Sacha swiped his hoody off the back of the door, shrugging it on as he ushered her out into the hallway.

When she handed the book back to him, their fingers brushed. His eyes flickered to meet hers.

Heat rushed to her face and she looked away.

They headed down the stairs.

'Where were you last night? I stopped by your room late – you weren't there.' His tone was too casual to be casual.

Taylor's heart skipped a beat.

'I fell asleep in the professor's office,' she said, and Sacha stopped abruptly and shot her a look she couldn't read. It almost looked like jealousy.

'What happened, then? You said you would tell me. Is he the one who hurt you?' He pointed at her bandage.

She shook her head so hard her curls flew.

'We found a demonic book,' she explained. 'The book hurt me.'

Creases formed in his forehead. 'A *book* hurt you?'

The scepticism in his voice made Taylor laugh.

'Welcome to alchemy,' she said. 'Even the books will kill you.'

♊

'Professor?' Taylor said as she pushed open Zeitinger's door. 'We're back.'

As he took in the crowded office, Sacha's expression was a complex mixture of surprise and doubt. If he had felt any jealousy earlier – which was unlikely – it had evaporated at the sight of the professor's deeply lined face and snow-white halo of candyfloss hair.

Still, he lingered in the doorway, clearly uncertain about all of this.

He'd been shocked by Taylor's story about the demon.

'It was that bad?' he'd said, searching her face.

'Worse.'

They'd stopped in the shadows of the quad so she could tell him everything he'd missed.

Taylor struggled to find the right words to explain how terrifying the incident had been.

'It was Hell, Sacha. Like, I think Hell is real.'

Their eyes had locked.

'And that's what we have to fight?' Sacha's cockiness had evaporated.

Taylor's hand throbbed – a reminder of the sheer power and hatred they faced. Fighting a sudden sense of hopelessness she wouldn't share with anyone, she nodded.

'That's who we have to *beat*.'

By the time they'd arrived at the history building, their mood was dark.

'Ah.' Zeitinger peered at Sacha over the tops of his reading glasses. His eyes glittered in the lamp light. 'You are Sacha Winters?'

'Yeah.'

The professor studied him intently.

'I am Professor Wolfgang Zeitinger. I knew your father.'

Taylor felt Sacha tense.

'He was a good man, I believe,' Zeitinger continued.

Sacha's expression was a complex mix of confusion and wistfulness.

'Yeah,' he said after a pause. 'He was.'

'Now we must try and finish the work he began.' Zeitinger held out one gnarled hand, palm up. 'May I see the book?'

Sacha hesitated for so long, Taylor feared he might refuse. At last, though, he pulled the battered volume out from the crook of his elbow and handed it over.

The professor set it down next to *The Book of Unravelling*. When he opened it he did so gently, respectful of the fragile old pages.

'I understand this book holds an account of the issuance of the curse,' he said. 'Please, could you find the correct page.'

Walking around the desk to stand at the professor's shoulder, Sacha asked, 'Do you read French?'

The professor shot him a look from under heavy white brows. '*Bien sur.*'

'*Alors.*' Sacha leafed through the book, stopping about forty pages in. The text was hand-written in faded black ink.

'It starts here.'

The professor read quickly, his eyes darting across the spidery script.

Taylor knew the book had been written in the seventeenth century by one of Sacha's ancestors, and the story of the curse was the tale of her own ancestor, an alchemist who had dabbled with Dark practice. She was burned as a witch. Her name was Isabelle Montclair. And she was the woman who first issued the curse that would now kill Sacha on his eighteenth birthday.

The book proved that her family and Sacha's had been intertwined by death and blood for nearly four centuries. Twelve first-born boys in Sacha's family had already died because of it. Finishing the passage, the professor picked up his empty pipe.

'Well,' he said. 'We have what we need.'

Sacha and Taylor exchanged a bemused look.

'What do you mean?' Taylor asked.

With the top if his unlit pipe, Zeitinger pointed at the first line. Taylor leaned closer to see what he indicated.

'Carcassonne 1763.'

The professor looked up at them.

'That is where you must go to undo this Dark practice that threatens you both,' he said. 'You must go to Carcassonne. And fight the demon.'

# SIXTEEN

'Where is Carcassonne?' Taylor looked back and forth from the professor to Sacha.

'In France. In the south.' Sacha turned back to the professor, searching his face for clues. 'I don't understand. Why do we have to go there?'

The professor moved his father's book to one side and, carefully, using the tips of two pens, moved another book to the centre of his desk. It was open to a page in the middle that appeared to be covered in bizarre symbols – half-finished triangles, broken suns, twisted, curving lines covered the thick, yellowed pages.

'This book was written by an alchemist who lived before the trouble that plagues your family first began.' Zeitinger spoke quickly, his accent thickening in his excitement. 'This man achieved what you are trying to do now – he broke an old and powerful Dark curse. He confronted a demon.' His gaze shifted to Taylor's bandaged hand. 'There are rules to unravelling Dark practice. Isabelle Montclair issued the curse. Therefore, Miss Montclair, as Isabelle's direct descendant, must perform the rite. Furthermore, the ritual must take place at the precise location where the curse was issued, and on the day the curse would otherwise be fulfilled.'

Sacha didn't like the sound of this. Taylor had told him about meeting the demon – how powerless she'd felt. It had hurt her too easily. They both understood the wounds on her hand were there as a warning.

Taylor jumped in before he could.

'How, professor? The demon isn't going to just do what we say.'

'With blood.' The professor tapped the book in front of him. 'It says "Blood will open the door to the realm".'

Seeing their expressions, the professor's brow lowered. 'Don't you understand? This is not alchemical science. We are out of our own world now. Dark power is a blood practice. You cannot undo demonology with alchemy. Blood calls for blood. This ceremony you will conduct is demonic.'

Sacha's breath caught. He'd known this, on so many levels, already. But hearing it said in this way made it even worse.

Next to him, Taylor had gone very still; some colour had left her cheeks.

'How can we conduct a demonic ceremony?' Sacha made himself ask. 'It seems impossible. We don't even believe—'

'I believe.' Taylor cut him off. She held up her hand so he could see the white bandage wrapped around it. 'And so do you. How could you not? After everything.'

She was right. But it was so hard to accept. Sacha fell silent.

'Professor, how can we get ready for this ceremony?' Taylor asked. 'The demon is so powerful.'

'I will tell you all you need to know,' the professor said. He studied the two of them over the tops of his glasses. His eyes were steely. 'You are ready. You know you are. There is Darkness in you. Both of you. You have the choice to remain one of us or to follow the path of your ancestor into Darkness,' the professor said. 'In Carcassonne you must choose. Darkness. Or light.'

As he said the last word he held up his pipe. The bowl, which Sacha had assumed to be empty, flared. A thin wisp of aromatic smoke curled upward.

The professor leaned back in his chair, and drew on the pipe.

For Sacha there was something inevitable about this moment. Some part of him had always suspected that what the professor was telling him was true.

It was almost a relief to have his suspicions confirmed.

Taylor on the other hand, looked as if Zeitinger had slapped her. She stood frozen, staring at him, her eyes too bright.

Sacha could believe what the professor had said about him, but she was different. There wasn't an evil bone in her body. It was ridiculous to even suggest there was Darkness to her.

'Are we ... evil?' Her voice was thin. 'Is that what you're saying?'

'No, my dear,' the professor said gently. 'You misunderstand me. Both worlds are open to you. The same is true of all of us in many ways, but for you it is different. For you, both worlds are very close. Because of your history. Because of who you are. The choice is more stark.'

He glanced at Sacha, including him in this assessment. 'When the time comes, you must choose.'

♊

Later that night, Taylor and Sacha walked back to the dormitory in heavy silence. There was much to think about.

Over and over, Sacha replayed the professor's words in his mind.

*There is Darkness in you. Both of you.*

Taylor kept her arms wrapped across her torso as they walked across the tiny lobby of Newton Hall, and up the stone stairwell. It smelled, as it always did, of floor polish and dust.

When they reached the first floor, Taylor stopped so suddenly Sacha ran into her. For a moment they were entangled.

'Sorry,' he said, trying not to notice the lemon fragrance of her hair, the softness of her skin.

There was some awkward shuffling as they stepped apart. Taylor reached for the door handle, and Sacha turned back towards the stairs to head up to his own room. Her voice stopped him.

'Do you want to come in?' she said, as if the thought had just occurred to her. 'To my room, I mean?'

Her cheeks were flushed, and she seemed anxious. Nervy.

Sacha's nod was casual, but inside he was filled with relief. The last thing he wanted to be right now was alone.

Taylor's room was neater than his, and considerably more

spacious, with a row of three arched windows on one wall; two of them were arrow-slim but the one in the middle was larger, overlooking the quad. Aside from a dresser, a desk and an almost empty bookcase, the room held nothing. It had the hollowness of a space where no one really lived.

It was a familiar feeling – his room was the same.

Neither of them had had a chance to put down much in the way of roots, but the empty bookcase bothered him. If ever there was a student whose shelves should have been overflowing it was Taylor.

'Do you want anything to drink?' she asked. 'I have . . . nothing.'

The hopeless smile she gave him then tugged at his heart.

'It's fine,' he said, dropping down on the bed. 'I'm not thirsty.'

When Taylor sat down next to him, Sacha hid his surprise. She always kept distance between them if she could – just a little, but consistently enough that he noticed. If there were four chairs at the table and one was next to his, Taylor would sit across from him.

'So we're going to Carcassonne,' she said.

Her English pronunciation of the town's name was charmingly off-kilter.

'I guess so,' Sacha shrugged. 'What is the American phrase? Road trip.'

'Yes,' she said distantly. 'Road trip. It'll be great.'

Suddenly, with little warning, she began to weep. Not great, heaving sobs but silently. Reluctantly. As if it was the last thing she wanted.

Sacha didn't know what to do. 'Taylor? What's wrong?'

He reached for her, then pulled his hand back.

'I'm sorry,' she said, swiping tears from her cheeks with her bandaged hand. 'This is ridiculous. I'm not even sad. Not really. Just scared. And what the professor said was ... not what I expected.'

Sacha loved her accent. The way each word was so precise and clear. Her curious way of putting things. He didn't think he'd ever heard anything more magical than Taylor talking.

Why hadn't he ever told her that? What was he afraid of?

'Hey.' He moved closer, still not reaching for her. 'What he said – he might be wrong, you know? That book is very old and we can't believe everything in it.'

'I know.' She took a deep breath. 'It just threw me. I mean, the idea that we could go Dark like, like Mortimer. That maybe that's who we are.' Almost pleadingly, she turned her face towards him. 'You don't believe it, do you?'

Tears clung to her eyelashes like tiny jewels.

Longing fluttered in Sacha's chest. Slowly, he reached for her good hand, taking it carefully in his. For some reason he thought she'd snatch it back, but she didn't.

'I don't believe it,' he said, not exactly honestly. 'Not for a minute. Not about you, anyway. You are the least evil person I think I've ever known.'

Taylor's smile was grateful. She clung to his hand as the seriousness returned to her eyes.

'He told me other things, Sacha,' she confessed. 'Before you came.'

Sacha's face darkened. 'What things?'

'He said there was a chance ... a good chance, that we would both die trying to undo this curse.'

She was afraid. He could hear it in her voice. And he knew he should be afraid too, but he felt nothing. Not for himself, anyway. He'd died so many times already, and the hammer of actual, permanent death had hung over his head for so long he no longer really feared it. Being threatened with death now was no worse than being threatened with detention. It was a nuisance.

But he didn't want Taylor to die. Taylor with her blonde curls and green eyes. Her heart-shaped face and huge brain. Taylor who might change the world if history didn't kill her first.

She couldn't die. He wouldn't let that happen.

'You won't die.' He said it flatly. A simple statement of inviolable fact.

She squinted at him dubiously. 'How do you know?'

'I just know,' he said. 'And I won't die either. Neither of us will die. We are too beautiful to die. And too clever.'

She stared at him for a second as if she intended to argue, and then gave up with a helpless laugh he felt in his chest.

'Sacha, this is serious.'

He shrugged. 'Everything is serious,' he said impatiently. 'Life has been serious for as long as I can remember. But you will not die, Taylor.' He took her other hand carefully, feeling the softness of the bandage as he turned her to face him. 'You are the best alchemist they have ever seen. Off the charts. That's what Louisa told me. You're powerful – that's what Jones said. You will be fine.' His voice had taken on a fervent note. One he hardly recognised. 'We will go to Carcassonne. We will do the thing we have to do, whatever it is. Then you will come back here with all your books. And I will ride my motorcycle around the world, getting into trouble. We will be *alive*. And we will be free. Believe it. It will happen.'

She held his hands, her eyes locked on his. 'I want to believe that, Sacha. More than anything.'

He ran his thumbs across the palms of her warm, small hands. Her skin was butter soft.

She drew in a small surprised breath.

He could feel the heat radiating from her skin. Smell the soft fragrance of her scent – soft and heady.

'Taylor,' he whispered, leaning towards her. 'You have to believe.'

'Sacha,' she said, raising her lips towards his. 'I . . . '

She never finished the sentence.

With an almighty crash, something huge burst through the largest of the three windows. Glass exploded into the room like tiny crystal daggers.

Moving on pure instinct, Sacha threw himself on top of Taylor, shielding her with his body as glass showered the bed. Shards cut through the thin fabric of his t-shirt, slicing his back, sending pain burning through him.

Before he could lift himself off the bed and get them both to the door, something grabbed him by the back of his t-shirt and swung him into the air like a toy.

It happened so fast – Sacha never had a chance. He heard Taylor scream. Felt her fingers slip from his. Then his t-shirt tightened across his throat, strangling him.

Kicking with all his strength, he twisted in the unseen grip, struggling until he caught a glimpse of the huge thing that held him – scorched skin bulging hideously, eyes mad with pain and rage.

The creature from the tunnel.

'Taylor,' he gasped with the last of his air. 'Run.'

# Seventeen

Taylor didn't mean to scream.

The speed of the attack caught her off-guard. She didn't even have time to get a grip on Sacha before he flew up into the air.

She jumped to her feet.

'Let him go.' She shouted across the room at the huge man – for it must once have been a man before all this happened to him.

Ignoring her, it blundered across the room, kicking the chair out of the way with such force it crashed to the floor, sending splintered pieces flying.

The thing didn't seem very agile – stumbling and bashing into furniture, as if its vision wasn't good, or its reflexes were slow. It was so huge it had to bend to avoid the ceiling. It kept colliding with the light fixture, sending light and shade swinging wildly around the room.

Sacha's face was turning purple.

She forced herself to think quickly. There was no time to call for help. What had Louisa and Alastair told her? They'd said alchemical abilities don't hurt them. But with no other weapons handy, she had to try.

Molecules of energy were all around her, golden strands from the electricity in the walls. Tiny dancing motes from the light particles in the air.

At the heart of it, the creature's energy was of a different nature entirely. Taylor sensed Dark power in him, but something else as well. Some residual alchemical gold, painful and tormented. A sickening kind of *emptiness* that she couldn't figure out. There was no time to think about what that might mean. Grabbing the biggest chunk of electrical molecular energy she could find, Taylor aimed it at the creature.

'Let him go,' she said again. This time her voice was a command, and she pushed the energy towards it with huge force.

Nothing happened.

The creature paused near the window, shuddering, a stupefied expression on its face. Its eyes were vacant.

Just like Louisa had described, it was taking in that energy, she realised. Absorbing it. *Feeding* on it.

Sacha dangled in its grip, choking. His hands clawed at the neck of his t-shirt in sheer desperation, trying to tear himself free. Before he could, though, the thin cotton gave way, ripping down the middle and released him.

He landed on his knees with a thud. His face was blue. He took great wheezing gasps of air.

Taylor rushed towards him.

The creature lumbered on towards the window, apparently momentarily unaware Sacha had escaped.

Her heart pounding, Taylor grabbed Sacha's hand, pulling him to his feet.

His black t-shirt was torn from the neck to the waist. The remnants of it fluttered loose around his lean torso as they stumbled towards the door.

Behind them, the creature, apparently registering what had happened, gave a roar of frustration. Taylor didn't dare look back as it crashed after them, its footsteps so heavy the walls shook.

'It's fast,' Sacha gasped, his voice hoarse.

Taylor didn't reply. She yanked the door open and they tumbled out of the room into the hall.

Slamming the door behind them, she spun around, seeking something to block it with.

'Don't bother,' Sacha rasped. 'It'll just . . . '

At that moment, the creature pulled the door off its hinges and threw it to one side with a shriek of rage.

'. . . do what it wants,' Sacha finished.

Taylor stared at the thing with horror.

It turned towards them, a kind of insane hatred darkening its distorted features.

'What do we do?' she asked.

'We run.' Sacha grabbed her hand, pulling her towards the stairwell.

They skidded into the staircase in perfect sync, thudding down to the ground floor. They were across the dimly lit lobby and out into the quad in seconds.

There, they paused, unsure of what to do next.

'We should get help.' Taylor reached for her phone. 'It could hurt someone.'

'Do it quickly,' Sacha said, poised to run.

It seemed to take forever for the call to go through. She waited, staring at the door of the Newton Dorm with fixed intensity. Finally, somewhere a phone rang.

Once. Twice. Three times.

'Taylor?' Louisa's voice on the line. 'What's up?'

'Lou . . . ' Taylor shouted, then the dormitory door flew open with a splintering crash, and the creature squeezed through it with a yowl of complaint.

She never had time to say another word.

'Let's go.' Sacha grabbed her hand, pulling her so hard she nearly dropped the phone.

They hurtled across the quad; the velvet grass cool beneath their feet.

'Where are we going?' Taylor shouted.

'I have no idea.' Sacha glanced over his shoulder, searching for the thing in the dark. 'Not the library. I don't want to be trapped in another library with this thing.'

Taylor didn't dare look back but she could hear the heavy footsteps behind them.

Ahead, the solid, ancient door to the dining hall loomed into view. The dining hall was never locked. The night porters used it as a break room, of sorts.

She pointed. 'In there.'

Sacha didn't argue.

They slammed through the doors, sliding the heavy brass lock into place behind them.

When it was done, they stepped back, watching it warily.

Seconds later something smashed into it from the other side. The doors shook from the blow, but held.

Sacha eyed the strong hinges warily.

'It'll get through,' he warned. 'They don't give up. We need to be ready.'

The thing crashed against the doors again. Plaster dust showered down from the ceiling. Across the room, the medieval stained-glass windows shivered.

Taylor heard a muffled frustrated roar through the thick wood of the door.

'I'll get a weapon,' Sacha announced, running towards the kitchen.

'Get one for me.' Standing behind a heavy, wooden chair that must have survived centuries in this glorious room, Taylor pulled the phone from her pocket and pressed the call button.

The creature crashed against the door again. The awful thud was followed by a horrible prolonged barrage of violence as its enormous fists bashed against the wood.

The portraits on the wall shivered. In the cupboard the crystal glasses vibrated, sending out an alarmed, unearthly chime.

'Where are you?' Louisa shouted. She was already running.

'The creatures from the tunnel,' Taylor said quickly. 'They're here.'

'I know. Are you in the dorm? That's where I'm headed.'

'We're not at the dorm anymore. We're in the dining hall. It's outside.' The thing crashed against the door again, and she added, 'But it's going to get in.'

'The *dining hall*?'

Taylor heard Louisa's footsteps stop.

'Alastair!' she shouted. 'They're in the dining hall. It's got Taylor and Sacha.'

In the distance, Taylor heard Alastair swear.

Louisa's footsteps began again, faster than before.

'On our way,' she said.

The line went dead.

The thing had begun pounding on the door relentlessly. Harder and harder. The building shook from the sheer force of it. The noise was maddening. It sounded like the creature would knock the whole building down.

Sacha appeared at her side. His eyes gleamed in the darkened room. In one hand, he held a carving knife. In his other, a long, slim knife with a deadly looking blade.

Flipping it over with surprising expertise, he held the latter out to her, handle first.

'Take it,' he said. 'Just in case.'

The carved handle looked like ivory, but was probably bone. It was cool to touch. The blade was deadly.

She set it down on the table beside her.

'Louisa's coming. We won't need these.'

The door shuddered under the monster's onslaught. The old lock began to bend.

'I hope she's fast.' Sacha didn't let go of his knife.

The thing pounded again. The assault was so loud, so vicious, Taylor could feel it in her chest. In her brain.

*Bangbangbangbangbangbang.*

Suddenly, the door splintered.

'It's getting in,' Sacha called above the cacophony. 'Get ready.'

Keeping her eyes fixed on the door, Taylor put her hand on the knife. Her heart hammered against her ribs.

Louisa was all the way over by the dorm. She'd never make it here in time.

How was she supposed to save Sacha – or herself – without her alchemical abilities?

Without them she was nothing.

Then something occurred to her. Something Alastair had said earlier that day. She looked down at the knife, her brow knitted, then back at the door.

A plan began to come together.

As the door sagged further, she reached for Sacha's hand. He looked up at her with surprise, his fingers tightening around hers instinctively.

'Help me,' she said. 'I want to try something.'

'Your energy makes it stronger,' he reminded her. 'You can't fight it that way.'

'I know. But I have an idea.'

Before he could reply, the thing threw itself at the door with unbelievable force. The door shivered and, with a screech of tearing metal, the lock began to give.

Taylor took a deep breath. Holding up her hand, she drew energy from all around, molecules of water, air, light and electricity. Attracted by the ancient connection between her and Sacha, it all flowed to her, rushing through her veins like alcohol.

All the fear left her.

She wasn't afraid of anything.

Staring at the door, she channelled molecules of golden energy towards it.

*Open.*

The bent lock straightened and slid back with a groan.

The thick double doors flew open.

The creature stood in the doorway, hatred burning in its eyes.

Snarling, it lunged towards them.

Next to her, Sacha flinched. Taylor gripped his fingers tightly with her good hand. The other, she raised, bandaged palm facing up.

*Knife.*

The slim, silver knife rose up from where it lay on the table next to her. For a split second it hovered in mid-air, glinting.

Taylor turned her hand, pointing at the creature lumbering towards them.

*There.*

The blade flew across the room like a bullet, sliding into its huge chest without a sound.

The creature stopped, looking down at the knife with an almost human grunt of surprise. Its deformed brow creased.

When it looked up at Taylor, she thought she saw pain in its eyes.

Unexpectedly, sadness washed over her. Whatever it was now, it hadn't started out like this. It didn't choose this existence.

Still. She had no choice. She had to finish this to stay alive.

Eyes still on the stunned creature, she raised her palm once more.

*Knife.*

The carving knife slipped from Sacha's fingers. He gave a gasp of surprise.

The blade hovered in front of them, shining silver and razor sharp.

Again, Taylor pointed at her target.

*There.*

The creature didn't try to run. The second knife plunged in beside the first.

Black blood fountained from the wound in its chest. The thing fell heavily to its knees.

Looking at Taylor with tormented eyes, the creature held up its thick arms. It seemed to want to tell her something but it couldn't speak. Instead, it made an inarticulate noise that sounded like a plea.

'I'm sorry,' Taylor whispered.

The creature's eyes glazed. Slowly, inexorably, it tumbled forward, hitting the polished oak floor with a crash that caused the chairs to jump.

It didn't move again.

# EIGHTEEN

The sun had turned the sky brilliant gold by the time Taylor and Sacha headed to the administration building the next morning. Each carried a small bag.

Taylor's feet felt light and odd, each step a moon-walk into the unknown. Neither of them had slept. They'd spent the night with the others, planning.

They couldn't stay in Oxford, that much was certain. Their presence put everyone in danger. Mortimer would never give up. Last night he'd sent one of his zombies to kill them. Tomorrow? Maybe he'd send twenty. Or a hundred.

Louisa and Alastair had arrived at the dining room seconds after the creature died. Skidding in the room, fists raised, faces flushed from running, they'd stared in astonishment at Taylor, who knelt next to the prone body.

Alastair spoke first. 'How the hell did you do that?'

'Knives.' Swiping a tear from her cheek, Taylor stood. 'You

told me Sacha killed one last night by stabbing it in the chest. So I tried the same thing. It worked.' She took a shaky breath. 'I think it really was human once.'

'Worse.' Louisa crouched down low, pointing to faded tattoos on the thing's arms. 'It was one of us.'

She held her arm next to it, so Taylor and Sacha could see they wore matching tattoos. Her well-toned bicep looked tiny next to the creature's thick flesh.

'We think Mortimer must have harvested the bodies of dead alchemists,' Louisa explained. 'God knows from where – the morgue. Cemeteries. Hospitals. He could have been doing it for years.' Her voice was bitter. 'He needed time. So they could grow.'

Her phone buzzed with angry insistence. She yanked it from her pocket. 'What's happening?' She listened for a moment. 'Good. It's dead. They stabbed it in the chest. I *know*.' Her gaze flickered at Taylor and Sacha. 'I'll be there shortly.'

She put her phone away.

'What's going on?' Sacha asked.

'The others are searching the grounds in case more of these things are sneaking around, but it looks like this might be the only one.' She gestured at the huge corpse. 'There's no sign of another.'

'Is it over then?' Taylor asked hopefully.

'For tonight, maybe.' Louisa turned towards the door. 'Jones wants everyone in his office. Alastair and I need to help wrap up the search. Will you two be OK?'

Sacha looked at Taylor.

'We'll be fine,' he promised her.

Once Louisa was gone, Taylor looked down at the huge body. 'What should we do about it?'

'They'll take care of it.' Sacha headed for the open doorway, stepping carefully over the rubble. 'Let's get out of here. We need to talk.'

His face was as serious as she'd ever seen it.

They'd stood out in the quiet quad talking for a while. It only took them a few minutes to decide to leave. By the time they reached the dean's office, their minds had been made up.

Jones hadn't been wild about the idea.

'We mustn't be hasty,' he cautioned, when they'd explained their decision. 'We need to formulate a plan. You have to be patient.'

'We can't be patient,' Taylor said. 'Sacha's birthday is four days away. It's time to go.'

'Do you truly believe you'll be safer out in the open than you are here?' Jones reasoned. 'Tonight when you were attacked, a dozen people ran to save you. Who will help you in France?'

'In the end, though,' Taylor reminded him, 'we saved ourselves.'

And so it went on – and on. Louisa sat quietly in a chair listening to them argue in circles. Until, finally, she'd had enough.

'They're right,' she told the dean. 'They should go now. But they shouldn't go alone. I'll go with them.'

They all turned to stare at her. She looked tired but resolute, her oval face still shiny from running, dark smudges underlining her exhausted eyes.

'Louisa, you're strong but you are not an army,' the dean

told her with surprising gentleness. 'You can't save everyone.'

'I know I can't save everyone,' she snapped. 'But I can save them.' She glanced at Taylor and Sacha. 'Alastair will come, too. We can travel separately, staying in touch. Make Mortimer think they're alone. If he believes he has them, they'll get farther.'

Once Louisa's mind was made up, the argument had ended fairly quickly. Giving in to the inevitable, Jones called for Zeitinger. If the German professor was surprised to be summoned in the middle of the night his expression didn't betray it when he bustled into the dean's office with an armful of books and papers.

Ignoring the others, he headed straight to Taylor, his eyes red-rimmed but alert.

'You are leaving now because of the attack?'

'Yes.'

'Good,' he said firmly. 'It is the right thing.'

'How far have you got with your research?' The dean had removed his tie. His jacket hung across the back of his chair, and his sleeves were rolled up to his elbows. A roadmap of France lay spread across his desk, and he'd been tracing a route with Louisa when Zeitinger walked in.

'I think I have the information we need,' Zeitinger told him. 'The book is difficult in places. Falkenstein's directions are not always logical. But the basics are clear.'

Dropping a notebook onto the table on top of the map, he pointed at a line of symbols. They gathered around him to see. To Taylor, they were frustratingly unreadable – triangles, circles, squiggly lines. But Zeitinger looked pleased.

'According to Falkenstein,' Zeitinger said, 'the most important thing is that the ceremony must take place at the precise location where the curse was issued.' He thumped his finger on his notebook. 'The exact spot.'

'Professor, the curse was three hundred years ago,' Sacha said doubtfully. 'How will we find out exactly where it happened?'

The professor beamed at him.

'You don't have to. I already have.'

Pulling a page out from the stack of papers, he flipped it over. It was a tourist map of Carcassonne. Its vivid colour scheme seemed incongruous in the muted room.

'This was the only map of Carcassonne I could locate,' Zeitinger explained. 'They don't seem to make maps of this town in normal colours. Now, places of execution were often chosen using pagan methods. Many were located intentionally on ground believed to have mystical powers. Later, churches were built on these very locations. The church wanted the old beliefs expunged completely, and what better way than to build a temple to your new god on top of the one for the old?'

Without waiting for a response, he pulled out a sheet of paper.

'This is the description of the execution from the book of Sacha's family. It describes the place of burning in the centre of Carcassonne. This book . . .' He grabbed a leather-bound book from the stack and held it up without opening it. ' . . . describes the same location – so the burnings at this time took place in the square at the top of the hill in the town centre within the walls of the old citadel.' He pressed his finger against a point on the map of Carcassonne. 'Without question, this is where you must go.'

When he lifted his hand, Taylor saw the cross beneath it. She leaned forward to read the words written beside it.

'The Basilica of St Nazaire?'

'A church,' the professor said, nodding. 'It was once very small. But it was expanded in the eighteenth century and again in the nineteenth. On top of the old gallows.'

'I can't believe they built a church on an execution ground,' Sacha sounded horrified.

'They sanctify the ground first,' Zeitinger told him. 'Claiming it for God. It's a kind of purification. Pointless of course. You cannot undo Dark practice with a prayer. But it is enough for priests.'

'And the ceremony?' Taylor looked at him. 'Once we find the place and get in the church, what do we do?'

At this, the professor's expression became sombre. 'Yes. This we must discuss.' He glanced around the room before turning back to Taylor. 'Let us talk in private, you and I. And leave the others to their planning.'

When no one objected, he'd led her out of the dean's office and down the hallway to a small office. It was clean and modern – a soulless cube. Taylor found herself wondering who spent every day here, surrounded by so much nothing.

'I did not want the others to hear what I have to tell you.' The professor shuffled through his papers until he found the one he wanted. He stared solemnly at her. 'The ceremony is very difficult and very dangerous. I am sorry to say, I am not convinced you will survive it. Are you certain you wish to go forward with this?'

Taylor's heart clenched. She didn't want to die. But she'd seen that creature last night. She'd killed it with her own hands. And she'd seen Bringers and a man with unimaginable Dark power.

There was no going back.

'I'm certain,' she said, determinedly.

He nodded, as if this was precisely what he'd expected.

'Well, then.' He cleared his throat, and peered at the page in his hand. 'You shall have to start with blood.'

Over a course of minutes that seemed to Taylor like hours, he explained the Dark ceremony she would have to conduct. His words were a series of terrors.

*'Cut deep enough to draw substantial blood . . . '*

*'You must call upon the demon . . . '*

*'It has hurt you before, it will hurt you again . . . '*

*'It will try to tempt you . . . '*

*'Remember: demons lie.'*

When he'd concluded, his eyes searched hers. 'There is one other thing you must understand.' He spoke with soft apology, like a doctor giving bad news. 'Performing a Dark ceremony leaves traces on your spirit. Sometimes these traces pervade. Sometimes they take over. They can act as a conquering army of Darkness. This could be what happened with Mortimer Pierce. He dabbled with Dark practices, and they *became* him.'

It took her a moment to realise what he was telling her.

'You're saying it's possible I could end up like him,' she whispered. 'I could lose my soul.'

'It is one of the possibilities,' the professor conceded regretfully. 'There are many others. Death. Survival. Perhaps you will fight off the traces of Darkness. I've told you before there is Darkness in you. But you are not, yourself, Dark. In truth, we know little about the realities of this. So much has been lost to time. This will be a very dangerous experiment.'

Taylor was very tired of being told how little they knew. When something goes horribly wrong, the last thing you want is for the world's most renowned experts to say, 'Oh yeah, that? We haven't really figured it out yet.'

She forced herself to stay calm. 'Are there things I can do, though? To protect myself?'

'Follow the instructions to the letter,' he said. 'That is key. Do not let the demon tempt you. He will try to persuade you he is on your side. Or that you are on his. He will be extremely convincing. Consider how normal Mortimer looks. How approachable he might seem if you did not know. Remember, no matter what happens, Pierce is not what he seems to be. He is not who he once was – he is absolutely not one of us. That part of him is dead. There is no humanity left in Mortimer Pierce. He is a monster. Never forget this. No matter what happens.'

When he'd finished, Zeitinger put his wrinkled hand on hers, his skin felt warm and dry.

'You must not miss a single step. Everything must be done precisely or all is lost. Do you understand?'

Her mouth was dry. She swallowed hard.

'Yes,' she said.

He held a piece of paper out to her. 'I have written everything down. Please memorise my words. Be ready.'

She took it from his hand, barely glancing at it before folding it up and putting it in her pocket.

She'd learned enough for now. 'I wish you good luck, Miss Montclair,' the professor said sombrely. 'What you must do now is the very hardest thing. You are a brave young woman.'

♊

Taylor walked numbly back down the darkened hallway past the pictures of all those former deans. She couldn't tell Sacha what Zeitinger had just told her. He'd never allow her to go through with the ceremony if he knew what it meant for her. The danger.

She'd have to keep this to herself.

When she reached the dean's office, the others were planning out the route. Sacha's gaze was focussed on the map spread across the glossy wood of the table.

'You must take the small back roads,' the dean said, tracing a route on the map. 'Avoid the motorways. Mortimer will be waiting for you. He knows you'll be going to Carcassonne, but there are many routes across France and he can't watch them all. Head south through the mountains. Avoid cities. Stick to small villages.'

They discussed the journey for hours, stopping finally when the sun rose and Louisa insisted it was time to depart.

It took Taylor about five minutes to pack a small bag with a change of clothes, and a handful of toiletries. She didn't know what to take, what to leave. What do you bring to an apocalypse? No need for mascara, surely.

When she picked up her hairbrush, she caught a glimpse

of herself in the mirror above her dresser. She looked wan but otherwise perfectly normal, and that seemed somehow ridiculous. Why wasn't her panic written on her face? How could she still look like her when everything had changed?

Forcing herself to look away, she yanked open the dresser drawer and grabbed some clothes, dressing for the journey in dark trousers and a short-sleeved top, and shoes she could run in.

A few minutes later, she met Sacha at the foot of the dormitory stairs.

When he saw what she was wearing, Sacha said, 'Wait here.'

He ran back to his room, returning a moment later with a battered leather jacket.

'It gets cold on a bike,' he said, holding it out for her. 'Even on a hot day.'

The sleeves were so long she'd had to roll them up. But the leather was soft and warm. And it smelled like him – like soap and fresh air.

It was comforting.

The dean was waiting for them in the quiet lobby, along with Alastair and Louisa – who each clutched large coffees and a bag of pastries. Taylor's stomach was too sour for food.

'I know I don't have to tell you how dangerous this is,' Jones told them. 'Or how grateful I am for what you're doing.'

'One moment, please.' The German-accented voice came from the front door, where Professor Zeitinger was hurrying towards them. 'I have something for Miss Montclair.'

The dean frowned, but waited with the others as the white-haired man approached breathlessly. Taylor could see that he carried something in his hands.

'It was very difficult to find this,' he told her. 'It was, I think, hidden. But you will need it.'

He pressed a long, narrow box into her hands. It was faded blue and covered in soft velvet, like a jewellery box, but oddly heavy.

'Use this for the ceremony.'

Taylor moved as if to open it, and he shook his head, pressing his hand against hers.

'Not now, Miss Montclair,' he said quietly. 'Perhaps, open it in private.'

Puzzled, she agreed, slipping the box into her bag. But the secrecy of it made her nervous. She felt its presence like a weight.

Whatever was in that velvet case, it scared her.

The professor took her hand. 'I wish you very good luck, my dear.'

His tone told her what she knew already – she'd need it.

Over his shoulder, Louisa caught Taylor's eye and gestured impatiently.

'Let's roll.' Without waiting for the others to agree, she hoisted her bag onto her shoulder, and with coffee in one hand, headed towards the parking garage. 'We've got a demon to kill.'

Taylor hurried over to join the others, and they walked together out to where the van and the motorcycle were parked side by side on the narrow drive behind the admin building.

'You should say "slay",' Alastair advised, striding next to Louisa. 'We've got a demon to *slay*.'

'Is that the correct terminology?' She shrugged. 'My bad.'

Alastair made his tone patronising. 'I know I've said this before but, you really should study more, Louisa.'

'Bite me, Alastair.'

Sacha snorted a laugh.

Taylor knew their joking was an act and that they were just as nervous as she was, but she was glad they were doing it. At least someone was being normal.

Normal seemed a long way away now.

# Nineteen

Sacha was driving too fast, but he didn't want to slow down. The motorcycle roared beneath him, Taylor's hands were warm against his waist, and a long, straight French highway stretched out in front of them.

He was free of that college. Free of Oxford. Free, for the moment, of Mortimer.

They'd been on the road for hours now. They'd caught the ferry without incident, and had been driving back roads ever since, without any sign of Dark energy around them. Louisa and Alastair were out there somewhere, taking a different route. Taylor checked in periodically to make sure all was well.

So far, the plan was working perfectly. The only problem was a very basic human weakness – Sacha was exhausted.

The road kept blurring in front of his eyes, and he found the handlebars harder to hold on to.

He hadn't slept at all the night before and it was now late afternoon.

'You OK?' Taylor called, shouting to be heard above the wind.

Keeping his eyes on the road, Sacha nodded. He was fine.

Absolutely fine.

He had to be.

They passed another road sign for Paris. One hundred and seventy-five kilometres – no distance at all. He could be home in two hours, sitting on the couch with his mother and Laura, telling them about the professors at St Wilfred's – making it all sound funny.

Paris was like a homing beacon, calling to him.

What if he did die? What if he never saw his family again?

The edges of the road blurred again, and he blinked hard to clear his vision.

He needed to stop thinking, but he was just so *tired*.

Lost in his troubled thoughts, he barely noticed they'd entered a small village until a red light loomed in front of him, and he slammed the brakes, narrowly avoiding a car crossing in front of them.

Taylor was thrown against him. Sacha dropped his foot to brace the motorcycle, which threatened to topple.

'Sorry,' he said, turning to look at her.

Worried green eyes peered back at him through her visor.

'You look really tired, Sacha.'

'I am tired,' he admitted reluctantly. 'Maybe we should take a break.'

Her helmet bobbed in agreement.

'What do you think?' He gestured at the town. 'Is it safe?'

The lone street light hung at a crossroads in what appeared to be a typical French village. All the houses were built of the same pale yellow stone. Bright roses hung over old walls. A church with a tall steeple sat squarely in the middle.

She pulled off her helmet, sending a tangle of blonde curls tumbling around her shoulders. Her cheeks were pink. A velvety sheen of perspiration covered the bridge of her nose.

They both looked around at the diminutive village square, its trees shivering in the summer breeze.

'Looks safe to me,' she said after a second. 'No bad guys.'

Sacha parked the bike on a narrow lane at the edge of the square. When he cut off the engine the silence was deafening. Gradually, though, as his ears adjusted he could hear the breeze blowing through the trees, and the birds complaining overhead. Children's laughter floated out from someone's garden.

When his stomach rumbled, they could both hear it. They hadn't eaten since they left the ferry hours ago.

'I'm starving,' he said.

'Me too.' Taylor stretched the kinks from her muscles. 'I think I spotted a bakery back on the main road. Let's see if they're open.'

They were both on high alert as they crossed the quiet square but everything seemed refreshingly normal.

An elderly woman walking a tiny dog on a long lead, nodded politely as she passed them. A burly man didn't glance at them as he rumbled through the town on a huge green tractor.

*Just a sleepy village*, Sacha told himself. But he couldn't stop looking over his shoulder.

The tiny bakery sat near the church, in a little stone building painted yellow and white. The bell above the door gave a cheerful jangle when they walked in.

The woman behind the counter set down her newspaper and looked up at them. She wore an apron over her jeans, and her weathered face creased as she smiled. Her shoulder-length hair was an unbelievable shade of red.

They ordered sandwiches and cold drinks, then waited as the woman put the food in bags, chattering brightly in rapid-fire French. Sacha found himself gazing longingly at the cakes and pastries – the whipped clouds of sugar, the bright glazes. He hadn't realised how hungry he was until now. He could have eaten all of it.

Taylor leaned over peering at the pastries through the glass. 'Which is your favourite?'

Without hesitation, he pointed to a narrow pastry covered in pale green icing, and sprinkled at one end with dark chocolate. 'That one.'

She studied the green lump doubtfully. 'Really?'

'It's delicious,' he insisted. 'There's this creamy custard inside which is, oh my God, it's amazing.'

Just talking about it made his mouth water.

He turned to the baker who was watching them with a look of amusement.

'Two *salambos*, please,' he said in French, pointing at the green pastry. 'And something else, in case she hates it.'

'She's never had a *salambo*?' The woman tutted as she put two in a cardboard box. 'How is this possible?'

Sacha could have told her they don't have *salambos* in

England, but he didn't feel like sharing any information with strangers, however innocuous, so instead he distracted the woman by ordering more.

Along with the pastry, he bought gooey chocolate éclairs, some cakes and a couple of mini lemon tarts because, as he explained to Taylor with a touch of defensiveness, 'Who knows when we'll get a chance to eat again? Everything closes early in the countryside.'

They paid up and strolled back outside. Sacha knew they should get going – they had to keep moving, that was the plan, it was safest and Louisa and Alastair were likely miles ahead by now. But he couldn't face it. Every muscle in his body ached.

'Let's rest for a second.' Spotting a bench in a tucked away corner of the empty little square, he made a beeline towards it.

Taylor didn't object. The dark circles under her eyes betrayed her own weariness.

The bench was warm, and they sat back with relief.

The late afternoon sun sent golden droplets of light scattering through the branches. A scrawny tabby cat bathed itself placidly in a puddle of sunshine.

'Are you as tired as me?' Taylor rubbed her eyes.

'Tireder,' he said, then paused to consider. 'Is that a word?'

'It is now.' She yawned. 'I could fall asleep right here.'

Sacha stared at the cat, which had stretched out and closed its eyes. 'I think I am asleep, perhaps, already.'

Shaking herself, Taylor reached for the pastry box.

'Maybe food will help. Can I have an éclair?'

'No,' he said firmly, pulling out one of the green pastries. 'First you must try this. It is wonderful.'

She made a face. 'Do I have to?'

'Yes.'

When she shot him a tragic look, he rolled his eyes. 'Look, if you hate it you can just . . . spit it out. The cat can have it.'

He held out the pastry.

With clear reluctance, she leaned forward to take a cautious nibble.

Her eyes widened.

'Oh my God. It's delicious. It doesn't taste anything like it looks.'

Grinning, Sacha ate half of the pastry in one bite, speaking with his mouth full.

'I told you.'

Taylor reached for the other one. 'Just one more bite . . .'

The sound of a car roaring into town drowned out the last of her sentence. They both ducked. A black BMW raced into the little main street, screeching to a halt at the edge of the square.

Sacha cursed. What had they been thinking? They'd been so stupid to stop. Idiotic.

Desperately, he searched for an escape route, but they were too far from the bike. They'd have to cross the square and there was no way to do it without being seen.

The car's door flew open. Instinctively, he reached for Taylor, not knowing quite what to do – how to protect her. But she was already on her feet, eyes trained on the BMW, energy crackling around her as she prepared for a fight.

At that moment, the bakery door opened with a jangle, and

the woman who'd served them earlier burst out complaining loudly. A balding, middle-aged man with a paunch emerged from the BMW, shouting back at her with equal ferocity. The two argued briefly – about his tardiness, how it was too late now to get the delivery of sugar she needed for the next day, and why was he so irresponsible? – until the man climbed back into the car and roared off, tyres spinning.

Still muttering to herself, the woman turned on her heel and went back inside, closing the door with an irritated thud.

His heart still racing, Sacha dropped back onto the bench.

'*Putain*,' he swore. 'That scared me.'

The colour had drained from Taylor's face. Clearly shaken, she sank down onto the bench and turned to him.

'I could have killed him, Sacha.'

Her voice quivered. She kept staring at her hands like she didn't recognise them.

Sacha wasn't sure what to say. How could he tell her that, in that brief, highly charged moment, he'd *wanted* her to kill that man?

Wordlessly, he reached for her hand; her fingers were sticky from the pastry, which now lay in the dirt at their feet.

'I hate this,' she said softly.

'Me, too.'

She looked up at him. 'What are we going to do?'

'We're going to Carcassonne,' he told her. 'And we're going to make this stop.'

Her fingers curved around his. Then, with a sigh of weary resignation, she let go and rose to her feet.

'We better get moving.'

The moment had changed everything. As they walked back to the motorcycle, Sacha sensed danger everywhere – in the dark, lengthening shadow of the church tower. In the loud music pouring from the windows of a passing car.

Why had they ever stopped here? There was no sanctuary in this town.

When they reached the bike he stuffed the bakery box into his bag, and tossed Taylor her helmet. She clipped it on in silence.

He knew she was as eager to get out of here as he was, but where to? The nearest safe house was at least two hundred kilometres away. They'd never make it that far tonight. He was just too tired.

'I think we should find a place to sleep,' he said, as she climbed on behind him.

To his surprise, she agreed immediately.

'Good idea. Where?'

Pulling a map from his pocket, he unfolded it on his lap. Taylor leaned over his shoulder to see.

'We're here,' Sacha said, pointing. 'There must be something nearby . . .'

He traced their planned route with his fingertip, stopping when it reached a vast forest-green sprawl.

'This national forest is about an hour away,' he said. 'We should be able to find someplace in there.'

'There wouldn't be any people in there at night,' Taylor said thoughtfully. 'No reason for anyone to think we'd be there.'

It wasn't ideal, but it would have to do. Sacha made up his mind.

'Let Louisa know that's what we're going to do,' he said, folding the map away.

Taylor pulled her phone from her pocket, and pushed the dial button.

# TWENTY

'This is a bad idea,' Alastair muttered as he turned the van around.

Louisa put her phone away. 'I'm not arguing with you. But I can't blame them. They're worn out. They haven't had any rest in more than twenty-four hours.'

'If they'd kept going just a few more hours, they would have made it to a safe house.' There was no anger in Alastair's voice, but his expression was troubled.

Secretly, Louisa was just as worried as he was.

They were so close.

'The spot they've chosen is smart.' She said the words as much to herself as to him. 'They can lose themselves in there for a few hours, get some sleep and head off before dawn.'

'But we can't be with them,' Alastair reminded her unnecessarily. 'And we both think Mortimer is following us.'

They exchanged a look.

'Why didn't you tell her?'

Louisa looked out the window at the thickening forest. 'What's the point? If he comes anywhere near them she'll know it. I don't want them to be more scared than they already are.'

She wondered if she'd made the right decision. All day long she'd been sensing faint hints of Dark power. It had begun about forty miles after they left Calais, and happened intermittently since then.

It was impossible to trace, always just out of their reach. It felt like they were being followed. They'd taken every evasive action in the book and still, periodically, they'd both sensed it.

'It's like he's following us at a great distance,' Alastair had speculated after the second time they'd spotted it. 'Or he's close and shielding himself, somehow.'

'It could mean he's following us, but not them,' Louisa decided. 'Which is what we wanted, right?'

'Winning,' Alastair muttered.

He looked so tired. Deep circles underscored his eyes and his dark blond hair stood almost on end.

He'd handled all the driving, because Louisa had never learned how – it hadn't seemed important before. She was a city girl and always would be. As long as buses existed, driving was for other people.

She must have been tired too, because, for some reason, that thought summoned images of her foster parents, packing the kids into their crappy brown estate car, and she hadn't thought about that in years. In her memory, she was the last one in, as usual. Always forgotten. Always in the way.

'She can squeeze in there,' her foster mother would say,

frowning, as Louisa tried to angle herself in between the baby seat and her foster brother, who glared at her if she touched him.

She'd hear her foster parents murmuring to each other about space and money, and 'now that the baby's here, maybe we need to see if there's someplace else she could go'.

As if she didn't have ears.

As if they didn't have hearts.

But then, they didn't care, did they? None of them did.

'This looks like the place.'

Alastair's words jolted her from her memories.

Blinking hard, she shook her head to clear it. Alastair was turning the van off the highway onto a narrow road leading into thick woods. The only indication that they were entering a national forest was a small sign with a list of forbidden activities.

'I think that says if we start a camp fire we're going to jail,' she observed.

'They have to catch us first,' he said. 'And this van is like the wind.'

'Uh-huh.'

The roads inside the park climbed steeply through forested hills. Although it was still quite light on the flatlands, in the woods, it was already dark as night, and Alastair switched on the headlights.

It was gloomy in the shadow of the trees, as they wound their way up, up, up, until they neared the hilltop and it was briefly light again.

Louisa looked everywhere for a black motorcycle but there

were numerous side roads leading off into the woods – Sacha and Taylor could have taken any one.

When she pulled out her phone to call and find out where they'd parked, there were no bars at all showing on the screen.

'Damn, no signal.'

Alastair steered the van around a steep hairpin turn, his eyes fixed on the increasingly rugged road ahead.

'What should we do? Keep driving?'

Biting her lip, Louisa considered the options. This was a good place to spend the night, but she hadn't realised the technology implications.

They'd be cut off from each other all night.

She kept searching the woods for any sign of Taylor's distinctive alchemical energy, but it was impossible. It didn't travel far – not even at her strength level. On the plus side, there was no Dark energy, either. As far as she could tell, they were all alone.

Alastair cursed as the road twisted again. There was no guard rail, and on one side the hillside fell away into darkness in a steep, sheer drop.

'These aren't roads,' he muttered, squinting into the shadows, 'they're goat trails.'

They were both too tired for this. It wasn't safe.

'We should park,' Louisa announced.

'Great. Where?' Alastair looked around as if a parking place might leap out at them.

'There's got to be a car park somewhere.'

'Lou . . . ' He shot her a sideways look, grinding the gears as he downshifted. 'You do realise we're in a forest, right?'

'I'm looking,' she said evenly, 'for a good place. Will you let me look?'

'How about there?' He pointed.

They'd reached the top of a hill – a flat open area stretched out just off the side of the road.

'I think I can get the van in there without getting stuck.'

It wasn't terribly sheltered but then they weren't really hiding. She doubted very seriously that French authorities searched the parks at night for errant vans. Besides, it had a good view of the valley below – if anyone came up, they'd see them long before they reached the top.

'Works for me,' she said. 'There's not a soul up here to complain.'

They bumped off the road to the spot near a cluster of trees.

Turning off the engine, Alastair leaned back in his seat with a sigh of relief.

'Thank God that's over.' He looked up to where the last of the sun's light streaked the sky with amber and russet. 'What now?'

Louisa held her phone up as high as she could. Still nothing.

'Give me a second.' She rolled down the window and climbed out, pulling herself up onto the roof of the van with one good kick.

'Lou . . .' Alastair leaned out his window to stare up at her. 'What the hell are you doing?'

'Just . . . give me a second, will you?'

She held the phone up far above her head, swinging it left, then right.

Nothing.

When it became clear there was nothing more she could do, she stood for a while atop the van, scanning the valley below. It was perfectly quiet. The only movement came from a hawk, which swirled slow circles against the clear blue sky.

Louisa swung herself down to the ground in an easy, athletic move. Alastair watched her with a look of bemusement.

'Now,' she said, 'we wait.'

# TWENTY-ONE

The spot Sacha and Taylor chose was at the edge of a lake, well off the road, and tucked away at the end of a rough dirt lane. They could not be more hidden.

In fact, they would have missed it altogether, had Taylor not spotted the tiny sign in the headlights. All it said was: '*Lac Le Bac*'.

An arrow pointed down through a thick wall of conifers.

'What about there?' Taylor had suggested.

Sacha had slowed the bike, then gave a shrug. It looked remote enough.

'Let's check it out.'

Cautiously, he'd turned down the steep track.

The bike felt different on dirt, more unstable, less safe. Taylor held tightly to his waist as he eased it slowly down.

It seemed to take forever but then, all of a sudden, the

branches thinned and ahead of them lay a wide expanse of crystal blue. The water was still as glass, its surface reflecting the darkening sky like a mirror.

Sacha gave a whistle of surprise.

'Now that's a lake.'

A flock of water birds had settled for the night near the water's edge. The cacophony of the engine disturbed them, sending them up again in a flutter of anxiety.

Still moving slowly, Sacha followed the rough track around the lake's edge for a short distance, before pointing to where a path led down to a tiny cove, sheltered by trees.

'I can hide the bike there.'

It was already getting chilly so Taylor offered to build a fire while he disguised the motorcycle. By the time he'd pushed the bike behind the trees and stacked loose branches around so not an inch of it was visible, she'd nearly finished piling dry kindling into a neat pile.

The soft dirt disguised Sacha's footsteps, and she didn't hear him approaching.

Her curls tumbled over her shoulders in wild disarray as she knelt on the soft earth arranging the twigs with elaborate precision. Her face was so serious – so utterly focussed – that, as tired as he was, Sacha still had to smile. Of *course* Taylor would build an obsessively neat pile for her fire. Of course she'd have a system.

He stood for a second, watching her. How could he keep her safe? Was there any way to protect her from what was happening?

Not for the first time, he was overwhelmed with the urge to

run. To leave her here, hidden away, and just turn himself over to Mortimer. To trade her safety for his own life.

But if the alchemists were right, giving up his life wouldn't keep anyone safe. It would just unleash destruction.

They were trapped.

Something in the air must have shifted, because she glanced up at him. Her eyes searched his face.

'You OK?'

Smoothing his expression, he knelt next to her in front of the orderly firewood stack.

'How do we light it?' he asked. 'I don't have matches.'

Stars had begun to appear in the sky overhead. The sun was nearly gone now. Her teeth flashed white as she smiled at him.

'You don't need matches. You have me.' She held her hands over the dry wood.

Sacha thought he could feel it – the rush of energy towards her, like the earth hurrying to do her bidding. But it could have been his imagination.

In an instant, a golden tongue of flame licked at the wood. A wisp of smoke rose skyward.

Holding her hair back from her face, Taylor leaned forward to blow on it, gently calling it to life.

The flame danced and shuddered, before catching properly on the dry wood, and beginning to grow. A tiny tickle of warmth emanated towards them.

'That is pretty impressive.' Sacha glanced admiringly at Taylor, who held her hands out over the fire, absorbing the heat. 'You have such control now.'

'It's going to save me a fortune in matches.' Her face alight from the flames, she glanced up at him. 'I'm starving. I wish I could create food, too. We could have a barbecue.'

'You don't have to.'

He scrambled to his feet, brushing dirt from his knees, and headed back towards the bike to grab the cardboard box from his bag. It was battered and crumpled, but still mostly in one piece.

'Bet you're glad I didn't leave the pastries . . . ' he began as he walked up to the fire.

His voice faded.

The fire was burning brightly, and Taylor was gone.

'Taylor?' He tried to keep the panic from his voice, but his hands squeezed the pastry box flat.

He'd only been gone a second. How could this happen?

'*Taylor?* Where are you?' This time fear flooded his voice, and he didn't care.

'I'm here.' Her voice floated out of the darkness from the edge of the lake. She appeared in the fire's glow, shaking water from her hands. 'I had to clean up. I was filthy.'

Her face was damp, and she'd twisted her curls back loosely. He could make out the curves of her figure, traced in flames.

Relief made his bones feel soft.

She was fine.

He had to restrain himself from grabbing her, pulling her into his arms.

Unaware of how glorious she looked to him in that moment, she rubbed her hands on her trousers to dry them.

‘The water’s so cold. It’s like ice. I wish we had soap. I think I smell.’

Sacha couldn’t seem to think of the right response. In desperation, he held up the crushed pastry box.

‘I’ve got dinner.’

# Twenty-Two

'We should have brought more food.' Louisa looked mournfully into the empty bag of digestive biscuits.

'We didn't know we'd be doing the Duke of Edinburgh's bloody Challenge, though, did we?' Alastair huffed. 'We're supposed to be in a safe house right now.'

'You're mean when you're hungry,' she told him.

He didn't smile. 'I'm cold and I feel cut off. I don't like this, Lou.'

'I'm not a fan either, you know,' she said. 'I had to pee in the woods. Like a *bear*.'

His shrug said he didn't really care about her pee.

'What time is it?' Louisa asked, although her phone was right there and she could have checked.

He glanced at his watch. 'Just after nine.'

'Nine?' Her eyebrows shot up. 'How can it not be later? It seems like we've been here years.'

'It's been two hours.' He crossed his arms. 'I'm sorry my company is so boring for you.'

She glanced at him, a line deepening above her eyes. They never quarrelled. Alastair never got cross.

Louisa knew they both needed sleep and food but adrenaline was keeping them awake, and their tempers were fraying.

'I thought you liked camping,' she said. 'You're the farm boy here. You should be in your element.'

'My *grandparents* have a farm,' he said with slow deliberation. 'I grew up in Chichester.'

She had no idea where Chichester was.

'Isn't that in the countryside?'

'Oh my God.' He slid down in his seat, resting his chin on his chest, like a little boy. 'It's a city in the south of England with a nice cathedral in it. I can show you on a map.'

'I don't need to see it on a map,' she said, not taking the bait. 'I'm just surprised I didn't know that's where you were from. How could I not know that?'

'You never asked.'

Silence fell. Louisa couldn't think of anything to say.

Alastair was closer to her than anyone. How had she forgotten to ask him where he'd grown up? She knew his favourite colour was green, and that he liked dogs and hiking. That both his parents were alchemists who'd gone to St Wilfred's when they were young. That he had a sister he adored who was just a little younger than Taylor. But that was all information he'd volunteered, the kind of thing that came up in conversation. She had never really asked him anything about his life.

'Well, I'm an arsehole then,' she announced decisively. 'Tell me about your family. I want to know.'

His eyebrows winged up. 'Are you OK, Lou? You're not sick or anything?'

'I'm fine. I'm just trying to de-arse myself.' She turned in the van's spacious front seat so she was sitting cross-legged, facing him. 'Tell me.'

'Well,' he said cautiously, 'my dad's a solicitor and my mother is a psychologist. I went to state school until I was twelve and then they switched me to a private school because I kept wanting to read more books than they had in the library.'

'That,' Louisa said with a smile, 'does not surprise me. Tell me more.'

'What is there to tell?' He held up his hands. 'We had a dog named Pepper, who died three years ago.'

'What's your house like?' she prompted him. 'Is it new or old?'

'Old-ish.' He looked out the window, as if envisioning it. 'It's one of those rambling 1930s houses that never gets warm, except in the kitchen. So everyone's always in the kitchen. You know the kind.'

She didn't, actually. She'd grown up in flats and squats, aside from the years with foster families in various places in the suburbs of Liverpool, and an early childhood she couldn't remember.

She would have killed to have memories of a rambling family house filled with love.

'I know the kind.'

Something in her tone caught his attention.

'Lou . . .' His eyes held hers. 'What's going on? Why are you asking me all of this?'

'I just . . .' She let out a breath. The quiet was unearthly. It was so dark. The night seemed to press against the windows like water.

'It's just, I've seen what Mortimer can do, and I think there's a chance I might not get through this.' She looked back at him. 'And if I'm going to die, I want to die knowing more things about you.'

He reached for her hand, taking it quickly and holding it with firmness, as if he feared she would snatch it away.

'You're not going to die.'

'I might,' she argued. 'And I don't want to die regretting the one thing I should have done. The thing I didn't do because I was scared.'

'What's that?'

His voice was low, and his hand was so *warm*.

'This.' Reaching across the distance separating them, she grabbed his t-shirt by the nape of the neck and pulled him over until his lips were pressed against hers. She kissed him fiercely, prepared for him to pull back at any moment and tell her how he didn't feel the same.

But he didn't pull back.

Instead, he wrapped his arms around and pulled her closer, kissing her just as passionately as she'd kissed him. Parting her lips with his tongue, with a kind of longing that took her breath away.

His hands were strong on her back – strong enough to hold

her. Strong enough, she suspected, to let go if that was what she needed, too.

When the kiss finally paused, Alastair let out a shaky breath, and stroked the edges of her face.

'What the hell took you so long?'

Louisa, her hands still on his broad shoulders, shook her head. How could she explain?

'Maybe I don't know everything about you, but you know about me. You know about my family, right?'

He hesitated, but then nodded. 'Aldrich told me at the start. He was worried about you when you first came to St Wilfred's. Afraid you'd run and end up on the street again.'

This didn't come as a surprise to Louisa. It was Aldrich who'd found her after she'd escaped from prison, where she'd been held for accidentally killing a man who'd tried to rape her when she was seventeen.

In Liverpool for a meeting, he'd spotted her on the street near the station. Her alchemical power, he'd always said, 'was shining like a star'.

It had taken a lot of work on his part to convince her he was who he said he was. At first she hadn't believed him. She'd threatened him, shouted at him, run away from him. But he wouldn't give up.

Gradually, he'd convinced her of who he was, and what she was.

Still, she wouldn't go back to Oxford with him alone. He'd had to send for his graduate assistant, a kind young woman named Joanne, who'd travelled all the way to Liverpool just to drive back with them.

Louisa had ridden in the back seat of Aldrich's antique Jaguar, clinging to the door handle, plotting her escape if the two had turned on her. But they didn't. Aldrich had hummed along to jazz streaming from the radio, while Joanne twisted around in her seat to reassure her that she was safe.

Even after they arrived in Oxford, and Louisa was ensconced in a warm, dry room of her own, they'd struggled to convince her to stay the night.

In the end, exhaustion won out – she simply fell asleep.

The next morning, Alastair had appeared in the corridor outside her room, posh as hell, more than six feet tall, wearing torn jeans and holding a cardboard cup of coffee and a bag of doughnuts.

'Aldrich told me to bring you these,' he'd said. 'The cafeteria food might kill you, and we don't want you to die before you get to know us.'

She'd always known it was a set-up. Aldrich hadn't sent the wisest, funniest student in his class by accident. He'd hoped they'd look out for each other.

And now, four years later, here they were.

She was desperate. Desperate not to lose him. Now that Aldrich was gone, he was all she had.

She looked into his eyes, shadowed with affection and worry.

'I don't know how to love anyone,' she confessed. 'But I think I love you.' To her astonishment, tears burned the backs of her eyes. Her voice trembled. 'Alastair, I don't know what to do.'

His hands tightened around her, pulling her closer until she was across the central console and sitting on his lap, his arms warm around her.

'You do know how to love,' he told her, pressing his forehead lightly against hers. 'And what you don't know, I'll teach you.'

Then they were kissing again, and, for a while anyway, Louisa forgot to be afraid.

# TWENTY-THREE

Taylor and Sacha sat next to the fire. There was no moon, and the darkness had a solidity to it, like you could almost reach out and touch it.

Sacha relished the peace. It reminded him of his aunt's vineyard. Crickets were singing softly. An owl hooted somewhere in the woods nearby. The air was filled with the pleasing scent of wood smoke.

And best of all, just for a moment, nobody knew where they were. It felt safe. After they'd eaten the sandwiches and some of the pastries, rationing the little water they had left, they settled down by the fire.

Taylor had put his leather jacket back on as the evening chill deepened, and it swung back as she looked up at the sky, revealing the pale arc of her throat.

'So many stars.' Her voice was barely above a whisper. 'I don't think I knew there were so many stars in the universe.'

Sacha looked up, too. Starlight frosted the dark sky with silver. Suddenly the night didn't seem quite so dark after all.

When he glanced back, she was still gazing up, her expression pensive. She'd been quiet all evening – lost in her own thoughts. She seemed so lonely.

'Tell me something about yourself,' he said, breaking the silence. 'Something I don't know.'

She turned her head, a bemused look on her face. 'There's nothing to tell. I'm boring. My family is boring.'

He made an impatient sound.

'Everyone's family is boring. I didn't say tell me something interesting. I just said tell me *something*.'

Straightening, Taylor threw fresh wood on the fire. The flames crackled and jumped, sending sparks shooting up towards the stars.

Aware that she was buying time, Sacha waited patiently.

'I stole something once,' she said at last. 'A lipstick. It was the worst thing I'd ever done until . . .'

She didn't finish the sentence but he knew what she meant to say: *Until now.*

'You stole something? I don't believe it.' He kept his tone light. 'You would never steal. It's not in your nature. I know a thief when I see one.'

'I did though,' she insisted. 'It wasn't my idea. My friend Georgie made me do it. She was obsessed with challenging yourself. Doing things you don't want to do. She was always saying, "Get out of your comfort zone, Tay. Live a little."' A smile flickered across her face. 'I think she was afraid I'd end up trapped in Woodbury forever, alone with my books.'

'Tell me about the crime.' Sacha shifted, moving subtly closer to her. 'How did it go down?'

'It didn't *go down*, Sacha. I'm not a gangster.' She glanced at him, half-smiling. 'It was nothing, I guess. But it still bothers me. I can remember every second of it. I walked into the local chemist. I knew it so well – it was where my mum bought all our plasters and hair bobbles. And I took a lipstick.' She looked off into the distance. 'I grabbed the first one I saw; I didn't even know what colour it was. My hands were shaking so hard I could barely hold onto it.' She looked down at her fingers, as if remembering that feeling. 'Then I walked out. No one even looked at me. Perfect Taylor Montclair would never steal. I felt horrible about it. Like I was stabbing the people who worked there in the back. But I did it anyway. To test myself.'

'You didn't get caught?'

'That was the worst part, I think. I got away with it.' She hugged her knees. 'I wanted to take it back, but Georgie said that would put me back in my comfort zone again, and that I had to take it and never give it back. I kept waiting for the police to come to my house and take me away. It never happened.'

'I'm sorry the justice system let you down,' he said solemnly.

She swatted at him. 'I was *fourteen*. Respect my trauma, please.'

He laughed, dodging her hand. 'It must have been very upsetting.'

'OK, smartarse.' She turned to face him. 'Tell me something I don't know about you.'

'I would tell you about my crimes,' he said. 'But we're only here for another eight hours or so and that's not really enough time.'

Taylor's laugh was soft and pleasing.

'Fine then. Tell me about your favourite crime. Or your worst. Or your most memorable. Choose one.'

Picking up a twig, Sacha traced it through the dirt as he considered which story to tell. He was only half-joking about his list of crimes – there were so many. He'd never told her about Antoine, for instance – about jumping off a warehouse to his 'death' for cash – but now wasn't the time . . . It would make her stop laughing and he didn't want that to happen.

'I got mixed up with these guys for a while,' he said after a long pause. 'I guess you'd call them a gang, maybe? Anyway, they were up to all kinds of things. I thought it was funny to hang out with them. They used to hold these high-stakes poker games. They would bet everything – their cars, houses . . . It was crazy. It's where I got the motorcycle.'

He gestured to where the bike was hidden behind a cluster of trees.

'You *won* it?' Taylor stared.

Sacha nodded.

'The guy who bet it was really drunk,' he explained modestly. 'He should have known better. I wasn't actually that good at playing poker, but I was good at knowing when other people were worse.'

'How much is that bike worth? It looks really expensive.'

'A lot.' He couldn't disguise his pride. 'It was one of my biggest wins.'

She looked at him with new suspicion. 'Is it legal?'

'That depends on your definition of legal.' Before she could ask more tricky questions he hurried into his story. 'So, anyway, one night these guys bet that I couldn't steal their boss's car. Their boss is this big guy, surrounded at all times by a swarm of bodyguards. It was impossible. But I did it.'

Intrigued, Taylor turned to face him. 'How?'

'Everyone in his gang knew me. I was always hanging around with them. So, one day, I walked into the garage like usual, and told them I was there to pick up a car for Antoine, one of the guys. I was super casual. Very calm. But I was *sweating* because, these guys are all armed, you know? They called Antoine to check and he said, "Yes, let Sacha have the car."' His grin broadened. 'I drove out of the garage in the boss's car instead. They were furious. Antoine got into a lot of trouble.'

'Did they come after you?'

'Of course. I gave the car back but . . . ' Sacha thought of Antoine, a gun in his hand, pointing to the edge of the warehouse roof. 'I had a few problems with them after that.'

Taylor turned until she sat cross-legged facing him, her elbows resting on her knees. 'Were these the same guys who . . . hurt you when I was with you in Paris?'

He hesitated, not wanting the conversation to go where he could see it heading.

'Some of them,' he conceded. 'But that was different. They were really after Antoine. Not me.'

Silence fell for a moment then Taylor said softly, 'Why do you do it?'

Sacha's brow creased. 'Do what?'

'Take all these risks? Hang out with criminals who want to kill you.'

Sacha threw a twig into the fire with a little too much force, sending red hot embers tumbling.

'I guess I didn't care how much pain I caused,' he said. 'I didn't think about anyone but myself.'

'What about your mum? Or your sister?' Taylor was watching him closely.

'What meaning does life have when you know the day you're going to die?' Sacha held her eyes – challenging her to argue. 'You have to understand – I was clueless back then. I didn't know *why* things were like they were. All I knew was it wasn't fair. Nothing mattered to me, Taylor. I didn't care at all – not about other people, and especially not about myself. And . . .'

He paused, unable to bring himself to finish his thought.

'And what?' she pressed him gently. 'You can say it. Whatever it is.'

He looked up at her. 'I wanted to die.'

She flinched, and he continued quickly.

'Can't you see? If I could die before my eighteenth birthday, then I would have had some control over my own life, over this stupid curse. I would have been a normal guy, not some . . . *monster* who can be shot in the face or stabbed in the heart and just get up and walk away. Someone who can open a vein only to watch it heal almost immediately.' He swallowed hard. 'I tried to change my destiny. And I failed.'

He hazarded a glance at her. Her eyes were bright with unshed tears.

'I get it.' She said the words so softly, for a second he thought he'd misheard her.

'What?'

'I get it,' she said again. 'I've thought about it, too. About finding a way out. A way to not be me – and my problems aren't anything compared to yours. Nobody ever told me I had to die, not until this week. But . . . ' A tear escaped, tracing a line down the curve of her cheek. '. . . I want you to know I will do everything I can to keep you alive.'

He reached for her then, unable to stop himself, pulling her closer until she nestled in the warmth of his arms. She wrapped her own arms tightly around his neck, pulling him closer.

'Don't die, Sacha,' she whispered fiercely. 'Please don't die.'

'I don't want to,' he said, his voice breaking. 'Not anymore.' He pulled back so he could see her face – those green eyes. 'Now I want to live. More than anything in the world, I want to live. With you.'

Taylor's breath caught. Then, as if making up her mind she tilted her chin, lifting her lips to meet his. It happened so quickly. Later he would try to remember the exact moment, but all he would remember was that little pause, when she didn't breathe. And then they were kissing.

Her mouth was soft and warm. She tasted of salt from her tears and sugar from the pastries.

Gently he parted her lips with his tongue. Her hands tightened against him, pulling him closer still, until the softness of her body pressed against his.

He heard himself make a faint noise in his throat, as his

hands slid under the leather coat, up the warmth of her back, brushing the raised ridge of her spine and the slim, horizontal line of her bra strap, before losing themselves in the velvet waves of her hair as they tumbled together onto the soft earth beside the fire.

Lapsing into French unconsciously, he whispered things to her. Telling her how beautiful she was, how much he had longed to kiss her, that he loved her. Kissing her cheeks, her forehead, her eyelids – each part of her feather soft.

Each kiss was proof that he wasn't alone anymore.

He rolled onto his back, pulling her with him until she was above him, kissing the sharp line of his jaw, up his cheek towards his ear. It was hard to think when she kissed him there. Hard to do anything except hold her close.

Without warning, an electric shock ran through his body, shaking him. Making it hard to breathe, the way it did when Taylor was using his energy to draw power.

At the same moment, the breeze intensified. The trees swayed towards them. Even the flames from the fire seemed to lean in a way that didn't seem entirely natural. His hair began to stand on end.

'Taylor,' he murmured, not wanting her to stop kissing him. 'Are you doing something?'

Puzzled, she stared at him, then glanced at the fire and the trees.

She jumped off of him and scrambled away, colour rushing to her face.

'Oh my God,' she said. 'I didn't mean to do that. I didn't know . . .'

'What happened?' He was trying not to smile, but she looked so cute, her lips red from kissing, hair wild, cheeks flushed.

'Nothing,' she said unconvincingly.

His eyebrows winged up.

With obvious reluctance she admitted, 'I think ... I think I was drawing your energy by accident.' She looked mortified. 'I don't even know how I did that.'

Laughing, he reached for her hand. She tried to stay out of reach, but eventually gave in, allowing him to pull her back towards him until she was in his arms again.

'You can have my energy,' Sacha told her, 'any time you want it.'

# Twenty-four

As the first faint streaks of golden light took the black from the night sky, Taylor woke to find herself curled up in Sacha's arms.

For a while, she lay still, watching him sleep.

He looked beautiful. Sleep swept all the cynicism from his face. He looked young and vulnerable. His thick, dark lashes lay against his cheeks like charcoal smudges.

She didn't know how long she'd studied him with a kind of wonder before he stirred, lifting a hand to shield his eyes from the light.

She wondered if anything would change between them now that they were more than just friends. Were *they* different now?

When he woke up, though, he was still the same Sacha. Rubbing his eyes and glaring at the birds cawing in the sky overhead.

'Stupid birds,' he said hoarsely, before shouting, '*Vos gueules les piafs!* Will you please just *shut up*?'

She laughed, and his attention swung from the birds to her. Raising himself on one elbow, he reached down to brush a curl from her cheek.

'Good morning,' he said. 'Did you sleep?'

'A little.'

The smile they exchanged then spoke volumes. He leaned down to kiss her, his lips soft and gentle.

The sun was warm against Taylor's face, a reminder that time was passing. Reluctantly, she pulled back.

'We better get going. Louisa wanted us on the road at dawn.'

'Slave driver,' he said, but he got up.

They cleaned up as best they could. There was very little bottled water left, so they brushed their teeth with lake water.

The whole time, Taylor felt giddy. She kept saying remarkably idiotic things.

'Hopefully there's no bacteria too deadly in here,' she heard herself say brightly.

She wondered, even as the words left her mouth, why she said things like that.

Sacha just smiled at her through a mouthful of foam, managing to look so endearing it completely nonplussed her, and she forgot to criticise herself for a while.

When they got back to the camp fire, she checked her phone once more for any sign of a signal, and found the battery completely dead.

'Bollocks,' she said, holding it up so Sacha could see the blank screen. 'Is yours working?'

He checked his phone and shook his head. 'It's dead, too.'

The first twinge of panic stirred in Taylor's chest. But Sacha was calm about the whole thing.

'We have the address of the safe house. Louisa will meet us there. It'll be fine.'

Taylor couldn't understand how he could be so sanguine. Nothing seemed to get to him. When he wasn't looking, she studied him, admiring his sharp cheekbones or the way his eyes were the same blue as the lake. She liked how tall and skinny he was, the way his straight brown hair fell into his eyes, the way he blew it back with a puff of air.

Once, when they were loading their things back on the bike, he caught her gaze. He didn't look away. She wondered if he'd been watching her when she wasn't looking, too.

Kissing him had been amazing. Better than she'd ever imagined. Maybe it was a French thing. Or maybe it was just Sacha. But kissing her last boyfriend paled by comparison.

He'd even managed to make the power surge thing less humiliating.

'You're like a girl-shaped rechargeable battery,' he'd said, trailing kisses down her neck. 'Plugged into the planet.'

She'd wanted to argue but she also didn't want him to stop kissing her.

The memory made her blush. Maybe she needed to stop thinking about kissing.

It took both of them to push the motorcycle out of its hiding place – its wheels had sunk in the soft mud. When she climbed on behind him, he glanced back. His eyes were even more beautiful through the visor.

'Ready?'

She wrapped her arms around his waist, holding him closer than she'd dared the previous day. Before he put the bike into gear, Sacha reached down to squeeze her hand. That simple gesture made her heart flip.

Whatever awaited them at the end of the road, they would face it together.

'I'm ready.'

♊

It was nearly noon by the time Taylor and Sacha reached the town they were looking for. Staying off the main roads made everything more complicated – the back roads were confusing, and they'd taken several wrong turns.

They finally ended up in a town where the narrow streets were all lined with houses in pale pink stone. Most had closed their shutters to the heat, giving the place a sleepy, abandoned feel.

The motorcycle engine sounded louder here, and Sacha quickly found a quiet spot on a side street to park.

Removing his helmet, he pulled a paper from his pocket to check the address.

'We're looking for Rue des Abbesses,' he said.

Taylor pulled off her own helmet and took a deep gulp of air. After being encased in plastic for hours, even hot air felt good on her skin.

'Are there more directions?'

He shook his head. 'It just says Rue des Abbesses.'

Taylor looked around. 'We'll have to go street by street.'

'Wait.' Sacha rubbed his chin thoughtfully. 'A street with a name like that is bound to be near a church or abbey.' He twisted around to point to where a church steeple rose above the green trees like a stovepipe. 'It'll be back there somewhere.'

'Makes sense.' Taylor pulled her helmet back on. 'Let's go take a look.'

They headed back the way they'd come, slowing for every street sign.

They found the grey-stone abbey after some searching, at the far end of a long lane behind a high wall with a forbidding gate. A sign mounted nearby read: 'Rue des Abbesses'.

'At last,' Taylor said.

Sacha slowed the bike to a crawl. They made their way down, checking numbers. The one they sought was a tall, narrow house, just outside the imposing metal gates of the abbey.

Taylor closed her eyes to *see* the place. Molecular energy was all around her – tiny golden threads from the plants in the gardens, thicker strands from the electrical wires overhead, and something under her feet – running water, she guessed.

Inside the houses, all was calm. In some, she sensed the red signs of human energy. In others, nothing at all. No sign of Mortimer.

'It looks safe,' she said.

Sacha cut the engine.

Like all the buildings on the street, this house was made of the same stone as the abbey – solid and grey. It was three storeys tall, its roof bristling with chimneys. Filmy curtains covered the upper windows, while the lower windows were shuttered tightly. A low wall surrounded it, with an old stable to one side. The front gate had been left open, as if they were expected.

Taylor could get nothing from the house at all – neither human nor alchemical energy.

'It's weird,' she said in a low voice. 'It's like the house is empty – only it's more than empty. I can't sense the electricity or water or anything.' She stared at the tall, old building. 'It's like the building isn't *there*.'

Sacha didn't like the sound of that. But it was definitely the place.

'Let's check it out,' he said.

Motioning for her to follow, he climbed off the bike. They didn't take their bags.

'Let's leave everything here. Just in case . . . ' he said.

They headed slowly across the little courtyard in front of the door. A fountain gushed to one side – a statue of a beautiful girl poured water slowly and forever from an urn.

They were midway to the front door when the gate swung shut behind them and latched with a solid clunk. Taylor's heart stopped.

They stood frozen, torn between running away and knocking.

'Maybe it's them,' Taylor suggested. 'They shut the gate to keep us safe.'

'Or it could be Mortimer,' Sacha pointed out. 'Shutting the gate to keep us in. Besides, my bike's on the other side.'

He didn't look happy.

'I think we should knock,' she decided. 'There has to be a

reason I can't sense anything from that house. Maybe it's just that a safe house is really . . . safe.'

'Just be ready to run,' Sacha cautioned her. 'And don't wait for me. If it's him, you go. Don't let him get both of us.'

Taylor reached for his hand. 'He's not getting either of us.'

They both heard footsteps approach. Taylor tried to sense what was coming but the house gave nothing away.

Her heart thudded painfully in her chest.

Sacha's hand tightened on hers.

'Be ready,' he whispered.

They both heard the locks turning, bolts sliding, and it was too late to run.

The door swung open soundlessly.

A man stood in front of them. Dark hair carefully combed back, a square, smoothly shaven jaw, a pair of fashionable glasses.

'There you are,' he said in French-accented English. 'We were worried.'

Sacha drew a startled breath.

'Mr Deide?'

# TWENTY-FIVE

'I'm so glad to see you both in one piece,' Deide said, handing Sacha a steaming mug of coffee.

Sacha accepted it numbly.

They stood in a bright, spacious kitchen at the back of the elegant house.

He didn't know what to think. The last time he'd seen his English teacher had been in his Paris classroom, warning Taylor that she was in danger.

He looked exactly the same – button-down shirt, trendy glasses, artful stubble on his jaw. But he looked a little older, as if the last few weeks had taken years off his life.

'I'm so confused,' Sacha said. 'I thought you were in Paris. What happened?'

'Yes, well.' Deide's eyes were hard to read behind his glasses. 'That's a long story.'

Standing a little apart, Taylor watched the two of them, a worried frown creasing her brow.

'Where are Louisa and Alastair?' she asked.

'They're fine,' the teacher assured her. 'They had some trouble with the van but they're on their way. Is your phone not working? They've been trying to reach you. We've been very worried.'

'Both our batteries died,' Taylor explained.

He nodded, and turned to pour steaming water from the kettle into a cup. The kitchen was straight out of a catalogue – the countertops were scrubbed pine; white cabinets lined the walls. The whole place was attractive and characterless.

'That is as we suspected.'

'Mr Deide,' Sacha said. 'I still don't understand what you're doing here.'

The teacher handed Taylor a cup of tea.

'I'll explain,' he said. 'Please follow me.'

He led the way back down the wide, main corridor to the living room. The room was big and expensively decorated, with polished wood floors and deep white sofas. Just like the kitchen it had an underlying forlorn air of emptiness.

Sacha and Taylor perched side by side on one of the sofas. He sat down across from them, a cup of coffee in one hand.

'When you left Paris,' Deide began, 'I wanted to go find you, Sacha. But St Wilfred's thought that was a bad idea.'

Sacha frowned. 'Why?'

'You see,' the teacher said, 'at the time, I was being followed. We now know it was Mortimer Pierce. Then, obviously, we didn't know who it was. All we knew was it was someone dabbling with Dark power. Aldrich believed I should stay in Paris to lure him away from you. We hoped if he thought I was hiding you, then you might have more of a chance. Unfortunately, that didn't work as well as we'd hoped. And then Aldrich, himself, was killed.'

He stopped then, his face clouding, and turned to Taylor. 'I was so sorry to hear about your grandfather. I met him only a few times, but I admired him greatly.'

'Thank you,' she replied, feelingly.

A momentary silence fell.

Taylor broke it.

'Mr Deide, are we safe here? Why couldn't I sense you in this house? The whole building gave me nothing at all.'

The teacher looked pleased. 'We've done our job well, then. This building, like all our safe houses is protected using the old methods.' He pointed above the window. For the first time Sacha saw the symbols carved there – triangles within a circle, a snake eating its tail.

'This particular combination of alchemical symbols acts as a barrier – no energy comes in and none goes out.'

'What about Mortimer Pierce?' Sacha asked. 'Would these protections stop him?'

Deide's face darkened. 'I'm afraid there's no way to know the answer to that question. He's dabbled in demonology. His power goes beyond anything we understand . . .'

His voice trailed off. Holding up a hand to silence them, he turned towards the window, listening. A second later, Sacha heard it, too. A car engine, growing closer. And then, stopping.

The teacher sprang up from the sofa and sprinted from the room. Without waiting for an invitation, Taylor and Sacha ran after him to the front door.

Alastair's battered blue van was parked out front next to Sacha's gleaming motorcycle.

The passenger door gave a rusty groan and Louisa climbed out, her turquoise hair sparkling in the afternoon sun.

'Dammit, you two,' she complained, throwing a leather bag over her shoulder. 'Where the hell have you *been*?'

'Louisa!' Taylor sped down the stairs and launched herself at her. 'I was so worried.'

Louisa hugged her back reflexively. It was the first time Sacha could ever remember seeing her genuinely flustered.

'No need for histrionics,' she said gruffly.

But Sacha could tell she was pleased.

Alastair emerged from the driver's seat carrying the rest of their things, his hair more dishevelled than Sacha had ever seen it.

'Bloody van overheated.' His cut-glass English accent made it sound kind of impressive. 'I thought Lou was going to murder it with her eyes.'

'It deserved to die,' Louisa said.

When Alastair reached Sacha he gave him a one-arm hug.

'Good to see you in one piece.'

'You as well,' Sacha said, grinning.

They were all talking at once, complaining about the roads, the van, when Deide held up his hands.

'Everyone, *s'il vous plait*. We're not safe out here. Move the vehicles into the courtyard, please. Lock the gate. Then we talk.'

♊

A few minutes later they were all settled in the living room, telling their tales of the night before.

'... so we just camped down by the lake,' Sacha finished. 'No sign of trouble. What about you guys?'

'Slept in the van.' Louisa gave a casual shrug. 'No baddies there either.'

'Well, that's not exactly true,' Alastair said.

He and Louisa exchanged a look.

'Oh, yeah,' she said. 'That.'

'That, what?' Taylor asked.

Louisa hesitated.

'All day long we kept sensing Dark power.' She glanced at Deide. 'It was off and on, never steady enough that I could get a handle on it or identify it. Maybe it was some other Dark power guy but I got the feeling we were being followed.'

'You didn't think to mention this before?' Deide did not look happy.

'Well, here's the thing,' Alastair said. 'After we entered the forest, we lost it completely. Never encountered it again. We thought maybe we just got rid of him.'

Deide leaned back in his chair, his expression was troubled. 'I do not believe it is possible to get rid of Pierce in this way. I don't like the sound of this at all.'

'How is he doing this?' Sacha could hear the frustration in Taylor's voice. 'How could he find us? How is he doing any of this? The zombies. The attack. It doesn't make *sense*. We did everything right. It's like he's not human.'

She bit her lip hard as if to make herself stop.

It was Deide who responded.

'You are not wrong. What he is doing was long believed impossible,' he said, choosing his words carefully. 'And I'm not certain how human he really is anymore.'

He glanced at Louisa, who inclined her head slightly.

Deide continued. 'We think the things he's doing – his power – it may mean he's closer to raising this demon than we'd thought. It's as if they're already working together.'

An icy shard of fear entered Sacha's chest.

'I thought the reason he needed me was to raise the demon. Isn't that what this is all about? What are you telling us? Has he done it already? Are we too late?'

'I think it's more that he's found a way to communicate with the demon,' Deide said. 'And now the demon is helping him.'

'Why?' Sacha stuttered. 'How . . . ?'

Alastair interceded. 'Why? Because it's in the demon's interest for Mortimer to win. How . . . ? Well. That's what we're trying to figure out.'

'We're not too late, Sacha.' Leaning forward, Deide rested his wrists on his knees. 'The demon is not in our dimension. But somehow his energy is filtering through. It's possible it's just a matter of time – it's only three days from the moment the curse is due to be fulfilled – the separation between our world and other dimensions could be losing strength. That would explain how Mortimer could make these creatures. And why they are not affected by our abilities. And why the traditions that usually protect us are failing.'

'What happens now?' Taylor asked. 'How long can we stay here? When do we move on?'

'I think it's safe for you all to spend the night here,' Deide said. 'Tomorrow, though, you must go to Carcassonne. There's another safe house there, waiting for you. It's more remote than this one – and better protected.'

'But we are safe here tonight,' Sacha asked. 'Right?'

The look Deide gave him was regretful.

'This is the best we can do. But I am sorry to say, nowhere is safe anymore.'

# Twenty-six

Later on, Taylor would remember that night they spent in the safe house as a hazy blur. After that first serious discussion, the mood lightened – becoming at times, almost giddy. The levels of stress they'd been operating under couldn't be sustained, and the tension finally broke.

They had dinner in the dining room, gathered around a long table, everyone talking and laughing.

To her own surprise, Taylor found herself enjoying it. For the most part, they all avoided talking about Mortimer. Instead, they talked about other things.

Louisa told them about the *ordeal* of spending the night in the van, and how Alastair snored.

'How dare you,' Alastair said, with faux umbrage.

'Like a bloody lawn mower,' Louisa said, demonstrating raucously until he threw a piece of bread at her.

Taylor and Sacha explained how they'd subsisted on

squashed pastries and brushed their teeth in lake water. Their stories grew slightly hysterical as they frantically avoided mentioning kissing.

'And the birds were so noisy,' Sacha exclaimed.

'So noisy,' Taylor agreed with too much enthusiasm. 'It was *crazy*.'

But no one seemed to notice.

Throughout it all, Deide listened and smiled, laughing in the right places, and pouring drinks when glasses looked low. Keeping everyone talking.

They were all exhausted, and it was still early when Deide showed everyone up to their rooms. Taylor and Louisa shared a spacious room on the top floor, with whitewashed floors and twin beds neatly covered in spotless, matelassé spreads. A small porcelain lamp sat on the tiny table between them, beneath an oil painting of a farmhouse under a vivid blue sky.

Dropping her bag by the door, Louisa threw herself onto the first bed.

'A real bed,' she sighed. 'I may never wake up again.'

Once they'd cleaned their teeth and changed – Taylor into sleeping shorts and t-shirt, Louisa into an outfit nearly identical to the one she'd been wearing before – they turned off the lamp. But, tired as she was, Taylor couldn't seem to rest.

Shadows skittered outside the window. Deide's words – *Nowhere is safe* – seemed to echo in her mind. Each time she closed her eyes, she saw Mortimer, destroying everything she loved. Monsters with scorched skin lumbering towards her. Bringers holding out their hands summoning pain.

She sat up.

In the next bed, Louisa was still – her breathing slow and even. The house was very quiet – she could hear a clock ticking somewhere, slow and methodical.

*I'll just have a look*, she told herself. *Then I can sleep.*

Careful not to wake Louisa, she slipped out of bed and tiptoed to the window.

Through the glass she could see the little courtyard out front. It was empty. Water still poured from the statue's urn.

Beyond the front wall, a single light illuminated a row of elegant town houses, and an empty street. Everything was quiet.

Taylor let out a long breath.

It was fine. There was nothing there.

She was just turning back towards bed, when something moved in her peripheral vision.

Hurriedly, she whipped around, pressing her face against the glass.

She watched with growing horror as a shadow detached itself from the abbey wall and stepped closer.

Still in darkness, it was hard to make it out. Then the moon moved out from behind a cloud and she thought she saw the long shadow of a walking cane.

Gasping, Taylor recoiled.

Swearing under her breath, she went back to the window and forced herself to peer outside again. Her heart thudded hard in her chest and she pressed her hand against it, as if it might escape.

There was nobody there. Suddenly a hand gripped her shoulder.

'Don't scream,' Louisa whispered. 'Is it him?'

Taylor couldn't seem to speak. Her entire face felt frozen. She had to force the words out.

'I thought I saw him. But now . . . '

Moving past her, Louisa looked out the window. Taylor stared at her, barely breathing.

'There's nothing there. What did you see?'

Taylor described the shadow. The way it moved.

'I thought . . . it was him. His cane.' She took a sobbing breath. 'But then he wasn't there anymore. He disappeared.'

Louisa thought for a moment.

'Come on.' Grabbing Taylor's hand, she dragged her from the room.

They ran down the stairs, their bare feet silent on the wood floor.

The ground floor was dark and quiet as they sped down the main corridor towards the front door.

They skidded to a stop.

Louisa pressed her hand against it, and the complex locks released with a series of loud clicks.

The door swung open.

The night was cool. The air smelled fresh, with a promise of rain. Nothing moved.

They stood side by side in the courtyard, scanning the street for any sign of Mortimer. Taylor found nothing – just a faint hint of Dark power, like an oil sheen on water, that could have been her imagination.

'What's going on?' Alastair appeared in the doorway behind them, barefoot in jeans and a St Wilfred's t-shirt, his face blurry with sleep. 'Are you running away?'

'Taylor thought she saw Pierce,' Louisa said.

Instantly alert, he strode out to join them. 'Where? Any sign of him?'

'It's like earlier.' Louisa gave him a significant look. 'Only faint traces.'

His face darkened. 'Dammit. How is he doing this? And what does it mean? Is he tracking us? Is it something new?'

'I don't know. But let's get Taylor inside, just in case.' Louisa took Taylor's arm and hustled her towards the door. 'Where's Sacha?'

'In our room, asleep,' Alastair said.

Even in the confusion, Taylor was relieved Sacha was fine. At least there was that.

Inside, Louisa grabbed a pair of shoes at random from a pile in front of the door and began yanking them on. Taylor watched her worriedly.

'Where are you going?'

'To take a look. I need to make sure he's really gone.'

'I'm going with you,' Alastair said.

'I'll come, too.' Taylor reached for some shoes, but Louisa stopped her.

'You can't come, Taylor,' she said firmly. 'I know you want to, but we have to keep you safe. That's the point of everything. Stay here.'

Taylor bristled. It was *her* power that had defeated Bringers and zombies. Her strength that saved them, over and over again.

But she didn't want an argument right now. So she bit her tongue.

Cautiously, with Alastair at her shoulder, Louisa opened

the door. Taylor got a brief glimpse of the quiet street outside. Smelled the cool night air.

And then they disappeared into the darkness.

♊

They were gone for hours.

Taylor waited for a while, moving to the living room as time ticked by, and eventually lying down on the sofa.

It was so quiet.

Despite the danger, exhaustion won out. At some point she must have fallen asleep because, when she opened her eyes, light was streaming through the windows and she could hear voices talking quietly.

Instantly wide awake, she leaped to her feet and followed the sounds to the kitchen.

Sacha, Alastair and Deide were sitting on tall stools around the kitchen island, clutching mugs of coffee. The only person missing was Louisa. The butcher block table top bore the remnants of a breakfast of bread, cheese and fruit.

'There she is,' Deide said, as she walked through the door. He wore a crisply ironed white shirt and jeans and looked relaxed. As if last night hadn't happened at all.

'Why didn't anyone wake me?' Taylor asked accusingly. 'What happened? Is everything OK? Where's Louisa?'

'Outside.' Alastair yawned, rubbing his eyes. 'Standing guard.'

'Everything's fine,' Deide said. 'No sign of Pierce.'

'I can't believe I missed all the excitement.' Sacha's expression was gloomy. 'You let me sleep through it all.'

'There was nothing to see,' Alastair said, swallowing his coffee.

'We're leaving as soon as Louisa gets back,' Deide told Taylor, handing her a large cup of *cafe au lait*.

Sacha slid a baguette and knife towards her. 'We saved you some food.'

His dark hair was rumpled. He wore a clean black t-shirt and jeans without a belt. Seeing him made her feel a little better. A little safer.

Pulling out an empty stool, Taylor sat down next to him and forced herself to take a bite of bread, but she couldn't taste it. She didn't have an appetite.

'If he wasn't there, what did I see?' she asked. 'Did I dream it?'

Deide took a seat across from her. 'We don't know for sure. We suspect he tracked Alastair and Louisa somehow. It's possible that your enhanced abilities just allowed you to process it all differently. They sensed Darkness, you saw shadows.' He shrugged. 'All we can hope is that our defences worked, and he couldn't detect your presence in the house.'

'What if he follows us today?' Sacha asked. 'If he followed us before, won't we lead him right to the next safe house?'

'Lou and I searched this town from one end to another,' Alastair said. 'If Mortimer's here he's completely invisible.'

Deide put down his cup. 'We must take different routes again. We'll all leave at the same time, making it impossible to follow all of us.'

'What should we do if we sense him?' Taylor asked.

'If you sense you're being followed, don't go to the safe house,' Deide said. 'That goes for all of you. Stop somewhere and call us. We'll figure out a way to get you back.'

'We can't lead him right to us a second time,' Alastair agreed.

The front door opened with a bang, and they all jumped.

Louisa's biker boots clumped on the wood floor as she stormed down the hallway. She wore a dark hoody with black trousers, her eyes were puffy from lack of sleep.

'It's raining,' was all she said.

Deide looked at her. 'All clear?'

'Completely empty,' she said. 'No sign of him. We should go now before the miserable bastard wakes up and starts stalking us again.'

Turning back to the table, Deide looked at his watch.

'*Allons-y*. It's nearly six o'clock,' he said. 'We should be out of this house in the next fifteen minutes. I suggest you pack quickly.

'It's time to go to Carcassonne.'

# Twenty-seven

Sacha and Taylor kept to the back roads as they headed south.

It rained all morning, making the journey treacherous and forcing Sacha to keep his speed down. They crawled through sleepy villages, and wide, empty pastures.

After the disturbed night, Taylor felt vulnerable and exposed. She had the constant sense of being watched but, whenever she turned around, no one was there. Not once did she sense Mortimer.

That didn't mean he wasn't there.

As planned, they'd all left the house at the same time. Louisa had given Taylor a quick, fierce hug before climbing into the van.

'Be safe,' she'd said. 'No chances.'

'You guys, too,' Taylor replied fervently.

Deide had climbed into a surprisingly smart black sports

car – nothing too flashy, but snazzier than you'd expect for an English teacher.

'I'll see you in Carcassonne,' he'd said, pulling on a pair of sleek sunglasses.

Sacha and Taylor had followed the others as far as the main intersection in the town, at which point they'd sped off in three separate directions.

Since then, there had been no communication from the others at all. Taylor could only hope they were all safe.

After the beauty of the French countryside, the unsubtle indicators of a busy tourist town were jarring as they neared Carcassonne. The roads teemed with tour buses and rental cars. The lush, green landscape was littered with billboards advertising cheap hotels, fast food, youth hostels.

The directions called for them to turn off the main road before they reached the town, and soon they found themselves back on a quiet country road. All around them gently rolling hills were covered in vineyards. Dark green grapevines heavy with fruit stretched as far as they could see in all directions.

They were on a peaceful stretch of road, when Sacha stopped the bike and drew the directions from his pocket.

Lifting his helmet off, he scanned the landscape.

'This must be the right place,' he said. 'But it says to turn left at a windmill. Do you see a windmill?'

The sun was dipping low in the sky, which was turning from blue to vivid magenta. A chilly wind blew off the long, low hills. Taylor could see nothing but vines.

'No sign of it,' she said.

Sacha rubbed his hand across his jaw. 'Maybe we took a wrong turn a few miles back.'

The thought was daunting. It would be dark soon. After that it would be even harder to find what they were looking for. There were no street lights out here. Few houses. No landmarks at all.

'Let's go on a bit further,' she suggested. 'Just to the next village. If we haven't found it by then, we'll turn back and try again.'

They continued on, searching for any sign of the elusive windmill. The sunset was flaming red on the horizon when Taylor thought she saw it.

She tapped his shoulder and pointed.

Far off the main road, down a rutted lane, a squat, ancient wooden windmill sat still and silent. It didn't look anything like the windmills she'd seen in England. It was so tiny and decrepit, it was hard to believe this was really what they sought.

Sacha stopped the bike.

Their instructions were to follow the lane past the windmill to the safe house, but right now they couldn't see anything behind the old structure except trees.

'This must be it.' There was doubt in his voice. 'I guess we should check it out.'

He turned down the rocky drive.

The old lane was so uneven, they slowed to a crawl. The low sun sent long shadows stretching out towards them like claws.

It wasn't until they passed the windmill that they finally saw the house, so overgrown it seemed to peer out from a thicket of trees.

Chateau D'Orbay was an imposing three-storey building with two long wings. It had once been a distinguished grey but its walls were so pitted and covered in dark green ivy, the colour was hard to identify.

Still on the bike, the two stared up at the towering front doors. A sun and moon had been carved into the stone on either side of the door. A triangle within a circle was carved at the very top.

There was no question this was the place. Taylor sensed a strange energy coming from the structure – it seemed to ... *hum*.

'It looks empty,' Sacha said.

'It's not empty,' she told him. 'I think it's ... alive.'

Before he had the chance to ask what she meant by that, the front door swung open and Louisa glared down at them, her hair aquamarine in the last of the sun's rays.

'Are you just going to sit there all day? Or are you coming in?'

♊

They stowed the motorcycle next to Alastair's van in a rickety outbuilding at the side of the chateau before following Louisa back around to the front.

The heavy main door swung open at the touch of her hand. Inside, it was dark as night, and smelled strongly of dust and mildew. It took Taylor's eyes a moment to adjust. What she saw, took her breath away.

The rooms were huge and filled with furniture that must once have been exquisite, but which now was falling to pieces. Priceless silk wallpaper was slowly rotting on the walls. The intricate plasterwork on the high ceilings was still beautiful, but was crumbling away to dust in places. The wood around the massive, floor-to-ceiling windows was water damaged and stained.

Ruined beauty filled every corner. Statues of shapely Greek nudes peered out from the gloaming, shoulders white and slim, blank eyes staring at nothing.

In the front lounge, a chandelier hung high overhead, its crystal brilliance muted by grey dust and a delicate netting of spider webs.

Through it all Taylor could feel the strange, underlying vibration she'd sensed from outside. It reminded her of being on an airplane – an odd sense of large engines working, unseen.

She and Sacha hung back, trying to take it all in, but Louisa walked briskly, as if nothing around them was at all unusual.

'This way,' she said, heading down a long shadowy hallway past a sweeping spiral staircase.

'This is the safest place we know of in this entire region,' she explained. 'There is no place as hidden as this. It may not look like much but, trust me, the locks are incredible.'

She turned off through a pair of wide double doors.

'What the hell?' Sacha murmured as they stepped through behind her.

Taylor couldn't blame him. It was like they'd stepped into a different house.

Here, the surfaces were clean and the floors polished. Huge windows gleamed. Ancient but serviceable chairs with fussy carved legs were clustered in groups. Candles in tall candelabra glimmered in every corner. Oil lanterns glowed on tables.

The scale of it was so overwhelming, Taylor almost didn't notice Alastair, stretched out on a sagging chaise longue in the far corner of the huge parlour. He was snoring softly, one arm flung over his eyes.

'We can only have candles back here,' Louisa explained, picking up an old-fashioned oil lantern. Its flame flickered, casting her face in moving shadows. 'The front stays dark. There's no electricity but there's water. Drop your bags here. Cup of tea?'

Without waiting for their answer, she headed towards a door at the end of the room. Exchanging a look of mute astonishment, Sacha and Taylor hurried after her.

'This place is massive,' Louisa said over her shoulder. 'Avoid the cellars. Those belong to the rats. But the rest is OK, as long as it doesn't rain. Oh, and the stairs are dodgy.'

'Where's Deide?' Sacha asked.

Louisa pushed open the door into the kitchen. 'In town.'

'In Carcassonne?' Taylor asked, surprised. 'By himself?'

'Looking for Mortimer.' She paused, frowning. 'I take it you didn't see any sign of him today?'

Taylor shook her head.

'No one did.' This fact didn't seem to please her.

The daylight had faded now, and the kitchen was dim – lighted only by Louisa's lantern – but Taylor could see it was a large, square room, with a sturdy oak table on one side. The other end of the room was dominated by an ancient cast-iron, wood-fired stove. An old-fashioned black kettle sat on top of it. The air smelled faintly of burning wood.

Setting the lantern down on the well-scrubbed counter, Louisa opened a cupboard and pulled out three delicate porcelain cups and tea bags.

'It's a bit dodgy using the stove,' she confessed, using a towel to pick up the kettle. 'Someone might notice the smoke. But we're English. We can't function without tea.'

After filling the cups, she rifled through a plastic cooler on the floor – it seemed jarringly modern in this setting – for milk.

'This place is incredible,' Sacha said when she handed him his cup. 'What is the story?'

'Yeah, I keep sensing this weird energy from it,' Taylor said. 'Like it's buzzing or something.'

Louisa tilted her head at the door. 'Let's talk in there where the lights are. We won't disturb Alastair. He could sleep through a Category 4 hurricane.'

Back in the parlour, she directed them to a quiet corner. They all perched on the spindly chairs, balancing fragile cups on their knees.

'This was once the home of a famous French alchemist and scientist in the seventeenth century, the Marquis D'Orbay,' Louisa explained. 'Have you heard of him?'

They both shook their heads.

'He was a friend of Isaac Newton – a scientist, an inventor. He was years ahead of his time. He invented things we still use today – a kind of early test tube, a process for distilling alcohol . . . ' She made a vague gesture. 'More importantly, he understood early medicine better than almost anyone – how to set bones, how to treat infections. He was hugely popular. In Paris, people lined up at his door to be treated by him. There were so many, he moved his practice out here to this chateau, which he used as a kind of hospital. Some people thought he had mystical powers . . . which, to be fair, he kind of did.' She waved a hand. Taylor felt the warmth of her drawing power and then the lantern on the table blinked out, coming back to life again with a flick of her fingers. 'Unfortunately, his success brought him to the attention of the French authorities. They accused him of witchcraft. Threatened him with a show trial and a terrible death. He hid this house to stay alive.'

'He *hid* the house?' Sacha's eyebrows winged up. 'How?'

'The windmill.'

Seeing the blank looks on their faces, Louisa smiled.

'The windmill draws water from an underground aquifer. There is tremendous energy in water. For us, it's like a nuclear power station. And he was sitting on top of it. Using a complex alchemical formula he invented himself, he drew the energy of the water to make it appear to normal people like there was nothing here but trees. To the rest of the world, it was as if this house disappeared overnight. The police searched for him, and it was a great mystery what became of him but, eventually, life went on and they forgot about him.'

She leaned her chair back against the wall, so the front two legs rose off the ground. It creaked alarmingly.

'After he disappeared, he could no longer treat the ill, of course, but he continued his research for the rest of his life. When he died, the house was bequeathed to the French branch of our organisation. They used it as a science institute for many years, but moved to a more modern building in the early twentieth century. These days it is mostly unused.' She flicked a glance at Sacha. 'Unless we have something to hide.'

Taylor put a hand on the wall to feel the humming more clearly. Suddenly the house made sense.

Next to her, Sacha was frowning. 'If he's dead, how is the house still invisible?'

'That's the weird part,' Louisa said. 'We can't figure it out.'

Taylor's hand dropped. 'You mean, you don't know how it works?'

'Not a clue.'

'But . . . wait. How can we not know?'

'He was an inventor, remember?' Alastair had woken without them noticing. He walked over to join them, rubbing his eyes. 'Glad you made it.'

Pulling up a chair next to Louisa's, he took the tea from her hand with a questioning look. She nodded permission. He took a sip.

'We think he invented a technique or device that operates in perpetuity,' he explained. 'It doesn't need us in order to function. We just don't know how it works. We were never able to find his plans for it. Maybe it somehow uses his energy after death. He's buried in the cellar after all.'

'He's buried *downstairs*?' Taylor shuddered.

'Apparently, being entombed in the house was his final wish.' Louisa yawned and stretched, letting the chair drop back to the floor with a thud. 'So there he lies.'

'If this house is really invisible then how come I could see it when we drove up?' There was a hint of scepticism in Sacha's voice.

'You could see it,' Louisa said, 'because we wanted you to see it.'

Draining the last of Louisa's cup, Alastair set it down on a spindly table.

'We can use our energy to counter the house's energy,' he explained. 'Revealing the house for short periods of time. As soon as we stop, D'Orbay's invention kicks back in again, and it disappears.'

Looking up to where the ornate ceiling disappeared into shadows, Taylor thought about the hunted marquis. She was beginning to know what it felt like to be pursued like that. To have death snapping at her heels. And why someone might want to disappear.

'It's a beautiful building to hide in,' she said.

'We've been fixing it up bit by bit,' Louisa said. 'But we have to be careful not to draw attention to what we're doing. The house must stay invisible. That's why there's no electricity. How could we hook it to the grid without telling someone the house exists?'

'Why can't we use the rooms in the front of the house?' Sacha asked.

'Water shifts and moves – its power is uneven,' Alastair explained. 'Besides, light has power of its own. The two can conflict. Very rarely, local residents have reported seeing lights and the shape of a house from behind the windmill.' A wicked smile crossed his face. 'They think the property is haunted. Which is fine with us. If they're scared, they stay away. Still, we have to take care not to draw attention to ourselves, especially now. Mortimer is out there somewhere, searching for us.'

Taylor's gaze darted involuntarily to the window. All she could see was the dancing candle flames reflected back at her.

Night had arrived.

# Twenty-eight

It was dinner time when Deide returned from Carcassonne. Alastair had cooked spaghetti on the old stove, and they were gathered around the kitchen table eating by candlelight when Deide strode into the room, dropping his shoulder bag on the floor with a thud. In a white shirt and khaki trousers, he looked for all thc world like someone's father coming home from work.

Spotting Taylor and Sacha, he smiled.

'I knew you'd make it.' Then he turned to the others. 'Any trouble?'

Louisa shook her head. 'Quiet as a tomb.'

'Good.'

They waited as the teacher spooned pasta onto a fine china plate. Taylor was learning there was nothing in the house that wasn't incredibly old and very beautiful. The fork in her hand was chunky silver, heavy as stone.

They all waited until Deide sat down at the table across from them and reached for the bottle of wine.

'How'd it go in town?' Louisa asked.

Deide took a sip of wine that looked black in the shadowy room.

'I saw no sign of Mortimer anywhere in Carcassonne,' he said, setting his glass back down. 'The town felt very strange. Too clean.'

'Nothing?' A crease formed on Alastair's brow. 'That doesn't make sense.'

'Exactly.' Deide met his eyes. 'I don't like it.'

'He's there.' Louisa reached for the wine bottle, her face set in grim lines. 'I know he's there.'

'I know it, too. But I can't find him. I can't find anyone. It's hard to explain, but the city feels empty even though it is very crowded. I think this is something he is doing to protect himself.'

Looking back and forth between them, Sacha asked the question that had also formed in Taylor's mind.

'Isn't it possible he isn't there? Maybe he's given up.'

'He's never giving up,' Louisa said. 'He can't. He's tied into this deal with the demon. Even if he wanted to walk away now, he couldn't.'

Alastair leaned back in his chair. 'I'm not surprised we can't locate him. He'll be doing as much as we are to stay undetected right now. He may have used some demonic weirdness to make himself invisible.' He glanced out the window into the dark night. 'I'm afraid if we don't find him soon, he'll find us. We can't wait. It's only two days until Sacha's birthday. He's got to be desperate to find us now.'

'Did you visit the church?' Taylor asked, thinking of the map in Jones' office. The cross marking the spot.

Deide nodded. 'It is even stranger than the town. There is a power there I couldn't identify. It wasn't Dark. It was . . . how should I say? Incredibly dangerous. I intended to search it, but I didn't dare. I didn't want to give away our presence too soon.'

He glanced at Louisa. 'We should go back tomorrow and search again. We have to find the precise location where Isabelle Montclair was executed before the ceremony can ever happen. It won't be easy – I am told it will be hidden. Everything about the ceremony must be so precise, we can't wait until Sacha's birthday to find it. We need to know where it is *now*. So, I think we must take the risk of going back together to look for it.'

*The ceremony.*

Taylor had been trying not to think about it. Zeitinger's instructions were still tucked away in her pocket – crumpled but disturbingly clear. She hadn't told Sacha what had to happen yet. That conversation was still to come.

His birthday was so close. She had to tell him the truth, soon.

'Fine.' Looking as if she'd lost her appetite, Louisa pushed her plate away. 'We go into town tomorrow together, and we somehow manage to search the church to find the special room. If the place is being watched, this will let Mortimer know we're here. He'll unleash all he's got on us. He'll want to get Sacha before his birthday, so if he can grab him tomorrow, he will.' She looked around at their faces. 'Am I the only one who sees the flaws in this plan?'

Taylor glanced at Sacha – he was listening to all this without expression – as if they were talking about someone else.

Alastair cleared his throat. 'I've been thinking. The key to everything is getting rid of Mortimer. So . . . we need to get rid of Mortimer.'

Louisa rolled her eyes. 'Yeah. And maybe Santa Claus will do it for us if we ask really nicely.'

'I'm serious,' Alastair chided her. 'Just hear me out. Mortimer doesn't expect us to attack him. He thinks all we want is to get Sacha to the church on his birthday and perform the ceremony. Everything he's doing is based on stopping us from doing that. So if we could find a way to draw him out and then kill him tomorrow . . . '

' . . . then there's nobody left to stop us when the time comes for the ceremony.' Deide straightened slowly. 'That's not a terrible idea.'

'But how?' Louisa looked unconvinced. 'We can't just say "And now we kill Mortimer Pierce" and have it happen. The guy won't want to die.'

'He won't,' Deide conceded. 'Still, as Alastair says, we are in a good place as he doesn't even expect us to try. We have the element of surprise.'

'Exactly,' Alastair said, excitedly. 'We can do this.'

The idea of killing Mortimer seemed to enervate them. All of their earlier tiredness had disappeared.

A cold shiver ran down Taylor's spine.

'How?' she asked, looking at the adults at the table. Their faces were hard to read in the scant light. 'We can't just . . . I don't know . . . shoot Mortimer. Can we?'

Louisa and Alastair exchanged a glance, but neither of them answered.

'It is easy,' Deide said simply, 'to kill.'

Picking up his heavy silver knife, he held it up so the flickering light caught it, and gave it a deadly shine.

'I could kill someone with this knife in two seconds.' He spun the knife off his fingertips and into his hand, thrusting it into the air.

'I will kill him,' Sacha said suddenly.

Taylor turned around to look at him. His eyes were fierce and filled with hatred.

'Let me do it.'

Deide set the knife down with a thump.

'We will all be involved in this plan,' he said. 'First, though, we must find him. And today, I could not do this. We have only two days left to find him. And then it will be too late.'

Louisa looked dubious. 'You said you think he's protected, in some way. How do we find him if he doesn't want to be found?'

Deide's gaze slid to Sacha and Taylor.

'We use bait.'

♊

The next morning, Taylor woke with a start in an unfamiliar room.

Pale light filtered through thick curtains that had once been yellow, with a delicate pattern of flowers, but that time had darkened to dull gold.

Blinking, she sat up slowly. The room was huge – four

times the size of her dormitory room at St Wilfred's. A marble fireplace dominated one wall, and an enormous armoire loomed across from it. The four-poster bed had the same yellow fabric the curtains were made from tied around each thick post.

It must once have been bright and cheerful, but the fabric was rotting in places and it smelled musty.

It had been late when they'd finally gone to bed. They'd carried candles to light their way as they made their way up the once-grand staircase. The steps creaked alarmingly, but Louisa insisted they were safe as long as they stuck to the edges.

'No one's fallen through, yet,' she'd said unconvincingly.

Sacha's room was on one side of Taylor's – Louisa's on the other.

As she'd got ready for bed she could hear the reassuring sounds of the two of them padding around their own cavernous rooms. Now, there was an uncanny quiet, but she thought she could smell coffee brewing downstairs.

She knew they'd be waiting for her; still, she didn't get up right away. She stayed in the surprisingly comfortable bed and went over the things they'd discussed the night before.

She needed to be ready when she faced the others. This was no time to look uncertain. No time for doubt.

After they'd eaten last night, they'd returned to the parlour. Taylor had curled up in one corner of a sagging sofa. Sacha sat stiffly at the other end. He'd been quiet all evening, his eyes dark with thought.

'Here's the plan,' Deide said. 'Tomorrow morning we go into

Carcassonne. You two ...' He pointed at Taylor and Sacha. '... go in together. Don't try to hide yourselves, but don't act obvious either. Blend in with the crowd. The rest of us will keep a safe distance away but we'll be there if you need us.'

'What are we going to do there?' Sacha asked. 'Aside from blending.'

'We have two aims. First, you will have to follow your instructions to find the precise location for the ceremony. You are looking for symbols, yes?'

'Professor Zeitinger said we look for an ourobouros – a snake, eating its tail,' Taylor said hesitantly. 'He said it would be carved on the stone where the ... Where we need to perform the ceremony.'

'Precisely,' Deide nodded. 'So you must find this stone. This is so you will be able to locate it easily the next night. At the same time, make sure you are seen.'

He glanced at Louisa and Alastair. 'The other goal for tomorrow is to be seen by Mortimer. We want him to know that you are here. We hope he will come out to try and take Sacha. When he does ...'

'We kill him.' Sacha said it flatly.

'Exactly so.'

'In broad daylight, though?' Taylor objected. 'There will be so many people around. How will that work?'

The teacher shrugged. 'We will do what we have to. Better to be thought a murderer than to end up dead ourselves, I think.'

When he put it like that it made an awful kind of sense.

'So. The plan.' Deide removed a map from the pocket of his blazer and spread it out on the scratched top of a tiny occasional table. He shifted a candle to cast its flickering light onto the page. They crowded around to see.

The room was warm, and smelled pleasantly of melted wax and burning lamp oil.

Pointing to a green space on the map, Deide said, 'There's a car park at the top of the hill near the citadel – Sacha and Taylor will park here. There's another at the edge of town but this is the one that will get you to the church the quickest. Mortimer will know this. He'll be keeping an eye on it. Move fast.'

'How can Mortimer watch the car park and all these streets at the same time?' Taylor asked.

Louisa lifted her gaze to meet Taylor's eyes. 'He won't be alone.'

Taylor's stomach tightened. 'How do you know . . .'

She never finished the sentence. Across the candlelit room, in Taylor's bag, her phone had begun to ring. It was Georgie's ring tone – her favourite pop song of the moment. The jaunty tune seemed wildly out of place in this setting.

'Sorry,' Taylor said, flushing.

She ran across the room and fumbled with the zipper on her bag, finally extricating it from the depths just as the ringing stopped.

Georgie's high-cheekboned, dark-skinned face beamed up at her. As the others resumed their conversation – a low rumble of tense discussion – Taylor stared at that beautiful face until it blurred.

Then she hit the ignore button. Switching the phone off, she shoved it back into her bag.

'Where were we?' she asked.

Louisa glanced at her.

'Once you get to the church,' she said, 'search for the room as quickly as you can. It could be in one of the side chapels located off the central nave. It might be in a crypt. It could be behind a locked door. Be thorough. It will be at the front of the building. Look for the symbol.'

Deide took over. 'There will be many tourists – the church is a popular attraction – so you should be safe. But you must endeavour not to become trapped in that church. You must be seen but not captured.'

Taylor swallowed hard. Trapped with Mortimer and his demons. The possibility hadn't occurred to her before now.

'From there, you will walk to your motorcycle as quickly as possible, and return here,' Deide continued. 'The rest of us will follow you all the way, hoping Mortimer takes the bait. If he does, we'll be ready for him.' He paused. 'I must be honest – I do not believe Mortimer will attack you in daylight. I hope he will, but I don't think he will. If he does not, we must return that night and try again. We will keep trying until Sacha's birthday.'

'We will never give up.'

♊

When Taylor headed downstairs, she found herself walking slowly, taking in the building in daylight. Last night it had been too dark to see much. Now, with the sun streaming through the windows, she could see all that she'd missed.

The hallway was broad and panelled in oak that must once have been polished to a high sheen, but now was faded and rough. Marble urns that would have held flowers, stood empty on plinths. The parlour was glorious, with tattered silk wallpaper, and huge mirrors above the two fireplaces that bookended the long, rectangular space. It might have been a ballroom at some point – it was easy to imagine it filled with women in luxurious gowns, dancing by candlelight.

By the time she walked into the kitchen a few minutes later, the others had finished breakfast.

Deide and Louisa were still at the table. Alastair stood at the sink, up to his elbows in suds, washing the dishes.

Taylor gaped.

They'd all dressed like tourists. Deide wore a baggy t-shirt and jeans. Alastair's cargo shorts exposed pale, muscled legs covered in fine, gold hair. Above it, he wore a t-shirt with a Union Jack on the front.

Seeing her expression, he held out his arms to show it off, soap dripping from his fingertips onto the stone floor. 'You like?'

'Very chic,' she said.

Louisa was the most transformed. A long-sleeved white top covered the tattoos on her arms. Full-length trousers disguised the ink on her legs. Her blue hair was hidden beneath Alastair's Oxford University baseball cap.

'You look horribly normal,' Taylor observed.

'Horribly normal is what I was going for,' Louisa said.

For her part, Taylor wore black shorts and a white t-shirt with the words 'Accio Book' on the front. But this was pretty much her normal look. She wondered if this meant she always sort of looked like a tourist.

Standing, Louisa gathered cups and glasses and ferried them to the sink for Alastair to wash. 'You missed breakfast. You better grab something quick if you want.'

'I'm not hungry.'

Taylor's stomach was tight with nerves.

'Where's Sacha?' she asked, noticing he was the only one missing.

'Getting the bike ready.' Louisa headed for the door. 'We're leaving in five. I'm going to grab my stuff.'

Taylor poured herself a glass of water and walked over to join Deide, who stood by the tall kitchen window looking out. The view was breathtaking. Dry hills rolled down into a deep valley. In the distance, Taylor could see an exquisite white castle, round turrets shining in the sun, looking like it had dropped straight from a fairy-tale.

It was almost too beautiful to be real.

'What is that?' she asked, pointing.

'That,' Deide said, 'is Carcassonne.'

# Twenty-nine

It was late morning when Sacha rolled the sleek black motorcycle into a barely legal parking space between a long tourist coach and a mini-van, and cut the engine.

The car park was packed. Rows of cars and coaches stretched across the hilltop lot in every direction. In fact, the whole town of Carcassonne seemed jammed with thousands upon thousands of people.

Removing his helmet, he glanced over his shoulder at Taylor. 'This is crazy.'

The air had the familiar tourist-town smell – a mixture of popcorn, burned sugar, and diesel exhaust. Hordes of tourists streamed by on foot, walking up from the town below.

'This is worse than Legoland.' Taylor handed him her helmet. 'I knew it would be busy but I didn't think it would be like *this*. Where are they all coming from?'

'Everywhere.'

A family gave the motorcycle suspicious looks as they skirted around it. Their three little kids ran ahead, clutching balloons in sticky hands and screaming with excitement.

Sacha shook his head. 'It's worse than I remembered.'

It wasn't yet noon but it was already hot. From where they'd parked, Sacha could barely see the town at the base of the hill – workaday limestone houses with red tile roofs. On the other side of the road, the castle towered – its formidable white stone walls flowing around dozens of watch towers, each with a fanciful pointed roof.

It looked timeless. Eternal.

Standing in front of those walls it was suddenly easy to believe in curses and alchemists, dungeons and public burnings.

'It's beautiful,' Taylor murmured, following his gaze. 'It's hard to believe a place like this still exists.'

Barely glancing up at the gorgeous edifice, Sacha hung the helmets from the handlebars.

'It's fake,' he said.

She looked at him in surprise. 'What do you mean, fake?'

'The castle.' He climbed off the bike, waiting as she followed. 'It looks medieval but it was rebuilt a hundred and fifty years ago by some lunatic. It's not medieval at all. It's fake.'

Taylor stood with her hands on her hips, staring up at the elegant castle shining on the hill.

'It's still an ace castle.'

Having a normal conversation broke some of the tension that had overshadowed their short journey from the chateau. As they made their way out of the car park, and allowed themselves to be absorbed into the crowds heading towards the huge arched gateway into the citadel, Sacha felt more confident. He'd been here once when he was a kid, on a school trip, and there was a familiarity to it that made it all a little less terrifying.

Maybe if he just treated this like a normal outing, he could get through this.

They passed through the archway, into a confusion of narrow, cobblestone lanes. Sacha glanced around with interest. Mostly he'd forgotten the old town – all he remembered of his first visit here were arguments in the coach and kids throwing up after eating too much junk food.

But now, as they were carried along by the throng onto the bridge spanning what had once been a wide moat, but which was now nothing more than a grassy dip, it felt familiar in a hazy way.

Although the castle had, as he told Taylor, been rebuilt, before then, it had been here for many hundreds of years, much as it was now. It was more than a castle, though. It was a city behind thick, fortified walls.

A whole community had lived here, and their houses still remained. These were the people who'd burned Isabelle Montclair. She'd been dragged past these houses the night she was killed.

Maybe his own ancestors lived in one of these houses.

It seemed as if he ought to feel some connection to this place beyond his visit here as a child. After all, he was so connected to his family's past, he might be about to die for it.

But he didn't.

The little shops selling candy and hand-made soaps, with their leaded glass windows and wooden signs – they were just stores. The narrow, stone-paved lanes, lower in the middle than at the edges, were pretty, but he didn't feel like he knew them.

He glanced over at Taylor to tell her about it, but her eyes held a far-away look of intense concentration. He knew what that meant.

'Do you sense anything?'

'It's very strange,' she said, a worried frown creasing her brow. 'I can't seem to sense much of anything.'

A man in a red t-shirt and shorts shoved past them, and Sacha pulled Taylor to one side.

'What? Nothing?' He gazed down at her, perplexed.

'It's sort of like the safe house,' she explained. 'Only more so. Like something's been done to it to make it unreadable. To protect it.'

She spun a circle, searching the faces of those around them before turning back to him. He could see the panic in her eyes.

'I can't describe it, Sacha. I can't *see* any of these people – their energy, I mean. It's not there. It's like they're not real. They're ghosts. I can't sense yours either. And I know it's there. It's like ... It's like I'm all alone on this street, but I know I'm not.' She took a quick, nervous breath. 'Someone's blocking me.'

'What does that mean?'

'I don't know.' She looked at him helplessly. 'I get it now, what Mr Deide said last night. There's no trace of Mortimer because there's no trace of anything.'

Sacha looked around the ancient street. There were people everywhere – families, couples holding hands, elderly people with canes. What she was saying made no sense.

Those people were real. The little nougat shop they stood in front of was definitely real. He could hear the conversation taking place inside ('Do you have a smaller box?' 'Of course, madam . . .'). The scent of icing sugar and almonds on the air-conditioned breeze flowing through the open door, that was real, too.

'There's something else.' Taylor bit her lip as if deciding how much to tell him, then leaned towards him, talking rapidly. 'There's something awful here, Sacha. Something Dark and horrible. I can't see it, but I can feel it. It feels like suffocating. It feels like . . . like death.'

Sacha leaned closer, lowering his voice. 'Is Mortimer doing this?'

Her reply came without hesitation. 'This is worse than Dark power.'

Sacha scanned the area as if he might find the source of what Taylor had sensed. Some instinctual part of him could sense a fraction of what Taylor felt. Or maybe it was just fear. Either way, every nerve was firing now.

Everything that had been benign appeared threatening. The splashing fountain where stone nymphs poured jugs of water into pools at their delicate feet. The small crowds of performers in medieval costumes across the square, performing magic tricks, juggling fire, rousing the crowds with their constant patter.

He wanted to get out of here, but they couldn't leave yet.

'We have to keep going,' he said grimly.

Taylor nodded, but he could see the icy apprehension in her face.

They stepped back into the stream of tourists with new caution. On a quiet side lane, the sound of hysterical laughter drew their attention towards a tiny stone cottage, set back in the shadows. It seemed to sell old-fashioned wooden puppets. A little stage, covered in black fabric, had been set up in front of the shop, and a small crowd of children had gathered to watch a puppet show.

Taylor and Sacha paused at the fringe of the crowd in the shade of a plane tree.

One puppet was dressed like a woman in a ragged black dress. The other, a man on horseback, played the villain. His little face was carved and painted with a thick brown beard. It took Sacha a second to realise what he was seeing. The man puppet was playing a judge. The woman puppet was on trial, accused of witchcraft and condemned to burn at the stake.

Grimacing, Sacha turned to explain to Taylor what was happening.

'I get it,' she said, before he could explain. 'It's horrible.'

Many witches had burned here, just like Isabelle Montclair. It wasn't hard in this ancient space, that had changed so little over the centuries, to imagine the sound of horses' hooves slamming on the pavement, the cries of the hunters, the terrified howls of the burning victims.

They hurried away.

The last they saw of the puppet show, the puppet woman was standing on a miniature pyre, as 'flames' of red-and-orange fabric scraps, stirred by a small fan, crackled beneath her wooden feet.

A few minutes later, Taylor stopped to point.

'Sacha,' she said. 'Look.'

Looking where she indicated, Sacha saw a symbol, carved into the ancient stone. A triangle within a circle. An alchemical symbol for security. He'd seen dozens of them at St Wilfred's.

'What's it doing there?' he asked.

'I don't know. It looks really old. Maybe alchemists marked the town in the past,' she guessed. 'They tried to keep it safe.'

They walked on, eyes scanning the buildings for more symbols. It turned out they didn't have to go far. The symbols were everywhere.

'There,' she said, pointing to a sun and moon carved above a shop. 'And there.' A few feet away, an infinity symbol was carved into the stone.

Each seemed to lead to the next.

Sacha's brow creased. 'It's like a trail.'

They followed the symbols down the old street, past shops and little restaurants. They were so involved in hunting for them, it took Sacha a second to realise where the symbols had led them.

They stood in a quiet stone square in front of the Basilica of St Nazaire – built atop the place where Isabelle Montclair had been executed. And where he was meant to die.

The hulking church towered above the low medieval cottages around it, its bell tower thrusting up against the clear blue sky. Hideous gargoyles with freakishly long arched necks stretched out overhead. They had human hands but faces like dogs, lips pulled back to reveal jagged teeth.

Cautiously, they made their way towards the church's open arched doorway.

'I guess we go in,' Taylor said hesitantly.

'I guess we do.'

Tourists still walked past them, but even so, Sacha had the strangest sense of isolation – as if he were all alone.

He didn't remember taking Taylor's hand, but he was holding it when they walked inside.

It was cooler in here – almost cold. And surprisingly dark.

The church didn't look dangerous. Everything was just as you'd expect – dark pews in neat rows. The altar at the front held a plain table covered in vivid cloth beneath sword-shaped stained-glass windows that sent purple shards of light across the stone floors.

For the most part, the crowds hadn't made it inside. A few people stood looking at the windows. Two sat in the pews, apparently praying. In the dimness, it took Sacha a second to notice that one of them was Alastair. He kept his head bowed over his hands, never looking at them.

Seeing him made Sacha feel safer. He could do this.

They began their search, starting with the vast nave.

Zeitinger had told them that the burning took place in the town square, and that the building had later expanded over that spot. That implied the room they were looking for was near the front of the existing building.

The front wall was lined with a series of small chapels dedicated to individual saints. They stopped outside each one, peering into the shadows, looking for the carved ourobouros.

They were so focussed on their search, at first they didn't notice the atmosphere changing. It had gone deathly quiet.

The perfume of incense and lilies lingered in the air, but now something new joined that – something unpleasantly sweet, and not unlike decay.

The air felt heavy and thick. Sacha fought a sudden urge to run.

Next to him, Taylor paled. Her fingers were clammy against his. He knew she could sense it, too.

Something was very wrong here.

At some point during their search, the church had emptied. Only Alastair remained. He stood up now, looking around in confusion.

Whatever was happening they could all feel it.

'What's going on?' Taylor whispered.

Sacha shook his head. He didn't know.

'Let's keep going,' he said, although his stomach was churning and his head had begun to pound.

They headed to the next chapel – they were nearly to the end of the wall, now, and so far they'd found nothing.

Without a word, Alastair joined them. He didn't look directly at them, and he was acting casual, but Sacha could see his alert posture, the way his eyes swept the room, waiting for an attack.

Somewhere in the building someone began to play an organ – the music seemed ominous, full of portent. The feel of the building grew increasingly oppressive. The smell of sweet sickness grew with each step. The air seemed to have weight, pressing down on them.

The music grew louder, building up and up into a disorienting wall of sound. The sweet deathly smell seemed to grow with it, until Sacha thought he would gag.

Whatever was in this church, it seemed to him that it recognised him, and reached out to him hungrily.

He had to force his feet forward, as if walking into a blizzard.

Somewhere a door slammed. An icy breeze blew through the building.

Suddenly a voice, deep and guttural, whispered in his ear.

'This is where it began with fire and blood. This is where it will end. Tomorrow night. In this room. On this floor. You will die.'

Bile burned Sacha's throat.

Suddenly, Alastair was behind them, urging them towards the door.

'Get out, *now*.'

Sacha didn't need more encouragement. Grabbing Taylor's hand, he ran.

As they stumbled out of the church and into the sun's purifying light, he thought he heard a mocking laugh fill the nave. He kept going, beyond the square, away from those hideous gargoyles, which seemed to watch them.

Then he fell to his knees in the shade of a tree and vomited.

When he stood up, wiping his mouth with the back of his hand, Taylor and Alastair stood next to him. Louisa appeared from nowhere to join them, eyes scanning the crowds.

'Are you OK?' Taylor asked, breathlessly.

'I heard it,' Sacha said. 'The demon's voice. I heard it. It said I was going to die.' His voice shook, and he fought for control. Looking at Louisa he asked, 'How can a demon be in a *church*?'

It was Alastair who answered.

'I don't know.' His expression was grim. 'But it's there. And it was waiting for us.'

# THIRTY

Back at the chateau that afternoon, the mood was subdued.

They gathered in the parlour, sitting on the old chairs at the back of the room.

'It was like there was this invisible wall between me and everyone else,' Taylor said. 'Mortimer could have been standing right next to me, I never would have known.'

'We felt it too,' Louisa said. 'Never experienced anything like that in my life.'

'The demon's getting stronger.' Deide's face was stony. 'We didn't find the room for the ceremony, and Mortimer didn't attack. He toyed with us. I'm sorry, but we must go back tonight and try again. We have to at least try to kill him. To end this before tomorrow comes and we run out of chances.'

The thought of going back made Sacha shudder.

He'd felt his own death in that room.

'How are we going to do that?' Taylor asked plaintively. 'The power in that church was overwhelming. We were helpless.'

Nobody replied.

Looking around at their despairing faces, Sacha realised with sickening clarity that no one had any answers. It was all much worse than they'd imagined.

'She's got a point,' Louisa said finally. 'How can we take Taylor and Sacha back there tonight if we can't even see what we're fighting? Mortimer could be right beside us and we wouldn't know. We're blind in there.'

'We don't have any *choice*.' Yanking off his glasses, Deide flung them onto the table. 'Don't you understand? We don't get to walk away from this. We must find that room before Sacha's birthday. We must kill Mortimer. So we go back into town and fight. Or else we die tomorrow.'

His words seemed to echo in the old mansion house, reverberating around them.

*Die tomorrow . . . die tomorrow . . .*

Sacha dropped his head. It all felt hopeless. The others had fallen silent, too.

It was Taylor who kept the conversation going.

'Fine then, Mr Deide,' she said calmly. 'We have to go back there tonight and kill Mortimer. How are we going to do that?'

The teacher pulled out a map and spread it on the table. Without glasses, he looked younger. His jaw was set.

'I've got a plan.'

♊

When the meeting ended, Sacha headed up to his room.

They'd discussed the plan for an hour. Everyone knew what they had to do.

Sacha didn't think one person in that room truly thought it would work.

He had said nothing to the others but, in his own heart, he believed the fight was over. The demon's voice in his ear had made that very clear.

Ever since he'd first met Taylor, he'd been able to convince himself that he had a chance. That he could fight this thing. That he could live. Now he knew that was a fantasy.

Alone in his huge bedroom, he climbed onto the tall, four-poster bed. He'd left the tattered curtains closed that morning, and the room was cool and dim.

He closed his eyes. He didn't want to be awake anymore. He didn't want to think.

Still, as it had for days now, sleep eluded him. His mind whirled through an awful series of possibilities and horrible images.

After a while, he sat up just to shut it off.

Grabbing his phone off the bedside table, he checked the time. It was just after three o'clock. They wouldn't go back into Carcassonne until late. So many hours to get through before it all went wrong.

Almost out of habit, he scrolled through his messages. As always, he had several from his mother. She told him his Aunt Annie was out of the hospital, and slowly recovering from her injuries at home, with her dog, Pikachu.

`The dog isn't the same. He barks at everything. He sleeps outside your old room. It's like he's waiting for you to come back. We all are.`

A single tear rolled down Sacha's cheek and he swiped it away with the back of his hand.

He'd avoided calling his mother ever since they left Oxford, waiting until he had good news to tell her.

There wasn't any point in waiting anymore. There wasn't going to be any good news.

He pressed the call button.

He didn't know what he was going to tell her, but it didn't matter. He just wanted to talk to someone who loved him.

It wasn't his mother who answered though.

'Hello?'

Sacha's heart jumped. 'Laura?'

His sister gave a small scream. '*Sacha.* Is it really you?'

'It's really me.' He forced a laugh. 'How's my favourite baby sister?'

'I'm your *only* baby sister,' she chided, and he could imagine her rolling her eyes. He heard her hold the phone from her ear to call out, '*Maman.* It's Sacha!'

He fell back on the bed, eyes closed. Behind his eyelids, he envisioned their apartment, flooded with the light on a summer day. Laura must be sitting in the living room on the old sofa, which was beginning to sag in the middle. Probably with the fluffy throw over her skinny legs, watching music videos.

In the distance he heard his mother exclaim. Maybe she was

working nights at the hospital again. If that was the case, she would have just woken up.

'Sacha?' His mother's familiar voice sounded breathless and so redolent of home and safety he thought his heart would fracture. '*Mon chéri*, I can't believe it. How are you? Where are you? We miss you so much.'

He took a shaky breath, ordering his voice to sound normal.

'I'm fine, *Maman*,' he promised her. 'I'm somewhere in France. I can't tell you where. But I'm well.'

'I'm afraid for you,' she said. 'Please come home. There's so little time and we want . . . I want . . .'

Sacha swallowed the lump in his throat.

'*Maman*, listen to me carefully, because there is a chance this is the last time I'll ever speak to you.'

At that, she fell silent.

'Everything is very complicated,' he continued. 'But I can't come home. Danger travels with me. You know that.'

She made a small noise of disagreement but she didn't argue.

'I'm with some people. Good people. They think they might be able to stop this thing from happening. I don't know . . .' He took a deep breath. 'I don't know if they're right. It seems . . . impossible. But we have to try. *Papa* knew them, and he trusted them. And now. Well. I have to trust them, too.'

'Is it that English girl?' she asked, suspicion in her tone. 'That Taylor Montclair?'

'She's here,' he admitted. 'But we're not alone. Others are with us trying to help. They're all doing everything they can.'

'Well.'

How could one short word be so expressive?

‘Put Laura on the phone, too,’ he said. ‘I want to tell you both something.’

‘He wants to talk to both of us,’ he heard his mother say. ‘How do you turn on that speaker thing?’

He heard Laura’s sigh of frustration. ‘I’ve shown you a thousand times, *Maman*. Push this button here.’

‘Uh . . .’ His mother’s voice, sounding further away. ‘Can you hear us?’

He smiled. ‘I can hear you.’

‘Hi Sacha!’ Laura’s excited voice sounded closer than his mother’s. ‘I hope you’re kicking the monsters’ asses.’

‘I am,’ he said, wishing it were true. ‘Listen, I can’t talk for long. I want you both to hear me make this promise. I swear I will do all I can to survive. And some day I will come home and hug you both. And we will celebrate my eighteenth birthday together.’ He drew a shaky breath. ‘If I can’t do it, please believe that I tried as hard as I could, OK? I’ll do everything I can to live. Because I want to see you both again.’

He heard a faint sound that might have been crying but he didn’t want to think about that.

‘Laura, if I don’t come back, please, look after *Maman*, OK?’

There was a long silence before she spoke.

‘I promise.’ Her voice was very small.

Sacha’s throat was so tight he could hardly say the next words. ‘I love you both. Remember that. Now, I have to go. The others are . . . calling me.’

His mother spoke rapidly. ‘We love you, too, Sacha. We will see you on your birthday.’

Sacha ended the call quickly, before he could hear any more.

Then he rolled on his back, one arm thrown across his eyes, and tried to think of nothing.

# THIRTY-ONE

Sacha wasn't the only one finding it hard to rest. One door away, Taylor lay on her bed, wide awake.

She was staring up at the dusty ornate plasterwork on the high ceiling, but her mind was everywhere – Carcassonne, the ancient church, the Darkness she'd felt the whole time they were there. And then Georgie, her mother, home, Oxford, St Wilfred's . . .

When the whirling thoughts became too much, she jumped to her feet and made her way down the creaky stairs in search of distraction. Her phone was in her hand. She longed to call her mother, but she couldn't. What would she say?

She couldn't seem to formulate the lies she needed to tell her. And the thought of saying goodbye hurt like fire.

Maybe it was better for both of them if she just didn't call at all.

The house was hushed. Dust motes danced in streams of

afternoon sunlight. From the corners, statues peered out at her with blank enquiry, as if they could hear her footsteps, and wondered what she was doing there.

The parlour was deserted. Alastair's baseball hat lay forgotten on a table. An empty wine bottle sat where it had been left the night before. Quiet seeped up through the floorboards. The silence was unearthly. As if nobody breathed in this house.

Taylor hurried a little as she made her way to the kitchen. It, too, was uninhabited.

A breeze ruffled her hair, and she noticed the back door had been left ajar. Curious, she pushed it open.

The warm day was cooling fast. The air smelled of lavender, which grew purple and wild around the back of the house.

Sitting on a battered wooden chair near the door, Louisa stared out across the valley at the white castle towers of Carcassonne.

Alerted by the sound of the door opening, she glanced up, her eyes toffee coloured in the late afternoon light. She'd changed out of her disguise, into a black, short-sleeved top and shorts. Against the pale backdrop of her skin, the dark ink of her tattooed alchemical symbols stood out starkly.

'Can't sleep?'

Taylor shook her head.

Louisa didn't seem surprised. 'Me neither.'

Lowering herself onto the doorstep next to her, Taylor pulled up her knees.

'The thing I can't figure out,' Louisa said, as if their earlier conversation had never ended, 'is how it's so strong already.

We should have more than twenty-four hours. Sacha's birthday doesn't begin until tomorrow at midnight.'

For a while silence fell between them. Then she spoke again. 'I never told you that, before we left St Wilfred's, I came across a book in Aldrich's office. It was a sixteenth-century translation of a thirteenth-century manuscript called, "To Bring a Demon Forth".'

Taylor turned to stare at her, and Louisa held up one hand in response to her unspoken question.

'I thought it was bollocks when I read it. But I've changed my mind. I think it explains what's happening here right now.'

'Why did you think it was bollocks?' Taylor asked.

'Aldrich had put one of his notes inside it,' Louisa said, as if that explained everything.

'What notes?'

Louisa glanced at her. 'You know how he had loads of books, right?'

Taylor nodded.

'Well, it got to the point where he'd read so many he could never remember his assessment of each one. Was this a book he'd read and agreed with? Or one he'd read and thought was ridiculous? It slowed him down; he was constantly re-reading. Finally, he started leaving a note for himself in each book. He had this whole system. "B" for Believable. "A" for Absurd. And so on.' A ghost of a smile flitted across her face. 'It was typical Aldrich.'

For a second her voice trailed off.

'What about this book?' Taylor drew her back. 'The one about the demon. What note did he put in it?'

'"U" for "Unlikely".' Louisa ran a hand through her hair,

sending blue sparks flying. 'That meant he didn't trust the author, but he didn't fully dismiss the theories, either. Anyway, the book said if a demon made contact with a human host, and an exchange was agreed, the space between our dimensions would gradually contract. The demon can't enter, but it can sense us.' She turned back to the castle. 'And we can sense it.'

Taylor's mouth had gone dry. She thought of the feeling she'd had in the town today – a low but overwhelming sense of dread. As if Dark power were all around her, oozing from the walls, sticking to her feet like tar.

Louisa wasn't finished.

'The book said on the day of the agreed exchange, a door would open.' She waved a hand. 'And the demon will walk right through.' She paused – her last words were barely above a whisper. 'And then we all die.'

Taylor's heart thumped hard.

'Do you believe that?'

Louisa turned the question around. 'Do you?'

With a sense of hopeless horror, Taylor realised she did.

Until now, it had been impossible to imagine what a demon was. The power of it. The monstrous empty violence it carried in its soul. It was something you read about in old books. Like dragons, or fairies. A fantasy.

Not anymore.

The red, half-healed claw marks on her hand said demons were real.

'Oh sodding hell, Louisa,' she said. 'What are we going to do?'

The other girl's reply came without hesitation.

'We're going back,' she said resolutely. 'We're going to find Mortimer Pierce, and we're going to kill him.'

'But how, though?' Taylor wouldn't let it go. 'You felt that power today.'

'I did.' Leaning forward, she put her elbows on her knees, and fixed Taylor with a steady look. 'But I've felt your power, too. I have told you before, Taylor. You are nuclear. Mortimer has been trying to kill you for weeks because he's *afraid* of you. Don't you get it?' She cocked her head to one side. 'He thinks you can win this thing.'

Taylor was speechless. 'I can't, Lou. I haven't had time to learn.'

'You don't need time,' Louisa said with conviction. 'You just need to not fear your own power. When you are in that church tonight and Mortimer comes for Sacha, let yourself be who you really are. Unleash everything you have on him. Open yourself to it.

'Kill Mortimer Pierce tonight, Taylor.'

♊

After that conversation, Taylor couldn't sit still. She haunted the dusty hallways of the house, wandering from room to room, restless and nervous.

Louisa's words kept playing in her head on a loop.

*Be who you really are. Kill Mortimer Pierce tonight . . .*

All this time she'd assumed Louisa or Deide would do the killing if there was killing to be done. Now it was clear that wasn't the case. She would have to kill Mortimer, as she'd killed the Bringers, and the revenants.

They believed she had murder in her soul.

Maybe they were right. But the power in that church today said she'd never get the chance.

If she was their only hope, they were going to die.

This realisation sent her into a tailspin.

She'd never finish her studies, never see the world. Never even learn to drive. Never do any of the things a human being is supposed to do in a lifetime.

It wasn't fair.

*I had so many plans.*

The thought of all she would never get to do was almost immobilising, and maybe that was why she kept moving. Forcing her legs to take step after step, keeping the blood pumping. Proving she wasn't dead yet.

At the very end of the corridor, she pushed open the last door on the left. Not because she really cared what was on the other side. But because it was there.

It swung open with a shriek of protest to reveal a tall, shadowed space, where the walls were lined, floor to ceiling, with the gilded spines of old books.

*A library.*

Taylor slipped inside, curiosity buzzing.

Even when her world was crashing down around her ears, a library still had the capacity to make her feel better.

The books were – of course – all in French. From a distance they looked beautiful – leather-bound with long, golden titles. Up close, though, she could see they were damaged – water-stained, sun-faded, bloated from humidity and poor conditions.

Still, they were books.

All the furniture in the room was covered in white dustcovers.

Grabbing a stack of interesting looking books at random, she settled down on the covered sofa, ignoring the cloud of dust that rose around her.

'*Je m'appelle Jacques*,' she read aloud, from the pages of a book that looked like it might be for children.

Curling up with the book in her arms, she began making her way through it, pausing to puzzle out the more unfamiliar words. She was so deep in the story of Jacques' journey aboard a whaling ship, that when a strange buzzing sound filled the air, she looked around, as if the source might manifest from a corner.

It took her a second to realise the sound was her phone. She'd shoved it into her pocket that morning out of habit and then completely forgotten it.

When she pulled it out, Georgie's face beamed up at her from the screen.

She stared into familiar brown eyes, and then hit the answer button.

'Oh my God.' Georgie's loud excited voice rang out in the silent house. 'I can't believe it. What is going on in Oxford? Do they have you tied up in a *cellar*? Why haven't you been answering my calls?'

To her complete astonishment, Taylor found herself laughing.

'I'm not in a cellar. Don't be so dramatic.'

'Well you better be tied up somewhere if you're ignoring me.'

'Shut up,' Taylor said automatically. 'Did you actually just call me to shout at me? I'm in the library and I'll get into trouble if they find me talking to you. Make it quick.'

She leaned back on the sofa.

Georgie gave an exaggerated sigh. 'Fine. I'm calling because I have news. My family and I are heading to Spain next weekend as you know, and – this is the good news part – my mum says I can bring you with us, if you want to come! They'll pay for you to come over.' Her tone shifted to defensiveness, anticipating Taylor's refusal. 'Now, I totally know you're busy. But you could come on Saturday and go back Monday morning and none of your weirdy beardy Oxford professors would even notice you were missing. What do you say? Taylor and Georgie, together again. Knocking the boys dead on the Costa del Sol. Can we make it happen?'

Taylor's chest ached with longing for a world in which friends could just go away together for a weekend. A world without monsters. Without death. Without alchemists or Mortimer Pierce.

Why couldn't she have that?

'Yes,' she heard herself say. 'Let's do it.'

Georgie gave a delighted squeal.

'Do you mean it? Oh my God, I have to tell my mum. Hang on.'

She dropped the phone. In the distance Taylor could hear the muffled thudding of her feet on the floor of her absurdly pink bedroom as she ran across the room and flung open the door.

'Mum! Taylor says she'll come with us!'

Far away, Georgie's mum made sounds of approval.

Seconds later, Georgie was back, breathless from shouting. 'This is going to be brilliant. Mum says, do you have your passport with you?'

Taylor nodded, smiling although tears had begun to fill her eyes.

'Yes,' she whispered. 'I have my passport.'

And she did. In fact, she hadn't really lied to Georgie once in this conversation. If it was the last time they ever spoke, she wanted most of what was said to be truthful.

And she really would go to Spain if she didn't die. She *would*.

'This is so awesome,' Georgie sighed. 'I miss you so much, Tay. I know Oxford is what you really want but I hate it here without you. I wish you could be in two places at once.'

'Me too.'

Georgie paused, as if she'd heard the unevenness of Taylor's voice. But when she spoke she sounded as cheerful as ever.

'I can't believe we'll see each other next week. My mum will arrange it all with your mum.' She gave another little cheer. 'I'm so glad you answered the phone at last. I've got to go. Mum wants me to go shopping with her. See you in a few days . . .'

'See you . . .' Taylor said, but Georgie had already hung up. So there was no one to hear her last words.

'I love you.'

# Thirty-Two

After her talk with Taylor, Louisa went looking for Alastair.

She checked the kitchen and, finding it empty, headed back outside again and made her way around the side of the building.

She found Alastair in the shed, under the bonnet of his beloved blue van.

'So this is where you've been hiding,' she said, leaning against a wall next to an old leather harness. 'I looked for you everywhere.'

Alastair glanced up at her. 'I'm not hiding.'

The shed was cool and shady, with a not altogether unpleasant smell of petrol and dirt. In one corner she noticed a worryingly large spider busily building a massive web, and made a mental note not to go over there.

The van – which Alastair had painted himself – looked battered and rickety next to Sacha's gleaming motorcycle and Deide's snazzy sports car. But she knew it was sturdy. Aside from the brief overheating incident on the way here, it had performed like a trooper.

'All I ask,' he said, 'is that it doesn't break down tonight.'

As he spoke, he kept working, hands methodically tightening some blackened part with an ancient wrench.

'Wishful thinking,' Louisa said. 'One whiff of demon and the old blue jalopy's going to faint.'

He straightened, wiping oil off his hands with a rag.

'Not if I have anything to say about it.' Through the open door of the shed, he glanced out at the quiet chateau. 'Are the others asleep?'

She shook her head. 'Everyone's restless. Finding ways to get through the day.'

'I can't blame them.' Alastair wiped his forehead with his hand, leaving a smudge of grease. 'How about you? Are you restless?'

'I'm worried, Al,' she said honestly. 'Today changed everything. We got a glimpse of what we're up against and it's not good. I'm giving everyone else pep talks, but the thing is, I've gone over and over this in my head. No matter how I play it, it doesn't end well.'

'Taylor and Sacha are pure power together, Lou,' he reminded her. 'They're like nothing we've ever seen. We have to give them a chance.'

'I know.' She sighed. 'But you felt it, too, today. That demonic power was off the charts. That was death.'

He shook his head hard. She could see the disapproval in his eyes.

'Come on. You know how this works. That's what the demon wanted us to feel. It wants us to give up hope. It's playing us.'

'How can you know that?' she said, trying not to show her frustration. 'You were there. You felt it.'

'Remember rule one,' he said gently. 'Demons lie.'

He reached a grease-stained hand out to her and she took it without hesitation, letting him pull her closer. When he wrapped his arms around her, she felt instantly safer.

There had never been a moment, since that first day in the corridor outside her dorm room, that she hadn't loved Alastair. She'd kept it to herself for years, harbouring a crush that made her heart race, and her stomach ache every time she saw him.

As the months had passed, they'd become allies, and then friends.

No matter how abrasive she was, no matter how hard her shell, Alastair seemed to find her soft side. Nothing she did put him off.

When she ranted, he laughed. When she broke things, he fixed whatever she shattered. Until Alastair, she'd never thought it possible anyone would want to do that for her.

Everyone needs someone to help pick up the broken pieces.

On this trip they'd finally crossed the barricades she'd raised around herself. She'd let him in.

And now she was going to lose him.

Today in Carcassonne, she'd felt death so close to them all. The sickening weight of it. The awful empty loss of it.

The demon was waiting for them. It was ready.

'We'll get through this,' Alastair promised, pulling her closer.

She gave a sad smile. Even now, when all seemed lost, he refused not to hope.

She pressed her nose against his chest, breathing in his scent of fresh air and oil and warm, sun-soaked skin.

'If that demon touches you,' she murmured. 'I'm going to kill it.'

She felt the rumble of his laugh.

'That demon has no idea what it's up against.'

Louisa lifted her head to see his face. 'How do we do this, Alastair? How do we survive this?'

He brushed his lips against hers.

'We follow the plan,' he said. 'We believe in each other. And we don't give up.'

# THIRTY-THREE

When they rode into Carcassonne late that night, they found a very different city from the one they'd visited that afternoon. Gone were the hordes of tourists who had packed the narrow lanes. Gone, too, were the coaches, the cars, and the locals.

The narrow winding streets were deserted.

Sacha's motorcycle was a roar in the stillness as they made their way up to the top of the hill.

Ahead, the huge castle was lit up on all sides. Dozens of spotlights were directed at the white stone walls from every angle.

All the parking lots near the citadel were empty, but Sacha ignored them, stopping the bike directly in front of the huge stone gateway, underneath a no parking sign.

As she pulled off her helmet, Taylor glanced at the sign.

Seeing the look, he gave a careless shrug. 'I don't think the parking police will be out tonight.'

The formidable gate, with its portcullis-like door, stood wide open, but they walked past it, turning left into the shadows. When they were well out of sight, they stopped to wait.

The castle was bounded on two sides by a steep, grassy slope that tumbled straight down to the modern town below. A rough footpath ran along the top of the hill on the outside of the castle walls. They stopped at the edge of it, waiting for their cue.

It didn't take long. Without sound or warning, all the spotlights around the edifice suddenly went black. For a tentative moment, all the town lights below flickered. Then, silently, they too blinked out.

All of Carcassonne was plunged into darkness.

Sacha gave a low, impressed whistle.

'*Felicitations*, Louisa,' he whispered.

Taylor tried to smile, but she couldn't. She was shaking like a leaf. Every muscle in her body was tense.

The night was still and very dark – there was no moon to light their way, and her eyes hadn't adjusted enough yet to see the stars. But that alone wasn't enough to explain the low ominous thrumming of fear in her veins.

Mortimer was somewhere on the other side of those walls.

'You ready?' Sacha looked at her expectantly.

He was so ready for this moment. Even in the darkness she could see that his blue eyes were utterly fearless.

To an extent, she could understand it. This time – this place – had tormented him his whole life. A sword forever poised just above his throat. Now the end was in sight. Soon they would either stop it for good, or fall onto the point of the blade.

Either way it would be over at last. And she knew how much he longed for that ending.

Taylor forced herself to nod.

Sacha led the way down the narrow dirt path. They moved carefully. The hill was steep, and the path ran right on the edge of it. One wrong step and they'd tumble down.

The walk had appeared short and simple in theory, but it seemed to be taking forever. Taylor lost track of time as they made their way around the edges of the old stone structure. She tripped on a stone and caught herself at the last second.

Sacha turned back. 'You OK?'

She nodded, then realised he probably couldn't see her. 'Yes.'

He turned back to the front. 'Good. I think we're almost . . .'

At that moment, crystalline in the silence, sirens rang out in the city below, cutting him off.

They both froze.

'*Merde*,' Sacha whispered.

Against the velvet black backdrop of a night without electricity, the flashing blue lights of the police car were vivid and clear. The wail of the siren was mournful and urgent.

Taylor held her breath, following its progress until, finally, it disappeared in the distance.

She inhaled. Her lungs ached in protest.

'Hurry.' Sacha was already a distance ahead – she hadn't noticed he'd walked away. 'We have to get in.'

She ran after him, catching up just as he reached a rusted metal gate at the foot of one of the round towers.

'Here,' Sacha whispered, pointing to where a heavy padlock hung from the door.

Taking a deep breath, Taylor placed her hand just above it. Closing her eyes, she searched for molecular energy. There was curiously little of it about. No water ran close by. No electricity coursed through the old exterior wall. But she pulled a fragile, golden strand from the grass beneath her feet and envisioned the lock releasing.

*Open.*

She wasn't sure there was enough power until she heard the click, followed by a hollow thud as the lock fell to the ground.

'Thank you,' she whispered to the earth, too quietly for Sacha to hear.

He wouldn't have noticed anyway, he was already opening the gate. It gave a screech of protest – it hadn't been used in a while – but opened, just as Deide had said it would.

They slipped inside.

The second they stepped onto the citadel's stone streets, Taylor's heart began to pound in earnest.

The demon's energy was everywhere. There was so much more of it now.

Closing her eyes, she searched for signs of life but, just like that morning, she couldn't sense anything. Not Sacha. Not the others. And certainly not Mortimer. They were alone.

Her throat tightened and she fought back the urge to panic. She had to stay focussed. They could do this.

Her eyes had adjusted enough by now that she could see

the old town around her. It looked much different than it had during the day. In the ambient light she could see the stone walls of the citadel were veined with age. The touristy shops selling candy and fake swords that had been bright and annoying in the sunshine seemed medieval and threatening in the dark.

A breeze blew her hair and sent the old-fashioned wooden signs overhead swaying. The air smelled of mould and death.

Sacha's brow was furrowed and his eyes focussed on the way ahead. His steps were absolutely sure – as if he'd walked these streets a thousand times. He took the most direct path, and only a few minutes had passed before the church loomed at them from the darkness, huge and eternal.

Taylor's teeth began to chatter as they crossed the square to the arched front door.

Unlike this morning, the big church doors were locked tight.

Closing her eyes, she felt for power. There'd been little at the gate. This time there was none at all. Not a single strand of alchemical energy.

Frowning, she focussed harder. Her hand was just above the door, trying to draw energy from somewhere, when the lock gave with a loud metallic click.

Taylor froze. A cold sense of dread filled her with ice.

Seeing the look on her face, Sacha shot her a questioning glance.

'That wasn't me.'

She barely got the words out before the church door slammed open, crashing against the stone wall with such violence it sent splinters flying.

Taylor ducked. Swearing, Sacha flung up a hand to protect his face.

Overhead, all the church bells began to toll in an awful disorienting cacophony that sounded not unlike screaming.

Dark power roared at Taylor from every direction, rolling in waves down the old stone walls.

She grabbed Sacha's wrist. 'We have to get out of here. *Now.*'

He didn't argue. They ran back across the cobblestones, the sound of their footsteps lost to the crashing bells.

They made it halfway across the square.

'There you are.' Mortimer melted out of the shadows ahead of them, nattily dressed and crackling with power. 'I've been looking everywhere for you.'

# THIRTY-FOUR

In his tweed jacket and neatly pressed trousers, Mortimer might have been on his way to a country fair. As always, his grey hair was hidden under a flat cap, and a slim silver moustache topped his upper lip. But his eyes burned with hate as they fixed on Sacha.

Watching him, Taylor tried to make herself breathe. This was what they wanted – Mortimer was here.

Now all she had to do was kill him.

He strolled towards them, his cane held loosely in one hand. He didn't appear particularly happy or excited about the situation. He looked like he always did – like a university professor on his way to class with things on his mind.

Taylor couldn't seem to make her feet work but Sacha stumbled backwards, pulling her with him.

'Stay away from us.' He glared at Mortimer.

'Oh dear,' Mortimer tutted. 'I was so hoping you wouldn't make this difficult. After all, fighting is so pointless when you've already lost. It would be vastly easier if you just conceded defeat and let us get on with our work.'

He held up his hand. Taylor sensed the Dark power flowing through him like a tidal wave of hate. Desperately, she flung up a hand in response.

'No!' she cried, reaching for anything in the air around them that could protect them.

There was nothing.

Stones have no molecular energy. There was no grass, few trees. No sunlight. No running water. And, thanks to their own plan, no electricity.

There was nothing to protect her. Mortimer's Dark energy coursed around her, unfettered. She tried to hold on, but Sacha's fingers slipped from her hand and she was flung backwards by a force she could not see.

There was no time to react. No way to protect herself.

She heard someone cry out, and then she hit something hard.

Everything went dark.

♊

When she opened her eyes for a split second she didn't know where she was. It was pitch dark. She lay on stone. Everything hurt.

In the distance she could hear shouts and screams, see flashes of light, a sharp retort.

*Was that a gun?*

She struggled to get up but her head spun and she had to lay still again.

Suddenly Sacha appeared beside her, his face white in the darkness.

'Taylor? Thank God. Are you OK?'

It took her several tries to form the words – her lips wouldn't seem to work. Finally, she made them say, 'I'm fine.'

Her head *ached*. When she reached up to see why, her fingertips came back wet and stained.

*Blood.*

Everything swung into sharp focus.

'I'm OK,' she insisted again, more forcefully this time although she wasn't at all certain this was true. 'Help me up.'

Relief suffusing his face, he pulled her to her feet. For a second, he held her close to his chest.

'I thought I'd lost you.'

She felt the warmth of him through their clothes. The world was swinging and she clung to his lean shoulders until it grew still.

His eyes skittered across her face. 'You're bleeding. Are you sure you can do this?'

'On your left, Alastair!'

The familiar voice came from the church square behind them.

'Is that Louisa? How long was I out? What's happened?' Taylor strained to see what was happening.

Her head thudded, but it didn't seem too bad now. She was sore, but otherwise fine.

'Get the lights on.' It was Deide's voice – angry and tense. 'I can't hold him for long.'

'I'm *trying*.' Louisa again.

A grunt of pain or exertion – the meaty sound of a fist hitting flesh.

'Goddamn it.' It was Alastair. 'This one's a fighter.'

*This one?*

'Mortimer brought friends.' Sacha's tone was dark. 'More of the *revenants*.'

Zombies. That was why she'd heard gunshots. They couldn't be fought with alchemical abilities. Deide must have brought a gun.

She thought of the huge, stumbling creatures that attacked them at St Wilfred's. Their freakish strength. The helplessness she'd felt facing them.

She struggled in Sacha's grip. 'We have to help them.'

'Louisa told me to get you out of here,' he told her, not letting go. 'You're injured. It looks bad.'

'It's not bad,' she snapped. 'It's just blood.'

Somewhere behind them a body – a big one – hit the ground with concussive force. Alastair swore colourfully. Taylor could hear the strain in his voice.

'Missed me, you wanker.'

Gripping her hand tightly, Sacha pulled her back towards the church square. They huddled in a doorway well out of sight. Across the square, Louisa knelt with her hands on a dark lamp post. She was clearly trying to summon enough energy to bring the electricity back, and with it waves of power they could draw on.

Taylor could see the sweat beading her forehead; sense her frustration.

As she watched, a huge, lumbering figure crashed towards the other girl, hands outstretched.

'*Arrete*,' Deide shouted, flinging a knife. It struck with unerring accuracy, slicing into the thing's back without a sound.

The creature stopped and fumbled for the knife, swatting at the blade like a human might slap a mosquito.

Taylor lunged towards Louisa, but Sacha held her tight.

'I've got to help her,' she said, twisting in his grip.

'Wait, Taylor . . . ' he began, but she was already gone.

She darted across the square, landing hard on her knees next to Louisa.

The other girl glared at her. 'What the hell are you doing here?'

Sacha crouched next to them. 'I couldn't stop her.'

'Dammit, Taylor.' Louisa fumed. 'It's like you're determined to die.'

'I'm going to help you. You can't do this alone.' Taylor rested her hands near the box at the base of the pole that controlled the power. 'Let's try this together. In three, two, one.'

Using all her remaining strength she sought.

Finding a fine strand of power from the few trees in the square, she urged it towards the light, summoning the city's electricity with all of her remaining strength.

It didn't work. The light stayed stubbornly dark. All the effort made her head throb alarmingly.

'Bollocks.' She wiped sweat from her forehead, and her hand came back tinged with red. 'Why isn't it working?'

Reaching over, Sacha took her hand. His gaze locked on hers. 'Try again.'

Taylor's breath caught. He was right. They could do this.

She reached for Louisa's hand, so that the three of them were physically connected.

'Once more,' she said.

This time, she felt the warm wave of Louisa's power.

Taking a deep breath, Taylor closed her eyes and called on the ground beneath her feet, the sky, every molecule of energy she could find, however fragile. She couldn't feel the stone path beneath her feet anymore, or the cold metal beneath her fingertips. Her head had stopped aching. She felt as if she was flying – floating above everything that was happening around her. She was strong. So strong.

She could sense the wires inside the walls around her. Even see them, empty and waiting to be filled. She would fill them.

She called everything to her.

*Light.*

From far away she heard a click, a buzzing sound and then . . . Blinding light.

'Oh thank God for that.' Louisa tumbled back on to the stones, as all around them lights flickered on. In the shops. Overhead. In the city at the foot of the hill.

The church blazed with light. Lights strung overhead burst into glowing life.

It was beautiful.

A cry behind her. 'Look out!'

Moving purely on instinct, Taylor and Sacha leaped out of the way. Louisa was right beside them.

Something crashed to the ground where they'd just been standing.

It was one of those things – its flesh bulging and swollen. Eyes small and empty. Clutching at its bloodied back.

As Taylor stared, it moaned and blinked at her.

It wasn't dead.

Heavy footsteps thudded towards her and they spun around to see a second creature swinging hard at Alastair. Blood ran down the thing's chest and face but it was still unbelievably strong.

Ducking the blow, Alastair whirled to face it, a carving knife in one hand.

'Why won't you die, you stupid bloody zombie? You've already done it once.'

Without warning, Deide leaped out of the shadows and slammed a knife into the thing's back. It stopped, roaring with pain and spun towards him.

'Where's Mortimer?' Sacha shouted at Louisa.

'Don't know,' she snapped. 'We need to find him. But we have to get past these things first. You and Taylor need to get out of here.'

Taylor shook her head stubbornly. 'I'm not leaving you.'

'The hell you're not.'

'Louisa, I'm serious ...' Taylor began, but then a voice carved from pure ice rang out across the square.

'This arguing is giving me a headache.'

As one, they whirled to find Mortimer standing next to them, as if he'd been there all along.

Louisa recovered first.

'Jesus, Pierce. You give me the creeps.'

Her voice was steady but she watched him the way you'd watch a rattlesnake, coiled to strike.

'Louisa!' Alastair called sharply from across the square. 'Mind yourself.'

Behind them, Taylor could hear Deide fighting furiously with the creatures but she didn't dare turn around.

Sacha took a step forward, fists raised, mouth opened to argue, but Mortimer shot him a look and he doubled over, as if he'd been punched.

'Sacha!' Taylor reached for him. He didn't look up. She hadn't even felt Mortimer use his power. It had been undetectable. She gripped his hand tightly.

Fury raced through her veins, washing the fear away.

'What did you do to him, you monster?' she shouted.

Mortimer tilted his head.

'You interest me, Miss Montclair,' he said. 'You seem so determined to prevent something that cannot be stopped. Aldrich thought you were intelligent. But isn't continuing to attempt the same task even after you are made aware of its impossibility a sign of lack of intelligence?'

'That depends,' Taylor said coldly, 'on whether you're right about it being impossible.'

Still holding Sacha's hand, she drew energy from the connection between them, and electricity from the wires under their feet – pulling it easily and propelling it towards Mortimer with all her strength.

If he'd been anyone else, it would have killed him. Instead, he knocked it aside with a flick of his fingers.

Louisa stood next to Taylor, angling her body so it was between her and Mortimer.

'Is that the demon juice, Mortimer?' Her tone was mocking. 'How did it feel to sell your soul, you disgusting pervert? Did you cry when it happened?'

His brow lowered. 'I don't think I like your tone.'

He raised his hand quickly but Louisa was quicker, fighting back the Dark energy he flung at her with astonishing speed and strength.

Taylor could smell the acrid scent of their power in the air.

'You can dish it out but I'll bet you can't take it,' Louisa taunted him.

But Taylor could see she was faltering. He was too strong.

'*Stop it.*' She shouted the words.

Mortimer's attention swung back towards her. In the shadows his eyes looked lidless.

'Do you have something to offer me, Miss Montclair? Because I can make this stop in an instant.'

'If you're asking for me to hand you Sacha, forget it,' she snapped. 'He's not for sale. I promise you will never have him.'

As she talked, her eyes skated the square, looking for something she could use to kill him. He'd already dodged her most powerful blow. She needed something else. Something creative.

She needed Sacha.

Keeping her eyes on Mortimer, she directed a delicate strand of electrical energy towards Sacha, hoping Mortimer wouldn't notice.

*Release.*

Mortimer smiled – thin lips curling up humourlessly as he studied her.

'Oh, I think you'll find that I will succeed. I have not come this far to fail, and you have delivered him safely to me.'

'You don't have me,' Sacha said. 'You never will.'

Taylor grinned. It had worked.

Mortimer eyed them coldly.

'You are all delusional,' he said. 'Well, let me show you the truth of the situation so we can move on.'

Before anyone realised what he was doing, he flicked his hand at Louisa. Caught off-guard, she shot backwards with a startled cry. Her feet left the ground, and she soared through the air high above them.

Mortimer made some small motion, Taylor saw it only out of the corner of her eye, and Louisa's body stopped moving. It just hung there, swinging sickeningly against the dark sky.

Mortimer stepped closer to Taylor.

'Now, do you understand, Miss Montclair? You have lost this fight.'

He made a slow loop with his finger, and Louisa's body spun in the air. Once. Twice.

Taylor heard herself sob.

Then, like a bird shot in flight, Louisa's limp body tumbled to the ground.

She heard Alastair cry out, and an awful crunching thud as she hit the cobblestone road many feet away.

Taylor felt that blow with her whole body. Tears burned her eyes, but she didn't dare look away from Mortimer long enough to see if Louisa was alive.

'You bastard,' she whispered. Mortimer held her gaze, unblinking.

'I take what I want, Miss Montclair. I should have thought your grandfather would have taught you that.'

Grabbing her hand, Sacha pulled Taylor towards him.

'Don't you touch her,' he said, but even Taylor could hear the fear in his voice.

Mortimer smiled.

Then footsteps thudded towards them. This time, Taylor did turn. She expected Alastair seeking revenge but it was Deide, a gun in his hand.

'Mortimer,' he shouted. Then he said something in French so rapidly Taylor couldn't catch it. Something about Hell and death.

Everything happened in slow motion.

Deide fired the gun. Taylor heard the concussion. Saw the flare of the muzzle. She even, she thought later, saw the bullet itself, moving in slow-motion.

Mortimer watched the bullet with interest. Then lifted one hand and plucked the shining piece of metal out of the air.

For a terrifying moment, he studied it. Then, he threw it back at Deide.

The bullet pierced the teacher's forehead, just above his glasses.

He crumpled to the ground and lay terribly still.

'*Non.*' Sacha lunged towards him, but Taylor knew there was no point.

Deide was dead. Maybe Louisa, too.

They'd all be dead if she didn't get Sacha out of here. Right now.

Stifling a sob, she flung up her hand, she pulled energy from the electricity around her – all of it.

*Protect.*

She gave it everything she had. She could almost hear Louisa's voice in her head: '*Give it a bit of welly, Taylor. Quit playing around.*'

The light post next to Mortimer exploded in a flash of fire and sparks.

All the lights went out again.

In the shelter of darkness, Taylor grabbed Sacha's hand and pulled him away from Deide's body.

'I can't leave him,' he protested, struggling in her grip.

'He's dead, Sacha.' She was holding onto him with strength she didn't know she had, tears streaming down her cheeks. 'We have to get out of here.'

# THIRTY-FIVE

They ran down a narrow side path, past the little cottage where they'd seen the disturbing puppet show that afternoon, past the shops and then straight out across the cobblestones and through the main gate.

The whole time, Sacha listened for footsteps following behind them, but all he could hear was the sound of their own feet hitting ancient stone, and their harsh breathing.

He kept seeing Deide's face, his look of disbelief as the bullet struck. The scene played out, over and over.

The motorcycle was right where he'd left it. Moving on pure autopilot, he leaped on the back, sweeping both helmets off the ground in the same motion. As Taylor climbed on behind him he glanced at her – she was trembling violently.

'Did Louisa and Alastair get away?'

She shot him an anguished look. 'I don't know.'

Sacha didn't ask any other questions. He fired up the engine with a roar, and they shot off down the hill. Somehow – he would never know precisely how he managed it – he forced himself to focus on the road ahead, not the carnage they'd left behind.

They wound their way through the town, driving without stopping until they reached the agreed meeting place by a wide, slow stream at the edge of the town.

Even with the street lights back on, it was dark in the shadows, but they stayed on the bike, poised to run. As they waited, Sacha stared down at his hands, trying not to see Deide's face in his mind.

He was heartsick.

They'd failed completely. Failed to kill Mortimer. Failed to find the room where the ceremony to undo the curse needed to happen.

All they'd managed to do was get a good man killed. And maybe more.

He could feel Taylor's body trembling.

'Mr Deide,' she whispered. 'Louisa.'

Sacha nodded, blinking back tears. 'I know.'

He had no idea how much time passed before they heard the van – probably just a few minutes, maybe even less. It felt like forever before it pulled off the road and skidded to a standstill.

Leaping from the bike, they both ran towards it.

Alastair didn't get out. He stuck his head out the window so the street light caught his blond hair, turning it white.

'She's alive.' His voice was taut. 'Barely.'

'Let me see her.' Taylor ran to the van, yanking open the back door.

Louisa lay on the seat, unconscious. Alastair had wrapped a t-shirt around her head to staunch the bleeding and strapped her head and neck so she couldn't move.

Sacha had never seen her look so small.

'Louisa,' Taylor choked, covering her mouth with her hands. 'Oh no.'

'I'm taking her to the hospital. I don't know if she has a chance, but I'm going to do all I can.' Alastair pushed his hair back from his face, and Sacha saw a purpling bruise above his left eye, blood encrusted around it.

'What happened with Mortimer?' he asked.

Alastair shook his head. 'I don't know. As soon as that light post exploded, I grabbed Lou and got out of there.' He let out a long breath. 'What are we going to do?'

For a moment, nobody answered. Then, closing the van door, Taylor stepped back to stand beside Sacha, slipping her hand into his. There was a calmness about her, as if she'd decided something in that van.

Sacha thought he knew what it was. He'd come to the same conclusion.

'Take Louisa to the hospital. Make sure she's OK,' she told Alastair. 'We'll handle Mortimer. You've done enough.'

Sacha squeezed her fingers.

'We'll be fine,' he lied.

There was regret in Alastair's eyes as he looked at them, but he didn't object.

'I hate that it worked out this way,' he said. 'You shouldn't have to do this alone.'

'It was always going to be us,' Taylor said. 'Wasn't it?'

'It's us he wants,' Sacha agreed. 'No one else should die for me.'

Alastair's lips tightened.

'Do me one favour,' he said, shifting the van into gear. 'Kill that bastard, will you? Do it for Louisa.'

The van spun its tyres, swinging back onto the road.

When the sound of the engine faded away, and they were all alone, Taylor leaned against Sacha.

'What *are* we going to do?'

He wished he knew the answer. All he knew was they couldn't stay here. He looked back at the bike.

'I guess we go back to the chateau.'

The suggestion made her shudder, and he couldn't blame her. The idea of going back to the chateau without the others was horrible. But what else could they do? They needed a safe place to regroup.

When they climbed on the bike, Taylor clung to him.

Sacha flipped his visor down.

He wanted to punch something. To scream.

But he wasn't a kid anymore.

So he pulled onto the narrow road, and headed away from Carcassonne.

♊

It wasn't until they got to the chateau that they learned how bad things really were.

Sacha had just turned off the road towards the windmill when Taylor felt it. She described the feeling later as like tar or something worse, sticky and tainted. It sucked the air out of her lungs.

She leaned forward urgently, her fingers digging into his sides.

'Turn around, Sacha. *Turn around.*'

He knew her well enough not to question. Wheeling the bike in a tight circle, he gunned it back towards the main road, tyres spitting gravel.

Only when he was a safe distance away, did he stop and look back to see what she'd sensed. The weathered, ivy-covered stone walls of the chateau loomed out of the darkness behind them, like a ship emerging from fog. There were *things* all over it – creatures of some sort, clambering up the walls. In the dark, he couldn't see what they were but they moved like spiders.

As he watched, sickened, flames began to leap from the ground floor, fast and eager. Soon, the entire building was burning.

Taylor sobbed, pressing her helmeted head against his back, as if she couldn't bear to look.

As they sped away, he could see the fire burning red in the bike's mirrors.

They rode aimlessly down the dark country roads. Sacha kept trying to think of what to do now but his head was spinning. First Deide, then Louisa. Now the house.

Mortimer was taking everything.

After nearly an hour, he pulled over and cut the engine, pulling off his helmet so he could breathe.

He twisted around on the seat so he could see Taylor.

'We need a place to stay safe until tomorrow night,' he said. 'You don't know of any other safe houses?'

Shaking her head, she wiped the tears from her cheeks.

'Only Deide and Louisa knew where they were. Maybe we could call St Wilfred's?'

He shook his head. 'I don't want anyone else to get involved. It's too dangerous.' He tried to think. 'I've got some money but I don't think a hotel would be a good idea . . . And we need to hide the bike.'

They sat for a while, trying to think. The motorcycle engine ticked as it cooled. In the distance, a night bird called out hungrily.

'What we need is an empty house,' Sacha said without much hope. 'An abandoned building or something. Just someplace we can hide for a while.'

Taylor blinked at him.

'I saw a garage,' she said. 'Back at the edge of Carcassonne. It had a "For Sale" sign and looked boarded up.'

Sacha remembered the dingy white garage, with the petrol pumps removed, its sign hanging crookedly.

'I know the one,' he said. 'I think I can remember where it was. Let's go check it out.'

♊

It was harder to find than he recalled, and they drove for quite some time before locating it.

It had been thoroughly secured. The windows were covered with boards. The door had three locks.

Taylor opened them in an instant.

Inside, the garage was mostly empty. The pile of junk mail on the floor – some of it yellowed with age – indicated nobody had visited this place in a while.

Sacha rolled the motorcycle into the repair shop, while Taylor looked around for food and water. There wasn't any. There was no furniture, no electricity.

Exhausted, they sat on the dirty concrete floor in the dark. Taylor wrapped her arms around her knees, shaking like a leaf.

'Hey,' Sacha said, pulling her closer. 'It's going to be OK.'

'I don't think so,' she said.

'Well.' He searched his tired brain for something positive to say. 'For the next five minutes or so, it's probably going to be fine.'

She forced a tremulous smile. 'At least we'll have five good minutes.'

They fell quiet for a moment. Then Taylor spoke the words foremost in Sacha's mind.

'Mr Deide.' She wiped away a tear. 'I just can't believe it.'

'I know.'

The memory of that bullet shooting from Mortimer's fingers sent a chill through him.

'I'm so scared for Louisa,' Taylor said. 'I want to call Alastair but I don't dare. What if Mortimer tracks us somehow? He seems to know everything we do.'

'Don't call,' Sacha said gently. 'We just have to hope.'

Taylor wiped the tears from her cheeks with the back of her hand.

'I don't think I know how to hope anymore.'

Wordlessly, he pressed his lips against her hair. It was sticky with dried blood.

'Your head.' Furious with himself for forgetting, he turned to face her, trying to see in the dark how bad it was. 'We have to do something about that. Is there a first aid kit here somewhere?'

He knew it was a stupid thing to ask – there was nothing but trash and uncollected mail. For some reason, the thought that she might be forced to spend the night on a dirt floor with blood in her hair was more than he could take.

'*Bordel*,' he shouted, pounding his fist on the hard floor. 'We can't live like this.'

'Hey.' Catching his hand, she lifted it to her lips. 'Stop.' Her breath was warm against his skin, soft as velvet. 'I'm fine. I promise.'

'No, you're not.'

He pressed his fists into his eyes, trying to think.

'I saw a 24-hour shop about a kilometre away,' he said. 'I remember the light in the window. It won't have much but it's better than nothing.'

She shook her head. 'Sacha, no. It's too dangerous.'

But he was already on his feet. 'We need water and food, and some bandages. They will have that much. I'll move fast and I won't take the bike.'

'Sacha . . . '

He held up his hand.

'I'm right, Taylor, and you know I am. There's more to surviving than just breathing. We need to be strong. And without food and water, we won't be.'

She bit her lip. 'Fine. But please, be careful.'

He tried to give her a rakish smile but his lips wouldn't cooperate. It just hadn't been that kind of a day.

'Lock the door,' he said. Seeing the anguished look in her eyes, he added, 'I'll be careful.'

# THIRTY-SIX

Sacha was only gone twenty minutes, but it was the longest twenty minutes of Taylor's life.

She paced the dark garage from one end to the other, willing him to return. Her heart felt cold as a stone in her chest. If Mortimer got him now, she'd never forgive herself.

When she sensed Sacha's presence outside the door she raced to it, commanding the locks to open while still several steps away. Bursting through before he could walk inside, she threw herself at him, sending him staggering backwards.

'Thank God. You're alive.'

He wrapped his arms around her, a plastic bag filled with supplies bumping heavily against her back.

'We're both alive,' he said.

When they were both back inside, she sat patiently on the floor while he cleaned blood from her wound with a bottle of Evian water.

'It doesn't look bad.' He peered at her head in the glow of a tiny pocket flashlight as he applied antiseptic.

It stung, but Taylor didn't really notice. All that mattered was they were both still here.

When he'd finished, he pulled bread and sliced cheese from the bag, creating makeshift sandwiches.

They ate without pleasure. They merely needed energy if they were going to fight.

Afterwards, they curled up together on the floor, resting their heads on a bag Sacha pulled off the back of his bike.

Taylor was so worn out her hands felt weighted down, but her mind still raced, flashing up images from earlier that night until she longed for unconsciousness.

Maybe if she just fell asleep, she'd stop seeing Louisa's body flying into the wall. And Deide's empty eyes as the bullet hit home.

'I hope Louisa's OK,' she said as exhaustion won out and her eyelids grew heavy.

'Me too,' Sacha whispered.

It was the last thing she heard, before she finally slept.

♊

When she woke, daylight streamed through cracks in the plywood covering the windows. Sacha lay on his back, one arm loosely around her waist. She was resting on his chest.

Every part of her ached. But her head felt a little better than it had the night before.

She was also incredibly thirsty. Careful not to wake him, she extricated herself from Sacha's arms and climbed to her feet.

It was very quiet outside – no sounds aside from the occasional car hurrying by – and she wondered what time it was as she tiptoed across the room and found the water bottle. After she'd had a drink, she pulled her phone from her pocket. Her battery was nearly dead, and the clock showed it was well after noon.

Her heart flip-flopped. Less than twelve hours left, until this was all over.

She wondered if she should wake Sacha, but he looked so peaceful that she couldn't bring herself to disturb him – he'd rolled onto his side, resting his head on his arm, and his lashes were soft and dark and perfect against his cheeks.

Stretching to loosen her tight muscles, she sat back down against the wall, checking her phone for messages.

One from Georgie:

I'm so excited about Spain!!! Your mum says get in touch about flights etc. xxxxxx

And then, at last, one from Alastair, sent a short while ago:

Still alive.

Taylor bit back a sob. Louisa had survived the night.

She hugged her phone tightly against her chest and fought back tears of relief.

*You keep fighting, Liverpool girl.*

It was the first tiny sign of hope she'd had in such a long time. And she was going to cling to it.

'What's going on?'

She looked up to find Sacha propped up on one elbow, watching her.

'Louisa,' she said, smiling through her tears. 'She's alive.'

'Thank God.' He held out his arms. 'Come here.'

Taylor's stomach flipped. He looked so beautiful, lying there in the dust, all cheekbones and lean muscles.

She knelt beside him, suddenly shy, but he pulled her down until she lay on his chest again.

'Every time I woke up during the night, you were like this.' His breath stirred her hair. 'I liked it.'

'Me, too,' she whispered.

It was easier to say that without looking at him, so she buried her face in his chest.

When he chuckled she felt the rumble through her cheeks. 'Why are you hiding from me?'

He pulled her up, until she lay on top of him, her face above his. No place to hide.

The way he looked at her, his gaze sweeping across her face like fingertips, made it hard for her to think of words.

'I'm not,' she insisted unconvincingly.

'Oh good,' he said softly. 'Because I like looking at you.'

His hand slid slowly up to cup the back of her head, and he pulled her down gently until his lips met hers.

The kiss was tender and soft, but that wasn't what Taylor needed right now. She pressed back against him, kissing him harder and more passionately. Parting his lips with the tip of her tongue, tasting him.

He let out a breath and then, wrapping his arms around her

protectively, rolled her over until he lay above her, braced on his forearms.

She looked up into his eyes.

'I'm so glad you're here,' she whispered. 'With me.'

Some of the brightness faded from his expression. He ran his thumb gently across her bottom lip.

'I wouldn't want to be with anyone else,' he told her.

Reaching up, she ran her fingers through the silk of his sandy brown hair. She stroked the sharp lines of his cheekbones, the soft straight brows, and the long line of his nose as if trying to memorise every inch of his face.

'You're so beautiful,' she whispered.

That made him smile. 'Don't be ridiculous.'

'You are,' she insisted. 'And the best thing is, you don't even know it.'

'It's funny,' he said. 'I've thought exactly the same thing about you.'

He kissed her then, hard and fast, pressing himself against her, holding her tightly. Holding nothing back. The kiss was desperate and filled with longing.

She ran her hands down his body until she could slide her fingers under his t-shirt, feeling the warmth of his skin.

She breathed in his breath, letting him fill her lungs.

They might have been facing the end of everything, but they were not alone. They had each other.

And for a little while they could forget the horrors that lay ahead, and imagine the life they wished they could have.

♊

Some time later, they sat tangled up together against the back wall of the garage, eating stale chocolate croissant.

Taylor's right leg was draped over his left, his hand rested possessively on her knee. She felt warm and safe for the first time in days. Even she knew it was an illusion but, just for now, she didn't care.

Alone in their hideout, time seemed to slow, and they found themselves telling each other things they'd never told anyone. Talking about family. And home.

'I called my mother and sister yesterday to say goodbye,' Sacha told her. 'In case I never see them again.'

'I couldn't call my mum,' she confessed. 'I thought if I heard her voice, I'd just run home. I didn't know if I could stop myself.' She ran a hand across her eyes. 'I better not die. Because she'd never forgive me. She thinks I'm going to Spain next Friday.'

'Maybe you will.'

Dipping his head down he kissed her hair. She pulled his arm tighter across her chest. 'How do you feel?' she asked quietly. 'Now that the time is finally here.'

He exhaled audibly.

'I never knew it would feel like this,' he said after a long second. 'That I'd be so afraid. I thought I'd walk into my eighteenth birthday like a fighter. Daring death to take me. Now I'm afraid I might crawl in, begging.' He wouldn't meet her eyes. 'I'm scared.'

Taylor pulled him closer.

'You won't crawl,' she promised him passionately. 'You are *incapable* of crawling.'

His blue eyes looked so old in that moment – older than his years. It made her heart ache.

'How can you know that? Maybe I'm not who you think I am.'

'I know you, Sacha Winters,' she told him. 'You're the bravest person I've ever met. You can do this.'

'*We* can do this,' he corrected her, pulling her close again. 'Together.'

When he kissed her, his mouth tasted of chocolate.

Later, as the sun began to sink in the sky outside, and the minutes ticked down, they worked out a plan.

'We can't be too early,' Sacha said. 'I think we should go right on time. Straight to the church. Let's not try to kill Mortimer. Let's just go do the ceremony.'

'We still have to find that chapel,' Taylor reminded him. 'If we can't find the right room, Zeitinger says the ceremony won't work. It has to happen on the right location.'

'We'll find it,' Sacha assured her. 'At least now we know where it isn't. We made it through most of the nave.' He paused to think. 'Hang on. By the time we left the church yesterday, we'd been to all the chapels on that side except the one right at the end. Do you remember it?'

Taylor paused to think. She'd been so worried about Sacha, the rest was a bit of a blur. But she did remember. A metal candle stand, with dozens of votive candles aglow. Behind it, a small, closed door covered by a velvet curtain.

'The one with candles outside it?'

Sacha nodded. 'It's the only room on that side of the church we didn't search.'

She stared at him. 'That has to be it.'

This was positive. That last side chapel could well be the place. If they went straight there, they could get to it before Mortimer found them.

They'd have to be focussed. But at least they knew where to look.

There was one thing left she had to take care of.

'We need to talk about what's going to happen in the church.' Reaching into her pocket, she pulled out the folded paper she'd carried from Oxford. 'You need to read this.'

Giving her a quizzical look, Sacha took the page of Zeitinger's hand-written instructions from her, and smoothed it out on the dusty floor. She waited as he read.

When he'd finished, his face was serious.

'Is he sure about this?'

'As sure as he can be.'

She pulled out the bag they'd used as a pillow, and felt in it until her fingers found the long, narrow box the professor had placed in her hands as she was leaving St Wilfred's.

Opening it, she set it on the dirty concrete floor.

'We have to use this.'

A silver dagger lay gleaming on a soft bed of blue velvet. Its handle was encrusted with alchemical carvings. An intertwined sun and moon formed the solid base of it. A hand, with symbols at the tip of each finger, was carved into the grip.

'That's what you're supposed to cut us with?' Sacha reached out a hand to touch the blade, but changed his mind, dropping his hand to his side.

'He said it would be best.'

There was a pause.

'Well,' Sacha said quietly. 'I guess we're ready.'

Outside, the sun hung low in the sky. There wasn't long to wait now.

Night was coming.

# THIRTY-SEVEN

When the time came, they left Sacha's bike in the garage, keys in the ignition. Their bags and helmets – everything they had – lay on the floor next to it. All they took with them was the dagger and Zeitinger's instructions.

As she closed the door, Taylor blinked back tears.

Everything felt so final. Everything felt like the end.

Hand-in-hand, they made their way through Carcassonne's dark winding streets. When they passed a church, the clock showed it was half past eleven.

Thirty minutes until Sacha turned eighteen. Thirty minutes to stop a process that had started three hundred years ago in a time of hate and fear. Thirty minutes to live.

*Not enough time.*

Taylor's heart skittered in a wild staccato beat. She was too scared to say anything.

Sacha squeezed her hand.

She couldn't imagine how frightened he must be right now. She was so terrified she couldn't take a breath. It had to be much worse for him. And yet he kept his eyes straight ahead, and put one foot in front of the other.

She squared her shoulders. If he could do this, she could do this.

She was curiously alert; hyperaware of every small sound – water dripping from a drainpipe, the flutter of a night bird overhead, their own footsteps thudding out of rhythm.

Her head didn't hurt anymore. Cold, transcendent fear had subsumed all other sensations.

After a few minutes, the citadel appeared above them. It was strikingly beautiful, with its round towers aglow in the spotlights – a perfect stage for their final performance.

They took a back route up the grassy slopes, far from the main tourist entrance. Taylor focussed on her feet, on breathing, on Sacha's hand in hers. She tried not to think about the dagger in the waistband of her jeans, pressing against the small of her back. Or what lay waiting for them at the top of that hill.

She was not thinking very hard when Sacha spoke.

'Do you sense anything?'

Taylor shook her head. The closer they got to the castle, the more her alchemical senses were muted. If Mortimer was there, she couldn't sense him.

The footpath took them straight to one of the side gates. It wasn't the same one they'd come through the night before – this one was oiled and modern. It opened silently at the touch of Taylor's hand.

They slipped through it like shadows.

Inside the old town, the street lights were all aglow – there was no Louisa to put them out. It was easy to find their way back towards the church square.

Glancing at Sacha, Taylor saw that every muscle in his body was tense. A nerve worked in the tight line of his jaw.

He knew, as she did, that their plan was tenuous at best. All they had was Zeitinger's guesswork and the ravings of a long-dead German scientist with a name too close to Frankenstein.

Not much to hang a life on.

*And each other*, she reminded herself. *We have us.*

Too soon they reached the square in front of the basilica.

Taylor tried not to look at the spot where Deide had died. She wondered what they'd done with his body, then tried not to think about it.

The square was filled with shadows that darted and danced dangerously. Maybe it was her imagination, but it seemed that the gargoyles clinging to the roof were writhing in hungry rage. For a second she even thought she could hear them snarl. The snap of their stony jaws.

Sacha drew in a sharp breath.

The church's huge front door loomed open.

Mortimer was inviting them in.

Sacha turned to her, holding her hand tight.

'Ready?'

She let out a long breath. 'Ready if you are.'

'OK,' he said grimly. 'Let's go kill a demon.'

They walked to the front door, and stepped into Darkness.

♊

They had only gone five steps when the door slammed shut behind them. Whirling, they ran back to it. With a thrill of horror, Sacha heard the distinct sound of the locks turning.

He pounded his fist hard against the thick wood.

'Hey.' Taylor's voice was gentle. 'You know I can open that door if you want me to. No need to beat it up.'

He forced himself to stop.

Thank God she was here. He wasn't to be alone at the end, after all.

'I'm sorry,' he said, and it wasn't at all what he wanted to say. *Thank you. I love you. Don't let me die.*

The look on her face told him she understood. She took a quick breath, as if about to say something but then a noise broke the stillness in the shadows behind them. A shuffling sound, like something big and slow, moving in the dark.

Apprehension ran cold fingers down Sacha's spine.

They both turned to look, but it was too dark. Anything could have been hiding in those shadows.

Taylor whispered something. Instantly, every candle in the room flared into life.

Now Sacha could see the wide central aisle between long rows of dark pews. Huge, heavy candleholders hung from the ceiling by chains, each with dozens of candles ablaze. Candles burned in wall sconces and on the altar, and in ornate candelabra in every corner.

They turned slow circles, alert for danger, but could see nothing.

'Where is he?' Taylor whispered, moving closer to Sacha.

'I don't know,' Sacha said. 'Let's find the chapel.'

Cautiously, they walked in perfect sync across an ancient stone floor pounded smooth over hundreds of years by the feet of worshippers and priests, nuns and believers.

How could Hell be in this place?

It felt wrong. Abominable. That made him angry, and anger was good. Anger was power. Anger wiped fear right out of his heart and replaced it with fire.

Taylor spotted it first.

'There,' she said, pointing.

Just as they'd remembered, the little door was tucked away behind a half-drawn velvet curtain. Rows of prayer candles glittered in a metal stand out front.

Sacha reached for the door handle, but Taylor grabbed his hand.

Giving him a warning look, she shook her head.

Behind them, the awful shuffling came again, followed by another clear, distinct sound: footsteps.

Sacha's mouth went dry.

'Quick,' he whispered.

Taylor held up her hand – the lock released and the door swung open.

Behind it, a narrow staircase led down into darkness.

Sacha swore under his breath. They were sure it would be a chapel. These looked like stairs to a cellar. Where they could be trapped.

The footsteps were gaining on them. Taylor shot Sacha a desperate look.

'Go,' he said, because there was no alternative.

They ran inside.

Taylor closed the door behind them and locked it with one smooth gesture.

At the top of the stairs, they huddled together catching their breath. The darkness was complete. Sacha could see nothing at all.

He felt Taylor move, heard her murmur something. With a sputtering hiss, torches mounted on the wall of the curving, old stairwell burst into life.

The stairs were narrow and ancient between walls of damp, grey stone. They couldn't see the bottom. But there was nowhere to go except down.

They picked their way down the uneven steps carefully, listening out for any sign that they were being followed. The sound never came. They were still alone when the steps ended at the edge of a large, sparsely furnished crypt.

The windowless room was cold, with a bare stone floor and walls. A table stood at one end, in front of two rows of dusty wooden pews. Tall candelabras provided illumination. The room had a graveyard smell of dust and isolation.

It looked like no one had been down here in many years.

'What is this?' Taylor whispered, looking around.

'I don't know,' he said. 'Can you feel anything? Like . . . sense anything?'

She closed her eyes, then opened them again immediately.

'There's something here.' He could see the excitement in her eyes. 'Help me. I think this could be the room we were looking for. I can feel its energy.'

Their footsteps echoed hollowly as they made their way slowly across the crypt, searching each stone. They crawled under the pews, and ran their hands along the stone walls, trying not to miss what they sought.

They found nothing.

Sacha was on the verge of despair when Taylor whispered.

'Oh my God, Sacha. Here it is.'

He ran to where she knelt in front of the altar table, dropping to his knees beside her.

Crouching forward, Taylor felt the carvings with her fingertips – a large ornate cross.

'Zeitinger said we'd know it was the right cross if we found the . . .'

Her voice trailed off and she pointed above the cross. Sacha squinted to see what she was indicating. Even in the dim candlelight, the snake symbol was unmistakeable – an ourobouros had been cut deep in the rock.

His heart stuttered. This was the place.

They were really going to do this.

Taylor looked at her watch.

'It's nearly time. Zeitinger said to start at midnight precisely,' she said. 'We have to get ready.'

Sacha looked over his shoulder. He didn't like how quiet it was.

'Where the hell is Mortimer?'

Her eyes met his. 'I don't know. Let's hurry.'

Reaching behind her back, she pulled the dagger from the waistband of her jeans. The ornate silver glittered ominously. Sacha couldn't take his eyes off it.

'We need thirteen candles.' She gestured to one of the candle holders, bristling with flames. 'Bring me those.'

Sacha pulled the glowing candles loose from their holders. Hot wax dripped onto his skin as he carried them to where she knelt, clutching Zeitinger's instructions in her hand.

She pointed at the carved stone. 'Set twelve of them in a star formation on this stone.'

As he watched, she demonstrated, drawing a large star in the dust with her fingertip.

'Put the last one in the centre.'

He did as she'd said, using the warm candle wax to hold each candle upright.

She pulled the dagger loose from its ornate sheath and lay the naked blade at the base of the glowing star.

'We have to cut ourselves,' she told him calmly. 'That begins the ceremony. Are you ready?'

'Taylor?' An English voice came from the stairwell.

Sacha leaped to his feet, fists raised, peering into the shadows. He hadn't heard a footstep. It wasn't Mortimer's voice. It was a girl.

Taylor still knelt on the stone floor. All the colour had drained from her face. She was staring into the shadows in the direction of the voice.

'No,' she whispered. 'Please, no no no . . .'

They both heard quick, light steps.

A girl stepped out of the shadows. She was about their age, in a short dark skirt and a fitted white blouse. She had dark skin, great legs, and thick black hair in a ponytail that swung with each step.

'Georgie,' Taylor whispered. 'You can't be here. This isn't possible . . .'

She looked utterly heartbroken.

Sacha looked back and forth between them. He'd heard Taylor talk about Georgie many times. She'd shown him a photo of her on her phone. This girl looked exactly like her.

From Taylor's panicked expression, he gathered it sounded like her, too.

But it couldn't be her, could it?

'I looked for you everywhere. I called and called.' Georgie stepped towards them. Her arms were folded tightly across her torso, she looked frightened. 'A man said you needed me. So I came with him. Taylor, who was he?'

'Sacha.' Taylor looked dazed. 'Is it really her? Or is it an illusion?'

'I think it's an illusion,' he said uncertainly. 'But I'm not sure.'

Georgie stopped a short distance away and watched them reproachfully. Her tears glimmered in the candlelight.

'Why are you acting like this, Taylor? I'm so scared. I don't know where I am. I don't know why we had to meet here in the dark.' She held out her hand. 'Help me, please. I'm so afraid of that man.'

Sacha felt Taylor flinch. Her hands twitched at her sides. He knew how badly she must want to reach out to her.

He didn't know what to do. What if it really *was* Georgie? They both knew Mortimer would stop at nothing.

Taylor had begun to tremble, but when she spoke, her tone was challenging.

'In Year Nine we hid notes to each other in a secret place. Where was it?'

Tears rolled down Georgie's cheeks. She held out a beseeching hand.

'I don't understand why you're asking me this, Taylor. I don't even know where I am. Why won't you help me? I'm *scared.*'

Taylor gripped the edge of the dark mahogany pew in front of her with such violence her knuckles whitened.

'Answer the question, Georgie,' she whispered.

'Why don't you believe me?' Georgie asked plaintively. 'How can you do this to me?'

At first Sacha thought Taylor wasn't making sense, but gradually he realised what she was doing. This was a test.

And Georgie had failed.

He could see Taylor's shoulders sag, just a little – whether from relief or disappointment, he didn't know.

'We hid them in the hole in the wall outside your house,' Taylor said. 'Every day for a year, we left each other notes. Georgie would know that. But you're not Georgie, are you?'

Mortimer stepped out of the shadows next to the girl, who had begun to sob.

He looked exasperated but otherwise exactly the same as always, shirt neatly buttoned, tie perfectly knotted.

'This is taking too long,' he said.

Sacha saw the blade in his hand at the last second.

Instinctively, he grabbed Taylor just as she lunged towards Mortimer.

'*No*,' she cried.

Mortimer's knife slid across Georgie's delicate throat with silken smoothness. Her blood splashed on the stones at his feet like falling water.

The girl clawed at her throat, looking at Taylor in bewilderment. She struggled to speak, but all that emerged was a hideous gurgling. Like she was drowning.

Sacha thought he'd never forget that sound.

Taylor screamed then, a horrible, heartrending cry that broke Sacha's heart. He wrapped his arms around her.

'Let me go,' she begged, struggling in his grip. 'I have to help her . . . Let me go, Sacha.'

'It's not her, Taylor. Look at her. Really *look*.' His voice was tight with fear but insistent.

He wasn't sure she'd heard him at first, but gradually she turned towards Mortimer, shoulders still heaving with sobs.

Her body sagged in his arms.

'It's not her, it's not her,' she whispered. 'It's Dark. Whatever it is it's Dark.'

Across the big, open room, Mortimer sighed. 'Well, that was a complete waste.'

He cleaned the blade with a white handkerchief, his movements fastidious and thorough.

Sacha stared at the body on the floor. Now he could see that it was obviously not a young girl – it was a man. He had grey hair and wore a black suit. He looked nothing at all like Georgie, and the realisation made Sacha's blood run cold.

How had Mortimer *done* that?

Taylor wasn't crying anymore.

'Did you think that was funny?' She called to him. 'Do you think this is a joke?'

'No, Miss Montclair.' Mortimer fixed her with an icy stare. 'I don't find any of this amusing.'

'I don't believe you.'

In a move so swift Sacha couldn't have even begun to prevent it, Taylor swooped down to the floor and grabbed the dagger.

'Maybe this is a joke, too.' She held up her left hand, the one marked with the demon's claws, and sliced her palm deeply with the blade.

Mortimer glowered.

'You're out of your depth, little girl. Playing games in a world she doesn't understand.'

'Sacha.' Taylor turned to him, her expression steely. 'I need your hand.'

Without hesitation, Sacha held up his right hand. Taylor took his wrist. There was no compassion in her eyes – no fear – only anger, as she brought the knife down.

The blade burned his skin like fire, and he flinched despite himself, but her grip on his wrist was tight and the cut was straight and true.

She dropped the knife carelessly – it clanged against the stone at their feet. She brought her bleeding hand up to clasp his.

'You're wasting your time.' Mortimer sounded bored. 'Playing little devil games with blood. This is dangerous, you know. Sacha would suffer more with you than he ever would with me.'

Blood dripped from their entwined hands, dark rain pattering on the floor. She'd cut deep.

Taylor didn't seem to feel the pain. Reaching into a pocket, she pulled out a strip of white cloth – Sacha couldn't remember seeing her pack that earlier.

Ignoring Mortimer, she wound the cloth around their hands, tying them together.

'Our combined blood binds us.' She spoke quickly as she worked, twisting the fabric around with her good hand. 'It makes your curse my fate, my powers your strength. Together we are each other and ourselves. Together we are twice what we were before.'

Sacha had seen those words on Zeitinger's paper; Taylor recited them like an incantation.

Tucking the end of the cloth in, she held his gaze.

'Do you accept my strength?'

She looked different. Her tears had dried and her green eyes were clear and filled with an awful fierceness.

'Stop this, now.' Mortimer's voice echoed across the room. For the first time, he sounded really angry.

At that exact moment, in the tower far above, the bells began to toll midnight.

Sacha's hand still burned, his heart was hammering against his ribcage.

There'd been a moment earlier when he wasn't scared.

He was scared now.

'Yes.'

But she must have heard the uncertainty in the voice because she paused.

'*Trust me, Sacha*,' she breathed, her voice nearly soundless beneath the bells.

'I do,' he promised.

She entwined her fingers through his, speaking quickly.

'Whatever happens, don't let go of my hand. As long as

we share our blood we are one person and the curse cannot be fulfilled. Montclair blood in Winters veins. Winters blood in Montclair veins. One can't die without the other. Do you understand?'

He nodded.

Then she raised her voice. 'Isn't that right, Mortimer? You can't raise the demon while Sacha lives. And the curse can't kill Sacha with my blood in his veins.'

'Temporary protection,' Mortimer scoffed.

He seemed taller all of a sudden. It took Sacha a moment to realise he was rising up in the air – his feet off the floor and floating just above the stones. He raised his hands out to either side, like a preacher delivering a eulogy.

'Do you see, Miss Montclair? The demon's power grows in me, even as you play your silly games.' He smiled. 'My companion is nearly here to convince you to change your mind. Can you sense him, Miss Montclair? He is most interested in meeting you. A direct descendant of the magnificent Isabelle Montclair. He wants to thank you in person. He enjoyed meeting you in his world. Now he would like to finish that meeting in yours.'

Cold horror ran down Sacha's back.

Taylor didn't reply. Bending down, she snatched up Zeitinger's paper from the floor. She took a breath but before she could read out the words, Mortimer gave a dramatic sigh.

'How tiresome.'

He flicked his fingers in her direction and the page in her hand caught fire.

With a gasp, she dropped it, stepping back as it burned to ashes at her feet.

Seeing the hollow look of terror on her face, Sacha tightened his grip on her.

'You don't need it,' he reminded her. 'You memorised it.'

But she shook her head mutely.

Somehow Sacha understood. It was more than the words. That paper had Zeitinger's handwriting on it. It was a piece of St Wilfred's. It had been her crutch and now it was ash.

The bells were ringing with such force, he could feel the vibration through his feet. It shook him hard enough to make his teeth chatter. He kept losing his balance.

Could bells do that?

Still clinging to him with one hand, Taylor flung out the other hand to grab the back of the pew.

'*Sacha*.'

It was all she said, and he knew.

'At last,' Mortimer sighed, rising up just a little higher. 'You waited too long to perform your little ceremony, Miss Montclair. The moment has arrived.'

He pointed to the floor in front of the altar. As Sacha stared, the stone began to tear down the middle like fabric, the crack widening into a chasm. He didn't want to look down into it. He didn't want to know what was about to crawl out of it.

Taylor stood next to him frozen in terror.

'Taylor . . . ' he said, raising his voice to be heard above the cacophony. 'Do it now.'

Their eyes met. For a moment, he thought she would be too frightened to remember the words.

But then she straightened, balancing on the moving floor with difficulty.

Squaring her shoulders, she raised their joined hands high.

Sacha felt the electricity instantly – it crackled through them, making his breath catch.

A breeze whose source Sacha couldn't identify, sent Taylor's curls into a cloud around her face. Her green eyes blazed.

When she spoke, her voice soared, above the bells, above the crash of stones falling and tearing. Above the howling that had begun to pour out of the chasm in the floor.

'I call on the demon dimension to honour the agreement of the ages. I am a daughter of Isabelle Montclair. This is a son of Matthieu L'Hiver. L'Hiver and Montclair, bound by blood. We beseech thee.'

She drew a breath, then continued with Zeitinger's words.

'I call upon Azazel and Lucifer. I call upon Moloch and Beelzebub. I call upon all the demons in Hell, hear my plea. Unbind this boy. Release this curse. Honour the agreement of the ages. I summon thee. I summon thee. I summon thee.'

'You summon me?' It was Mortimer's voice but deeper now. And they both looked up to where he hovered above their heads.

He held out his hands, his eyes black as the abyss behind him. 'Daughter of Isabelle Montclair. I am here.'

# Thirty-Eight

A howling wind hit them both like a fist. Every candle in the room blinked out, save for those placed in a star pattern on the stone at their feet. If anything, those glowed brighter now.

The ground swayed, and Taylor struggled to stay on her feet.

When she'd met the demon in the darkness back at St Wilfred's, she couldn't see it. She'd wondered then what form it might take. What a demon would really look like – would it be a lizard or some horned goat creature?

She should have known it would simply take human form. Zeitinger had told her once Mortimer was his vessel, but that hadn't sunk in until now.

This was the horrifying reality of Mortimer's bargain: that he would *become* the demon.

Now she could see death in his coal black eyes. The cold

ruthlessness of it. She could feel the overwhelming predatory power. Pure undiluted and devastating.

Long ago, Deide had told her that, to humans, demons would be the equivalent of nuclear war. Now she knew he was right.

It took everything in her to force herself to look into Mortimer's inhuman gaze. To make herself not fear him.

*Trust your power*, she imagined Louisa telling her. *Know your strength.*

She did feel strong. Mixing her blood with Sacha had increased her power exponentially. She had known it instantly – she'd felt the rush of electricity, like a drug. This was different than just holding hands. This power was god-like.

But was it enough?

'We meet again, daughter of Isabelle,' the Mortimer demon said. It was still floating, unbound by gravity, several feet above the stone floor. Its oily voice made her skin crawl. 'Why do you dare summon me?'

'I summon you to unbind this boy,' Taylor called above the winds, using Zeitinger's words. 'According to the rules of the ages. You are required to—'

'Required?' The Mortimer demon laughed. 'I am not *required* to do anything.'

His laugh was filled with hate, and Taylor felt the Darkness of it wash over her, subsuming her.

Gritting her teeth, she kept going. 'You are *required* by the rules of the ages to unbind the boy from this curse. Our combined blood proves the undoing.'

Mortimer smiled. It looked ghastly. Unnatural.

'Do you really believe you have the power to fight me,

daughter of Isabelle? Did your German professor tell you that you could win?' He tilted his head to one side. 'He is a fool. And when I am finished with you, I will take care of him.'

Taylor shivered.

*Demons lie*, Louisa's voice reminded her.

'Do you deny the power of the unbinding?' Taylor forced herself to sound cold and unafraid. 'Do the rules of the ages not apply to you? Do you think you are greater than the others?'

'*Enough.*' Mortimer met her gaze directly. 'When we met in my dimension, did I not warn you of the consequences if you followed this path? Did I not put my mark on you?'

He lowered his gaze to her arm, where the claw marks had nearly healed. Instantly they tore open again, sending burning pain up Taylor's arm. Blood poured out of the wound.

She bit back a scream. Forcing herself to show no fear.

'Now who is playing games?' she heard herself ask, and wondered where that audacity came from.

Mortimer demon's black eyes narrowed.

'Oh, daughter of Isabelle. You have no idea of my games. Allow me to demonstrate.'

He lifted one hand and Sacha's fingers slipped from hers.

His body flew across the room at huge speed, crashing into the wall above the altar with a sickening cracking sound, before sliding slowly to the floor and lying still.

It happened so fast, Taylor had no chance to react. Not even an instant to cling to him.

He was there. And then he wasn't.

'*No.*' She stared at her empty hand in disbelief. The

bloodstained fabric that had bound them dangled loose and torn, fluttering in the wind that swirled around her.

Her hand felt so cold.

She stared across the room at his crumpled body. He hadn't moved since he landed. He lay so still. So horribly, horribly still.

'Sacha.' It came out as a whisper.

Her chest felt hollow. She kept trying to draw a breath but her lungs wouldn't function.

She forgot Mortimer. Forgot even where she was. All she could see was that figure, its arms flung out to block a blow that had already happened.

'I warned you, daughter of Isabelle.' Mortimer's voice boomed into the church. 'I told you the boy was mine. And yet you dare try to undo a curse of the ages?'

Some part of Taylor knew she had to go through with the rest of it. She had to at least try to fight. But she couldn't seem to speak.

Besides, what was the point?

Zeitinger's book was wrong. The words had had no effect on the demon.

'Sacha,' she said again, despair in her voice.

Grief threatened to tear her body to pieces, and she took an unsteady step towards him. She just wanted to touch him. To see if there was any life left in him.

Mortimer stepped in front of her. At some point, he'd landed. She hadn't even noticed.

'It's over now,' he said. 'The curse is fulfilled. The end begins.'

Finally, Taylor lifted her eyes to him. Some catalyst inside her had begun to turn her pain into rage. She felt anger and hatred in every part of her being. It penetrated her soul like blades.

If Sacha was dead, she would avenge him. She could do that much.

'I told you,' she said, stepping towards him, 'I would save him.'

He opened his mouth to speak and she raised her hand.

*Silence.*

He stopped.

'I told you,' she said again, letting the anger fill her with its cleansing heat, 'I would destroy anyone who tried to harm him. Did you not hear me, then?'

He cocked his head to one side, studying her with new interest.

'You are stronger than I thought, daughter of Isabelle.'

'Yeah,' Taylor said. 'I am.'

She held up her hand.

*Blade.*

The ceremonial dagger jumped from the floor to her hand.

She looked at Mortimer's chest, right where his heart would be if he had one.

*Kill.*

The blade shot at him with unimaginable force. Faster than any bullet.

He flicked it away with his fingers. It clattered harmlessly to the floor.

Still, he watched her with those dead, black eyes.

'You interest me, daughter of Isabelle. Why are you still fighting? The boy is dead.'

She held out her arms. And let the power of the room flow into her. It seemed to pour from the star of candles atop the stone near her feet.

'*I summon you.* Moloch and Beelzebub.' She began again. 'I summon you to unbind this boy. According to the rules of the ages . . .'

'This boy is *dead*, Miss Montclair.'

Taylor paused. Black eyes scorched hers.

'You should join me, Miss Montclair. The power is . . .' Mortimer's head dropped back, further than was natural, before snapping up again with sickening suddenness. '. . . unimaginable.'

'I will never join you,' she growled. 'Never. You are despicable.'

Taking a step towards him she spat in his face.

Time seemed to stop. When he spoke again, the demon's voice was inside her head.

'You go too far. I warned you, daughter of Isabelle.'

And then, without warning, she was flying. She felt her feet leave the ground. The air whistled in her ears. For a fleeting instant she was weightless, but she knew what it meant.

*Now*, she thought hazily, *I'll know what death feels like.*

She hit the ground at the base of the altar so hard all the breath left her body. Searing pain shot through her ribs and she heard something snap.

When she managed to draw a breath, her chest burned. Air whistled into her lungs. She knew it shouldn't sound like that, but she couldn't seem to think clearly. Her ears rang and she wasn't entirely certain where she was.

Everything was a blur but one thing was clear. It was over.

She'd failed.

With effort, she forced her eyes open. She'd landed not far from Sacha's body. She could see his hands – fingers curled like a child's.

She didn't know where Mortimer was. It didn't really matter to her anymore.

Only Sacha mattered.

Slowly, agonisingly, she dragged herself across the rough stone floor. Each movement sent pain shooting through her. Finally, when she had no more strength, she collapsed beside him, resting her hand against his.

His skin was so cold.

'Sacha,' she whispered. 'I'm so sorry.' She drew another shallow, whistling breath. 'I tried.'

There was no response. His face was turned towards her, lashes long and dark against cheeks that could have been carved from marble.

Behind her she thought she heard Mortimer shouting something but she didn't know what. All she cared about was right in front of her.

Then, Sacha's eyes opened.

Taylor stared, her breath whistling faintly through the hole in her lung.

She was dreaming. She was unconscious. Maybe she was even dead already. That would explain it.

But if she was dead, why did everything hurt?

Sacha's eyes searched hers, like he was looking for something. Neither of them moved a muscle for a long second.

Very slowly his fingers tightened around hers. His grip was so tight it hurt.

*I'm not dreaming.*

Electricity rushed through her, and she drew in a gasping breath at the force of it.

She heard a *click* and felt the snap as her rib healed. Instantly, her breathing became easier.

Warmth suffused her scalp as her skull knitted. She hadn't even realised it was fractured until then.

The whole time her body was healing, Sacha held her gaze, sea-blue eyes intelligent and aware, as if he knew what was happening inside her.

'Winters blood,' he breathed, nearly silently.

And then she understood.

It *had* worked. The binding had been completed. She hadn't failed. Not yet.

*Demons lie.*

It had wanted her to believe Sacha was dead. That the fight was over. So she would give up.

It wasn't over at all.

Suddenly, she could see alchemical energy all around her. Thick, golden streams of it flowing around her like rivers, pooling like lakes.

It was everywhere.

The basilica seemed to be made of it.

Whatever the demon had done had hidden that from her before. But now it was clear.

Sacha was aware of it as well. In fact, he knew everything that was going through her mind. She didn't know how she knew that, but she knew it. And she knew what was going through his.

He wasn't afraid. He wasn't in pain.

He was *furious*.

His lips curved up just a little as he watched her catch up.

'Ready?' he whispered then. 'We have to do it now.'

Taylor didn't need to ask what he was talking about.

She knew.

Closing her eyes, she pulled strands of energy to them and felt Sacha doing the same. She imagined it lifting them up off the ground.

*Rise.*

In an instant, they were standing, their feet on the floor. Then they were hovering above it, their toes barely brushing the stone. Power coursed through them both, swirling around them in a protective nucleus. Rushing through their fingers, moving from one to the other of them.

Across the room, Mortimer had lifted one of the stones and was rummaging underneath it, his back to them.

In unison, Taylor and Sacha frowned as they both wondered what he was doing.

When Taylor spoke, Sacha spoke with her. 'We summon you to unbind the curse of the ages.'

Mortimer spun around, a look of almost comic surprise on his face. In his hands he clutched a tattered, ancient book. Looking behind him, into the hole he'd uncovered, they saw a skeleton holding a sword in the fractured remnants of an ancient coffin.

'The rules of time command you to unbind this boy,' Taylor and Sacha said as one. 'You must release him from the curse.'

Mortimer recovered quickly.

'These games,' he said, 'are so tiresome.'

But he was nervous.

He raised his hand and Taylor saw his power as oily black globules. She and Sacha watched with curious interest as it moved towards them with what seemed like incredible slowness.

They waved their free hands and the alchemical power around them deflected the globules away.

Mortimer stared at them with blank disbelief.

'This is not possible.'

*The dagger.*

It wasn't Taylor's thought, it was Sacha's. But she heard it in her head like her own. They both looked to where Zeitinger's ceremonial knife lay forgotten on the floor.

They each had the same thought.

*Blade.*

It flew to them and hung in front of them, steady and deadly.

They both looked at Mortimer.

'No,' he said, taking a step back. 'We had an agreement.'

'Unbind this boy,' they said. And their voices filled the church like a choir. 'According to the rules of the ages. We command thee. We command thee. We command thee.'

The dagger shot across the room and embedded itself in his chest. The force of it lifted him from the ground and threw him against the back wall where he dangled, impaled.

Black blood ran down his chest and pooled at his feet in a viscous puddle.

He opened his mouth to scream and the sound that came out was like a thousand tortured voices. It was deafening.

He stared at them with an expression of utter disbelief.

The book slipped from his fingers.

A long black shadow poured from his open mouth. Foaming and writhing, it slithered across the stone floor.

It had no recognisable shape but Taylor and Sacha both knew, somehow, *this* was the soul of the demon.

They watched, disgusted, as it slid into the gaping chasm in the floor.

Seconds later, a tremor shook the foundations of the ancient building, sending stones tumbling from the ceiling. Overhead, the bells rang a discordant peal.

When they looked back, the floor was whole again. But the ground was still shaking.

A chunk of the wall broke loose and landed near them, shattering into a thousand pieces, and sending shards of stone shooting in all directions.

Sacha pulled Taylor towards the stairs.

'We have to get out of here.'

He didn't need to say it aloud – he spoke out of habit. She knew what he was thinking.

Together, they ran across the crypt, dodging fallen masonry. When they reached the door to the stairwell, Taylor looked back.

Mortimer's impaled body swung slowly as the earth shifted. He seemed to be decaying incredibly rapidly, his flesh already hung loose from his bones. As if he'd died a long time ago.

'Come on,' Sacha called, tugging on her hand. She hurried after him.

They stumbled up the stairs, as the building shuddered around them. When they reached the nave, a fire flickered where candles had fallen. A heavy cross on one wall swung violently but did not fall. Columns swayed dangerously around them. The bells rang with wild, deafening fury.

'Quick,' Sacha shouted, pulling her past the row of side chapels to the huge arched doorway. It had been locked when they arrived, but now was flung open, and they hurtled through it, just as one of the stone gargoyles crashed to the ground behind them.

Outside in the church square, people had begun to pour out of nearby hotels and apartments, most of them in pyjamas or dressing gowns, all talking excitedly.

'It's an earthquake,' one exclaimed.

'Stay clear of the walls,' a man shouted in French.

'What did he say?' someone with an American accent asked in English.

'Run really fast?' his friend suggested.

Clutching Sacha's hand, Taylor stumbled through the crowd, dazedly.

Had these people heard nothing when the world nearly ended? Did they have any idea how close they'd come?

They stopped a short distance away, blending in with the crowd.

When the earth finally stopped shaking a few minutes later, the tourists cheered.

‘I want to come back to France again next year,’ someone said. ‘They know how to put on a show.’

Taylor had forgotten the crowd by now. Sacha stood close, his body warm against hers. His eyes were sea blue and clear.

She reached up to touch his face wonderingly.

‘Promise me you’re really alive.’

‘I promise I’m alive,’ he said.

‘I thought I’d lost you.’

He pulled her closer, pressing the palm of her hand against his chest so she could feel the steady and very real beating of his heart.

‘Never.’

# THIRTY-NINE

'You might as well come in.' Louisa raised one hand and gestured impatiently.

Her hospital room was bright white and clean as a laboratory. The sharp tang of disinfectant tickled Taylor's nose as she and Sacha stepped inside.

Louisa lay in bed, her head immobilised by a complex metal and plastic brace strapped to her forehead and chest, that looked for all the world like a cage. A long line of stitches snaked down the hairline on one side of her battered face, but her eyes were alert.

Suddenly self-conscious, Taylor smoothed her hair with a nervous brush of her hand. Sacha's hands were shoved deep in the pockets of his jeans, shoulders loose and slouched.

'Hi.' Taylor bit back the 'How are you?' that threatened to come out of her mouth and sound ridiculous. 'Alastair said you were doing OK, but we had to see for ourselves,' she said instead.

Louisa scanned her face, taking in the dark bruise on her temple. All Taylor's other wounds had healed already. Sacha had explained that the bruises always healed last.

'Might as well stop by when you're in the neighbourhood.'

Louisa's tone was mild, but Taylor could tell she was glad to see them.

A nurse in green scrubs bustled in, pushing buttons that set a trio of plastic machines beeping in a panicked chorus then, muttering to herself, pushing more buttons to stop the cacophony.

Louisa rolled her eyes. 'She keeps doing that. I've been in quieter roller-derbies.'

The woman breezed from the room, saying something in rapid French.

Sacha failed to suppress a grin.

'What did she say?' Louisa demanded, glaring. 'She keeps doing that to me. All that talking.'

Sacha's smile broadened. Taylor could sense that his affection for Louisa matched her own.

'She said, "This one's trouble".'

'Well.' Louisa tried to scratch under a metal pole connecting to her head. 'I guess she's smarter than she looks. Ouch.'

Sacha reached towards her instinctively before shoving his hand back into his pocket.

'Perhaps it would be best if you didn't do that?' he suggested.

'What does it feel like?' Taylor gestured hesitantly at the metal contraption. 'To have a broken neck, I mean.'

'It feels great,' Louisa said dryly. 'I'm having a party in here.'

Taylor grinned. 'I'm willing to admit it was a stupid question.'

'It wasn't stupid.' Louisa sighed. 'I'm just sick of being in this place. It's making me tetchy.' She touched the metal bars with a rare hesitancy. 'It doesn't actually hurt that much now. It just feels like someone's holding my head hostage.' She shifted gingerly. 'Just a couple more months to go and I'll get this thing off. Nothing to it.'

'I got your coffee but they simply don't believe in mocha in this country . . . ' Alastair hurried into the room, a cardboard cup in each hand. Seeing Taylor and Sacha, he skidded to a stop so suddenly he had to wave the cups around to keep them from spilling.

'There you are.' A pleased smile lit up his ruddy face. 'Alive and well.'

'You expected anything else?' Sacha's shrug was cocky.

'Of course not.'

Handing Louisa her coffee, Alastair perched on the edge of the bed next to her. The two of them studied Sacha and Taylor with expectant expressions, as if waiting for some big announcement.

'What?' Taylor asked, although she knew already.

'Don't be coy.' Louisa waved one hand with open impatience. 'Jones called this morning and gave us the news. Is it true?'

Sacha and Taylor exchanged a look.

*Here we go*, they both thought.

'It's true,' Taylor said finally.

'I don't believe it.' Alastair shook his head. 'It isn't possible.'

'That's what everyone keeps telling us,' Sacha said. 'But somehow . . . it happened.'

'Show us,' Louisa demanded. 'We won't believe it until we see it.'

Taylor and Sacha had expected this. They didn't bother to object.

Setting down her bag, Taylor lifted the flap and pulled out a candle. They'd found it in the hospital chapel, and brought it with them, just in case.

She handed the candle to Sacha and stood back. 'Show them.'

*This is silly*. Sacha's voice was clear in her head.

*I know*, she replied silently, arching one eyebrow. *Just do it and make them happy*.

Holding up the candle, Sacha looked at it fiercely.

It flickered into life, the flame tall and true.

Louisa exhaled audibly.

Alastair twisted around to see her face. 'This is mental.'

'How?' Louisa asked, although she was perfectly aware that nobody could answer that question with any certainty.

'Montclair blood in Winters veins.' Sacha spoke quietly, holding Taylor's gaze.

The way he looked at her made her shiver.

'Jones is going to lose his mind.' Louisa said it with satisfaction, as if a mindless dean was the best possible outcome.

'I don't understand this.' Alastair's expression was clouded. 'You can't *make* an alchemist. You can't alter DNA in this fashion. It's scientifically impossible. How did this happen?'

He looked at them with worry, and a hint of what looked to Taylor not unlike fear.

She wasn't surprised. They'd already gone through this on

the phone with St Wilfred's. In fact, at this point, everything they said freaked people out. So they didn't dare tell the whole truth.

Taylor had Sacha's healing ability now – every wound sealed itself within minutes. She didn't know yet if she could die – it wasn't anything she wanted to test.

'We don't know,' she said. 'Zeitinger doesn't know, either.'

She thought about what the German professor had told her about Dark ceremonies before she left St Wilfred's: *Performing a Dark ceremony leaves traces on your spirit. Sometimes these traces pervade. Sometimes they take over.*

Was there Dark power in her now? She didn't know. If it was there, she couldn't detect it.

The reality was – they both liked the way they were. They weren't Dark or evil. They were just stronger.

Better.

'What happens now, you two?' Louisa asked.

'We're going to Paris.' Sacha said it simply, a statement of fact.

'Sacha promised his mother he'd come home when this was over, and that's what we're going to do,' Taylor said. 'And after that, I'm going to Spain. To see my best friend.'

Louisa studied her. 'Then back to St Wilfred's?'

'Probably,' Taylor said. 'Back in time for term, anyway.'

She'd kept her expression neutral, but Louisa always could read her. She leaned forward now, looking at Taylor, a hint of suspicion in her gaze.

'Is something else going on?'

Taylor hesitated. She didn't want to lie to Louisa. But she

didn't want to tell her everything right now. There would be time to decide how much to share. Time to try and understand what had happened.

This wasn't that time.

'Everything's fine.' Crossing the room. She took Louisa's hand. She could feel the warmth of the blood moving in her veins, the strength of the muscle tissues beneath the skin. Mortimer's violence hadn't diminished her at all. She would recover from her injuries.

Then maybe it would be the right moment to tell her the truth.

'I promise.'

It wasn't a lie. Everything was fine.

*We should go.*

From across the room, Sacha caught Taylor's gaze. His motorcycle was outside, packed with their bags. At the thought of it, Taylor's heart leaped. Their life was just beginning.

Mortimer was gone. No one could stop them now.

'We have to go.' Leaning down, Taylor gave Louisa a gentle hug. As she did, she plucked a delicate strand of energy from the electricity buzzing around her and directed it at her fractured neck.

*Heal.*

Louisa started.

'What was that?'

One hand drifted towards her neck, tattoos dark against her pale skin.

Taylor didn't know how well her abilities projected yet. But she'd wanted to try it. Just in case.

'It was a hug, Lou. Nothing more.'

She headed to where Sacha stood waiting, her bag in his hand.

Turning to say goodbye to Louisa and Alastair, Taylor felt unexpectedly homesick for Oxford's tall, stone spires. For Zeitinger's book-lined office and days spent in the library reading dusty old parchment.

She would go back there in the autumn – this time as a proper student. She would work hard. And one day she would understand exactly what had happened during that ceremony in the crypt.

They paused for a moment in the wide doorway.

'See you at St Wilfred's,' Taylor said.

Before they could reply, she and Sacha walked down the wide hospital corridor, their steps in perfect sync, and headed out into the sunshine.

It was time to begin.